SPECIAL MESSAGE

THE ULVERSCROFT
(registered UK charity)
was established in 1972 to provide funds for
research, diagnosis and treatment of eye diseases.
Examples of major projects funded by the
Ulverscroft Foundation are:

- The Children's Eye Unit at Moorfields Eye Hospital, London
- The Ulverscroft Children's Eye Unit at Great Ormond Street Hospital for Sick Children
- Funding research into eye diseases and treatment at the Department of Ophthalmology, University of Leicester
- The Ulverscroft Vision Research Group, Institute of Child Health
- Twin operating theatres at the Western Ophthalmic Hospital, London
- The Chair of Ophthalmology at the Royal Australian College of Ophthalmologists

You can help further the work of the Foundation by making a donation or leaving a legacy. Every contribution is gratefully received. If you would like to help support the Foundation or require further information, please contact:

THE ULVERSCROFT FOUNDATION
The Green, Bradgate Road, Anstey
Leicester LE7 7FU, England
Tel: (0116) 236 4325

website: www.ulverscroft-foundation.org.uk

THE SILENCE OF WATER

When Fan's mum Agnes announces that the family is moving to Western Australia to take care of Agnes's father — a man they've never spoken of before now — Fan finds herself a stranger in a new town, living in a home whose currents and tensions she cannot read or understand. Resentful of her mother's decision to move, Fan forms an alliance with her grandfather, Edwin Salt, a convict transported to Australia in 1861. As she listens to memories of his former life in England, Fan starts snooping around the house, riffling through Edwin's belongings in an attempt to fill the gaps in his stories. But the secrets Fan uncovers will test the family's fragile bonds forever, and force Edwin into a final reckoning with the brutality of his past.

SHARRON BOOTH

——————◆——————

THE SILENCE
OF WATER

Complete and Unabridged

AURORA
Leicester

First published in 2022 by
Fremantle Press

First Aurora Edition
published 2022
by arrangement with
Fremantle Press

*A catalogue record for this book is available
from the British Library.*

ISBN 978-1-3991-3678-5

Published by
Ulverscroft Limited
Anstey, Leicestershire

Printed and bound in Great Britain by
TJ Books Ltd., Padstow, Cornwall

This book is printed on acid-free paper

For Caroline

*And dedicated to the memory of
Mary Ann Hall*

Home from the Indies and home from the ocean,
  Heroes and soldiers we all shall come home;
Still we shall find the old mill wheel in motion,
  Turning and churning that river to foam.

You with the bean that I gave when we quarrelled,
  I with your marble of Saturday last,
Honoured and old and all gaily apparelled,
  Here we shall meet and remember the past.

Robert Louis Stevenson, 'Keepsake Mill'

Contents

Contents

Letting go

Fan

Adelaide, October 1906

Fan awoke to a seagull calling to her through the open window. The air was already warm, which meant the ocean would be as flat as one of Ma's oatcakes.

Her bathing suit gaped a bit around the arms and chest — 'up top' as Aunty Florence so delicately called it — but Ma reckoned there was no money for a new one and it would have to see out the summer. Under her bare feet, the floorboards crunched with sand. So much for Ma and her 'sweep up that mess, young lady'. Fan probably still had sand in her hair and up her nose and goodness knew where else, but Ma didn't have a broom for those places.

In the kitchen, Ma was reading a letter.

'Ma, I can't find my hat,' Fan said.

'Isn't it on the back of the door?' Ma asked.

'I looked.'

'You should be more careful.'

'Aunty Florence usually brings a spare.' Fan noticed an envelope on the table. 'Who's that from?' She reached for it, but Ma snatched it away.

'None of your business.' Ma shoved the envelope into her apron pocket and pressed it to herself like she thought Fan might dive in for it. 'You planning on leaving the house in that state of indecency? Where are your clothes?'

'I was hoping you'd let me go for a quick dip on my own, early, 'cos it's already warm. Please, Ma. I'll look

3

after Tom and Ned all day for you. Promise.'

'All day? You must be keen. All right. Just this once and only' — Ma pointed her finger at Fan — 'only if there's somebody else on the beach.'

Fan stared open-mouthed at her mother.

'Don't die of shock, Fan. I said just this once. Don't go in if it's rough. Or where you can't touch the bottom.'

'It won't be rough, but yes, I know, I know,' Fan said. 'You worry too much. I'm the best swimmer in the whole of Semaphore.'

'I wish you'd stick to dry land,' Ma said. 'Your dad says you're more fish than girl.'

'You should try it one day, Ma.' Fan kissed her mother's cheek. 'I might be a fish, but you're chicken.'

Fan ran past the corner shop where she'd once nicked an apple on a dare, only to spit it out because she'd felt so guilty. Past the butcher, whose window had cracked years ago but which he'd never bothered to get fixed. Past the apothecary's shop, whose newly painted walls were already peeling from the salt and wind and blinding summer sun. She ran past the houses that got bigger the closer you got to the seafront, and over the road that divided where she lived from where she swam. Fan took a flying leap across the dunes, reaching through every inch of her arms and legs towards the bright blue sky. Then one big breath in, and the more-fish-than-girl was underwater, opening her eyes, nothing but the heartbeat of the ocean thudding in her ears.

The water held her steady and her hair spilled like ink as she surfaced. Floating on her back with everything bright and sparkly, Semaphore Jetty looked

4

so close. Fan knew she could swim and swim and look up and still feel like she'd got nowhere. One day she'd do it — she'd swim from Semaphore to Largs and barely come up for air. Bloody hell, she'd swim all the way to Brazil, as Ma and Uncle Ernest would say. Ma would huff and bluster, no doubt about it, but Uncle Ernest would talk Ma round as usual and say, 'Agnes, don't worry about Fan. She's a good swimmer,' and then he'd make a big fuss about swimming with her even though Fan wouldn't need the help. And Ma would no doubt hurry along the sand shouting at her from the beach, 'You stay close to Ernest or God help me I'll throttle you myself!' Funny how Ma only ever talked about God when she was mad as a snake about something, and then it was always assumed that God would be on Ma's side.

Fan licked salt off her lips. Why would God have given her these long arms, these strong legs, this mermaid hair, if she wasn't supposed to be at home in the water? Fan let herself sink to the bottom. She dug her hands into the seabed and opened her eyes and watched brown seaweed float by. Surely this was all the God anybody could want.

★ ★ ★

From the end of the road, Fan could see somebody sitting on the front step. She ran, to make it look like she was in a hurry in case it was Ma waiting to yell at her. It was Dad, sitting where he'd sat most of last week and the week before, whittling a piece of wood. He hardly acknowledged her, didn't even tell her off for trailing sand into the house. Maybe Dad was having a summer holiday, although Ma hadn't said anything. Fan would've thought somebody on holiday would smile a bit more, but she hadn't seen Dad smile for weeks.

6

Agnes

Adelaide, October 1906

When the letter had arrived a few days ago, the shock of seeing her name and address on an envelope from Western Australia had made Agnes cry out. She scanned the page and skimmed news of a move to a new house away from the stench of the East Perth river, a place with a tram line and the promise of electric lights. She hurried through the weather, an arthritic hip and a fickle milking cow. She re-read the pages looking for one word: Walter. It wasn't there.

I can no longer live with your father for various reasons. His heart and mind are failing and the drink has ruined him. I have asked him to leave. You must take him on.

Agnes's head ached between her eyes. After so many years of silence, it was the same old Annie, pointing out the mess and asking someone else to clean it up. She wondered if Annie had meant to write take him in.

'Is he dead?' George asked.

Agnes shook her head.

'Is it Walter?'

'I wish there was something, anything, about Walter. But it's just chitchat, and . . .'

'What, love? What's wrong?' George rested his hand on hers.

'She says she can't live with him anymore. She's thrown him out and expects me to do something about it.'

7

'How can a woman throw her husband out?' George took the letter from Agnes and began to read.

'Annie's never been one for doing things the usual way.' Agnes rubbed her forehead. 'And you don't know my father.'

George kissed her hair, spoke in a soothing voice. 'So she thinks he hasn't got long.'

'However long he's got is too long,' Agnes said. 'I don't know why she thinks it's got anything to do with me.'

In the distance, the bell rang at the port.

'There's the bell, love,' George said. 'Here we go again.' He flexed one arm up like a circus strongman. 'Who needs those young wharfies, aye?'

Agnes kissed his forearm. 'I'm sure things will pick up soon, love.'

In an hour, George was back, grim-faced and silent.

'Tomorrow will be better, I'm sure.' Agnes rested her hand on his shoulder, but he flinched and pushed it away.

* * *

'You're all the family I need,' Agnes was fond of saying to Ernest, Florence and Sarah, but today the trip to Rosewater made her feel nauseous. She'd barely opened the door before her news spilled into the room: the letter, Annie, her father, the throwing out and the taking on.

'Annie was always so tolerant of your father's . . . temper,' Ernest said.

'He was on his best behaviour when you lived with us,' Agnes said. 'Walter and me hardly recognised him. He didn't want our cousin saying anything bad

8

about him.'

'Ernest, darling, what do they do in the west with the old men who have no family or nowhere to go?' Florence asked.

'They sleep rough. In the streets,' Ernest said. 'Boarding houses. The churches do what they can.'

'Well then, it's settled,' Florence said, patting Agnes's hand. 'Annie can find him a room in a boarding house.'

'You must have known this day would come.' From the armchair, Sarah tapped her walking stick on the floor. 'He must be nearly eighty, Agnes. He's outlived all his brothers, including my dear Sam. Do you want your eighty-year-old father sleeping on the street?'

'It won't come to that, Mother.' Ernest put his arm around Agnes's shoulders. 'Poor Ag. Florence is right, you know, as always.'

'He's an old, sick man with nowhere to go,' Sarah said. 'Perhaps he's outlived all his mistakes, too. He's still your father, Agnes.'

'I'm not going back, and Annie's not shipping him here like some kind of cargo.' Agnes smiled at Florence. 'You're right. It's settled.'

★ ★ ★

A week later, George fell into bed in the blackest part of night and rolled over to give Agnes a whisky-kiss. She curled around him. He stroked her hair and whispered, 'Guess what, Agnes, love, I asked around. I know where I can get all the work I want. Plenty of it.' And the way he fumbled with her, well, Agnes knew he was his old self again.

'Fremantle, love,' George said. 'Word has it there's

9

loads of work there. Other Sunderland men say so. Shifts every day. Wages every week.'

'I told you, I'm never going back.' Agnes pulled away from him.

'Your old man could pay us something for board and lodgings. You want it to keep going like it is here?' George's voice had a flinty edge. 'We need the money.'

Agnes rested her head on his chest. 'Annie can find him a room in a boarding house or one of those places the church has for old men down on their luck.'

'Agnes, love.' George sat up on his elbows. 'I know you said things were bad when you left Perth, but what kind of daughter leaves her father to die on the street?'

'It's not like that.' Agnes's eyes welled. 'I'm not a monster, George.'

'I know, love. I'm sorry.' George held her. 'Maybe the old man's mellowed with age.'

'Not him.'

'We could give it a go in Fremantle. I know I can earn good money there.' George kissed her hand. 'I tell you what, if it doesn't work out, we can always come back.' He stroked her hair. 'I promise.'

★ ★ ★

Semaphore beach was crowded with families in colourful hats. The water teemed with swimmers and beyond the jetty, tiny white waves flickered and disappeared. Fan and Tom ran ahead to their usual sheltered spot in a shallow dip of dune. Ernest and Florence's children followed in a straggly line. Ned was last of all. Agnes, Ernest and Florence followed the trail of footprints until they caught up to the

10

children. The sky was bright and clear but beyond Largs, around the blind curve of coast, Agnes noticed the horizon was stained with purple cloud, and she shivered. Perhaps there was more than one storm coming today.

Florence pulled a hat out of her bag. 'Please don't send this one to Fan's Mysterious Hat Graveyard.'

'Oh, Aunty Florence, it's beautiful.' Fan put it on. The hat itself was plain, but Florence had tied two white ribbons around it and they danced in the breeze. She pulled the brim down low and tight, then just as quickly tossed it on the sand. 'Race everyone to the water!'

'I'm swimming with you all today,' Florence said, 'so none of the usual tiresome rules will apply.'

The scramble of arms and legs and bathing suits began and the children disappeared into the water. Even from this distance Agnes knew the bony curve of Tom's spine, Ned's lopsided walk. And, of course, Fan's unruly hair, her sweet, clear voice shouting some order at the others, always with her head half-turned towards Agnes and half-turned towards the open sea.

Agnes had packed marmalade sandwiches and brought enough money for ice-creams. The children stayed in the water much later than usual, long after the breeze began whipping the waves up, and Agnes resisted calling them in. Fan declared she was the last person in the whole of South Australia to leave the water that day.

'The best day ever, Ma. The best.' Shivering and dripping, she pressed a small stone into Agnes's hand. 'I got it way out there. Aunty Florence didn't mind how deep I went.' Fan twirled. 'See? I'm still here, it didn't swallow me up.'

11

'Florence has eyes in the back of her head, young lady.'

'I got that stone 'cos it reminds me of you. See how dark it is? But when the sun warms it up it goes lighter and you can see lots of pretty colours.'

'Thank you. I think.' Agnes put the stone in her pocket and took George's old jumper out of her bag. 'Put this on.'

'Best day ever,' Fan repeated, and pulled the jumper over her ears. The arms hung almost to her knees. 'Ma, I'm thinking about something important.' Fan bit her lip like she always did when she was nervous. 'I know you think I can't, but I want to swim between the jetties. I know I can do it.'

'It's a long way, Fan. And dangerous. Most grown men can't do it.'

'Can't I at least try?'

Once everyone was dried off and dressed, they walked back towards the tram. Ernest and Florence herded their children on board.

'How about next time?' Agnes said to Fan. 'Next time we all come here for a Sunday beach day, you can try the swim.'

Fan threw her arms around Agnes. 'You're the best, Ma.'

★ ★ ★

That evening, the rain crashed loud and shrill on the tin roof.

'I bloody well hate you.' Fan's eyes blazed.

'Mind your language,' Agnes said.

'I'm not going.' Fan kicked the leg of the table.

'That's enough,' George said.

12

'I knew something was up. Marmalade sandwiches. Ice-cream. Swimming between the jetties. I hate you, Ma.'

'I said that's enough.' George's jaw tightened. 'Watch how you speak to your mother, young lady.'

'What about Ma? Why don't you tell her off for all her big, fat lies?'

'Shut up, Fan. You're making it worse,' Tom said. Ned's bottom lip trembled.

Fan ran from the kitchen. Down the hall, a door slammed shut.

Agnes did her best to answer the tide of questions from Ned and Tom. Things were tough on the Port Adelaide docks and there would be more work for their father in Fremantle. Her father — their grandfather — had fallen ill and his wife, Annie, couldn't look after him anymore. He would be coming to live with them. Ned mouthed grandfather, a word he didn't know, and Tom repeated it slowly. Tom said a grandfather was some kind of family but Ned still didn't understand.

'What's he like?' Tom asked. 'How come you never said anything about him before?'

'There was nothing to say before.' Agnes reached for George's hand. 'My father came out from England many years ago for better prospects — to seek his fortune, like so many men did, when things were bad in England. Your dad did the same.'

'That I did,' George said. 'Never wanted to go back.'

'I left Western Australia when I was young,' Agnes continued. 'I met your father in Adelaide, and here we are.'

'Is there a beach?' Ned asked. 'Will it be like here?'

'A port, a beach, a roof over our heads,' George

said. 'Just like here.'

Agnes lay awake long after George had gone to sleep. It wasn't long before the rain slowed, but the low sobbing from behind Fan's closed door made everything feel damp.

Edwin

Perth, October 1906

Edwin struggled. His back had ached constantly for the better part of a week. He lined the wooden trunk with newspaper and put in a pair of boots, his tailoring bits and pieces. He covered all that up with another layer of newspapers, then put in his few remaining books. A couple of waistcoats and shirts. His good jacket.

He coughed with the effort, but he was determined not to ask Annie for help. The days of helping each other were long gone. After so many years, he could usually tell what she was thinking, but not today.

He pulled on his threadbare socks. These days he was grateful for cooler mornings, because his feet and ankles always swelled up in the heat. Years ago, Annie knitted him a new pair of socks each winter. He made her a dress each summer. It was one of the little things they had begun to do after Walter had left and there was an unspoken need in the house for kindness. Edwin would say how warm the new socks were and Annie would twirl and unpin her fine, grey hair and parade like a tailor's model. He couldn't remember when they had stopped these exchanges. Just that one winter, he'd pulled on a pair of socks and realised how old and full of holes they were. He was wearing the same pair now.

He put the almost-full rum bottle in his pocket. He'd need it to help get to sleep if Agnes's children

15

were noisy. He'd need it if Agnes's children were quiet, if truth be told.

'Don't forget that.' Annie pointed to an old brown leather bag. It was no bigger than something you'd keep a pair of boots in.

'I'm unlikely to forget it.'

'Good. I don't want nothing of you left behind.'

'Except the house,' Edwin said. 'You're happy for me to leave that behind.'

'It's the least I deserve after serving my sentence with you.'

It had been Annie's idea to sell up and buy a little plot this far south of the river, with its promise of trams and electrics, and he took joy in blaming her whenever something went wrong. Despite the stench from the slaughter yard and the often-stagnant river, he hadn't wanted to leave East Perth. Even after that terrible winter when Smith deserted his family for the goldfields and Mad Molloy shot two blacks and then himself, Edwin refused. Told her all her talk of land and curses meant she'd been talking to lunatics too long. It was only when she'd said, 'What if Eddie comes back? If we stay in East Perth, he'll always know where to find you,' that he'd felt a tightening in his guts. He felt it now, although it was probably just too much rum and not enough dinner.

'No need to watch me pack,' he said to her.

'Oh, but it's the last pleasure you're ever going to give me, Edwin. I want to make sure you're really going.'

'By God, you are the worst of all my punishments.'

'My dear Edwin.' Annie folded her arms and smiled. 'Despite my daily prayers, you ain't dead yet. You could have years left. Who knows what punishments the good Lord's still got up his sleeve?'

After she left him alone, he drank more rum and tried to remember the last time he felt anything for Annie but sour contempt. It had been years since she made up a bed for him in the sleep-out and locked the door to the house at night. Edwin opened the brown leather bag and took out a bundle of letters. Sometimes he read them and sometimes he didn't, but he needed to know they were there. He opened the tobacco pouch and held the lock of straw-gold hair to his cheek.

He drank more rum. Would he recognise his daughter? Agnes was barely eighteen when she left and now she had children of her own. Edwin stared into the blank years and tried to imagine an older version of his brown-eyed, gritty daughter, better than Walter at all the things that mattered, the only girl who'd lived. His eyes burned, his heart burned, he rubbed his chest — the damn drink.

Annie shouted some insult or other from the next room. He thumped the door in reply. He drank more rum and unfolded the blue cloth and traced his calloused fingers over the embroidered image of Lichfield Cathedral. There were moth-holes around the cloth's edges, and the white thread had yellowed, but Eliza's stitching had lasted. His sister had always been so much smarter and better at everything than he was. He could imagine her examining his life and finding shoddy workmanship: 'The tailor's son had all the advantages, but in the end everything he made fell to pieces.'

Edwin

Lichfield, 1840

His skill, Eliza once said with a grin, was that he could put decapitated men back together.

Edwin ran his fingers around the collar. His stitches were small, perfectly spaced. They would give the shirt an uprightness no amount of starch could imitate.

'Three more before you're done,' Mum said. The pins she held between her lips wobbled up and down.

'You said that three shirts ago.' Edwin yawned. Not even midday and the tiny room at the back of Thomas and Samuel Salt, Gentlemen's Tailors Since 1800, was hot and airless. Eliza hummed and stitched cuffs to sleeves. James, pimply and butter-fingered, was trusted only with buttons. Mary, old enough to be married, squashed her sausage-fingers into scissor handles. As usual, Sam Junior was nowhere to be seen, and Mum didn't seem to care.

Eliza poked out her tongue. Edwin stuck his finger in his mouth and mimed vomiting.

'I'm warning you two,' Mum's voice cut like scissors. 'Your father needs those shirts finished today.'

'It's Edwin's fault,' Eliza said. 'He pulls stupid faces.'

'You pull stupid faces,' Edwin said. 'Or is that your normal face?'

Mum clipped him over the back of his head. Eliza smirked.

Six twelves are seventy-two. I before E, except after

18

C. The longest river in England is the Severn. Edwin silently repeated what he'd learned at the school for tradesmen's sons, a rosary of facts to save him from the sameness of sleeves and collars.

'Eliza's too slow,' Edwin said. 'Get Mary to help her. It takes two girls to do the work of one man.'

'Don't be daft. I'm all thumbs,' Mary said.

'That's not what I heard from William Neville,' Eliza said. Mary's cheeks flushed deep red. Edwin sniggered.

'Young lady!' Mum said, and pins rained from her mouth.

Eliza threw her finished shirt at Edwin. 'Beat you again. First to the cathedral gets all their sins forgiven.'

'You're too young for sins,' Edwin said.

'It'd be a sin if I beat you again.'

Edwin dropped his half-finished shirt. The collar gaped like its throat had been cut. Edwin shoved Eliza out of the way to get through the door first.

It was a quick sprint down Sandford Street to the Crown Inn, the smell of hay and horses in his nostrils and the clip-clop and rattle of departing coaches in his ears. The sky was hazy and the air was sweet and ripe with late summer. Edwin was not a natural runner. At fourteen, his calves were already stocky like his father's, and his arms were ropey with muscle. Since Eliza turned twelve, she'd grown taller, developing grace and speed. Her cotton skirt swished behind him.

'Women's vestments slowing you down?'

'Never.'

They ran past an inn, the butcher, the milliner with a faded pink hat in the window. The Birmingham coach trotted past in the opposite direction and as

19

always, Edwin couldn't take his eyes off it: the whip rippling against the horse's flank, the driver's shouts. He caught sight of a black-gloved hand waving to him from the carriage and in the few seconds it took for the coach to pass, he invented a life, a story, a reason for this passenger's journey.

Eliza passed him in a blur of blue dress. 'You stop for the coach, but the coach isn't stopping for you!'

He took off again. Up ahead, Lichfield Cathedral loomed. He pumped his arms hard, his fists fighting through the air. His feet jarred on the lumpy cobbles.

They passed Minster Pool and sprinted to the cathedral. They were neck and neck. He could see Eliza's skirt tangling around her knees. She scowled, her lips pressed hard together, the same expression she always had when she tried hard at anything.

Edwin made noises like he was giving the run everything he had, but he let her fly past him. Eliza hurled herself at the ground under the biggest tree, their imaginary finish line. Edwin lunged forward and flung himself down next to her.

'Another victory for the little sister,' Eliza said, panting.

'Hardly. By an inch, if that.'

'An inch is as good as a mile, old man.'

Edwin stared at the cathedral's three spires. He squinted and tried to make them merge into one. Lichfield Cathedral was unique in the whole of England, he had learned, because of those three spires. They made shadows that lengthened and shortened across nearby fields like a sundial. On a hot July day last summer, he and Eliza had sneaked in and touched the tomb of a long-dead bishop. It was as high as Edwin's waist and wide as two coffins, and even though the

20

blue-and-yellow stained-glass windows split the sunlight into a million pieces, flooding the cathedral with light, Edwin had shivered in the presence of death.

'He's stone dead,' Eliza had said, and he'd admired her wit and been afraid for her intelligence at the same time.

'Look.' Eliza pointed at a cloud of birds. 'Swallows. Wish I'd brought my charcoals.'

'Me too. At least when you're drawing, you're not talking so much.'

Departing swallows meant the end of summer. Before long, the sky would be dark at four in the afternoon and it would be cold enough for the milk to freeze. Mum had already told him there'd be no new coat again this winter.

'I might sneak in, see if I can wake up Saint Chad,' Eliza said.

'Best of luck. He's been dead for six hundred years.'

Eliza sat up and leaned on her elbows. 'Just think about something else, when you're doing the tailoring.'

'I do. Birmingham. Liverpool. London. Sometimes I forget I'm even here.'

'You know he wants to put your name on the sign.'

'Not my name. He wants to paint out Grandfather Thomas and write *Samuel Salt and Son.*' Edwin picked at the dirt. 'Invisible. Worse than being dead.'

'I don't want to be helping Da forever,' Eliza said.

'You'll have to, at least 'til you get married. That's if any man's ever mad enough to ask you.'

'Shut up.' Eliza whacked his arm. 'They'll let women be teachers one day. Young ladies. I'm good enough. And when the railway comes, who knows where I'll go? I might go to London, become a great artist or

21

a . . . a thinker.'

'You already think too much. They'll never let the railway near Lichfield, Eliza. You've heard Da. The coachmen, the innkeepers, the tailors — they'll all vote against it because they don't want to lose their customers. Rich ladies and gentlemen have got to come to Lichfield now because it's halfway to somewhere else.'

'The tailor's children will be hemmed in while the world passes them by.'

'Well, I'm leaving the first chance I get.'

Eliza stood up and brushed dirt off her skirt. 'We'd better get back. Mum'll have our guts for garters.'

'You go.' Edwin watched the swallows circle the three spires. 'I've got something to do first.'

'Are you meeting a girl?' Eliza slapped her hand to her heart and blew a loud, spit-filled kiss into the air. 'Ooh, Edwin, take me away from this drab life!'

Edwin threw a handful of dirt at her, but Eliza had already run off down the hill.

* * *

In the coldest, darkest months of a bad winter, Stowe Pool had been known to freeze over, but today it was glossy and still. Edwin rolled up his trousers and waded in. The water stank a bit, but he didn't care. He peered into the nettles growing in the shade of an overhanging tree. He picked up a stick and poked around.

In a flash of brilliant white, the bird appeared. It moved towards him on its stick-like legs and looked at him with black eyes. Edwin stood as still as he could. In all his summers he'd never seen a bird so strange.

22

Its feathers were bright white, its beak flat and round at the end as if it was holding a spoon. He could tell just by looking that it didn't belong among Lichfield's mud-coloured ducks or the swallows and starlings that nested under the eaves of Saint Mary's church.

The bird scooped mud from the edge of the pond. Edwin inched towards it. He expected the bird to flee, as it had done yesterday and the day before and the day before that. But it did not move.

Edwin fumbled in his pocket for the stale bread he had brought. He lobbed it towards the bird.

A plop and a splash. The bird grabbed the bread.

Edwin took off his shirt and tossed it up onto the bank. Without it he felt daring, transparent, an exotic animal made for somewhere else. He took a careful step forward and tossed another lump of bread. Then another and another. Mum would kill him for being so reckless with any kind of bread, even the stale stuff. The bird jabbed out its beak and gobbled every piece.

He took another step forward. He was so close that, if the bird had been a man, they could have shaken hands. It lifted its beak and they stared at each other. He marvelled at its elegant neck, its foreignness. Where was it from? Would it be leaving with the swallows?

Edwin stretched out his hand and dropped the last piece of bread as close as he dared.

The bird flapped its wings and a deep pain worse than the stab of a needle shot through Edwin's fingers. He took a fast swipe with his fist, his fighting fist as William Neville had christened it after a scrap. The bird screeched and Edwin felt warmth, and the softness of feathers.

The air was heavy and still. The bird had nipped the ends of his fingers and they were bleeding. He swore, and pressed his hand under his armpit. The bird floated close to him, half-submerged, its black eye glassy. Edwin nudged it but it didn't move.

He waded towards the opposite bank, kicking the water to help propel the lifeless bird back to the place where he was used to seeing it appear. He willed it to flutter or squawk or even try to bite him again, but there was nothing. He bent down and peered into a dank clump of plants, parting them with his uninjured hand.

'Damn!' He felt the burn of nettles.

Edwin picked up the dead bird and lobbed it deep out of sight. He scrambled out of the water.

'Damned bird. I was only trying to feed you.' He looked up at the cathedral's spires and squinted, but he couldn't make them merge. He turned away. He couldn't stand them looking down on him.

★ ★ ★

'For pity's sake, Edwin.' Samuel Salt was a short, squat man, but his voice was whiny and thin. He lifted Edwin's swollen hand, wrinkled his nose at the stagnant, swampy smell of his son. 'How will you do the collars?'

'There are machines that could do it in half the time,' Edwin mumbled.

'The hands can feel, the hands can judge, they help the eyes see how to make a man look more than he is.'

'Da thinks the machines are a fad.' Eliza fetched a jar of ointment. 'Just like the railway.'

'How could you be so careless?' Mum said.

Edwin flexed his hand. His fingers still throbbed. The nettle sting on his arm was red and lumpy. His

24

heart thudded in his chest. The clock on the wall said he'd been at Stowe Pool only an hour, but it felt like a week. He might be hurting, but by God he knew he was alive.

★ ★ ★

Mum threatened so often about stopping him going to school that he finished five collars most days before sunrise and begged her to reconsider. She showed Da his fine workmanship.

'See what Edwin can do when he'd rather be somewhere else?' Mum said. 'If you want his best work, looks like we'd better keep him in that confounded school.'

Sometimes Edwin wondered if the threatening and the giving in was more for Da's benefit than for his. Now he was late. He slunk into an empty desk at the back.

'The railway will bring the world to your front door.' A woman stood at the front of the schoolroom. A woman. In front of the boys' class as ordinary as if it happened every day. She had skin the colour of peaches and a voice sweet as church music.

'One day, for just a few pennies, ordinary people like you will be able to travel to Birmingham or London. And beyond.' She traced an imaginary line on the map from Lichfield to Birmingham. She tickled the blank fields of Coventry and slid her finger lower until it rested on the black circle that was the capital city of the British Empire.

Edwin trembled so violently he was afraid she'd hear his knees knock together.

Who is she? Edwin mouthed to William Neville.

William licked his lips crudely.

'Better late than never.' The woman waved her hand at Edwin. 'What's your name?'

'Edwin Salt, miss.'

'See me afterwards.'

★ ★ ★

She smelled of lavender. The room was cold enough to see your own breath when you coughed but Edwin felt bathed in sunshine.

'Edwin Salt.' She looked closely at a large book of handwritten notes.

'Sorry I was late, miss. My Da — the shirts.'

'Never mind that.' She looked up and smiled. 'My husband's mother has been taken very ill and he has travelled with her to Derby, where her people live. I have stepped in until he returns.' Her vowels were cultured and southern and made the dullest thing sound important. 'Mr Atkins tells me you are one of his brightest boys.'

So this was the schoolmaster's wife.

'I like arithmetic. And reading, miss.'

'With hard work, a bright boy like you could find a clerical position. Work with your mind instead of your hands.'

'My Da wants me to be in the shop. Samuel Salt and Son.'

'I'm sure he wants the best for his sons, and his daughters, too.' She patted his hand and all the blood in his body seemed to rush to his fingers to take full advantage of the moment. 'The railway is changing the world,' Mrs Atkins whispered, as if she and Edwin were the only ones who could grasp the enormity of

26

this fact.

'But the Lichfield councillors voted against the railway.' Edwin was finding it difficult to concentrate. 'The new line only went to Tamworth and that's nine miles from here.'

'The railway will stop for no man.' She let go of his hand and all the blood flooded back into his body: arms, legs. Other places.

★ ★ ★

The back room of the shop felt even smaller and more airless than usual. He tried to concentrate on the latest batch of collars but his hands were clammy.

The railway will stop for no man.

Work with your mind instead of your hands.

Edwin imagined long lines of neat stitches, miles of track stretching from Da's cottage in Sandford Street, up past Minster Pool, circling around the cathedral a couple of times and then running south to Birmingham, London and beyond. He blinked and imagined himself as the map on the schoolroom wall, unfolding under Mrs Atkins's fingertips, her gasps of delight. The famous Edwin Thomas Salt, the brightest boy at the school for tradesmen's sons, the tailor's son made good, the new centre of the Empire.

Six sevens . . . The longest river in England . . . His thoughts unravelled. He couldn't concentrate.

A few hours later, when the air was icy and tasted metallic as it does before snow falls, Edwin crept outside to the freezing privy where, for a few agonising minutes, his desire for railways and London and lavender and peaches grew white-hot until it disappeared into blindness.

Months passed. Edwin finished shirts more quickly and accurately than his brother and sisters could manage in twice the time. He cut generous allowances for flabby arms and sagging bellies. While he worked, he memorised the capital cities of countries he knew he would never visit. Then, once he had done with the times tables, he started on the square roots and the cubes. He let Mrs Atkins's words roll around in his mouth like a sweet reward for the numbness of the work. His father unfolded Edwin's shirts for the gentlemen's inspection and joked about his own father, himself and his eldest lad. Thomas, Samuel and Edwin Salt. 'Cut from the same cloth,' he'd say, and Edwin's neck would tighten with irritation.

'Here's an arithmetic problem for you. How many hours d'you think you've done for Da this past twelve months?' Eliza asked one day, as they walked back from one of their races to the cathedral.

'More than the rest of you put together,' he retorted.

'And you think you're the smart one,' Eliza said wryly.

Edwin's brown eyes were always watchful. He knew that something would come along one day, just like Mrs Atkins had promised, and despite the blisters and pinpricks on his hands, he would be ready to grab hold of it the moment it emerged.

* * *

In 1845, when Edwin was more or less nineteen, gangs of men arrived out of nowhere and began to cut open old Parkin's fields, a mile and a half out of town. The men all looked the same, faces grimy with sweat and dirt. They worked the same, too: cursing, lifting, digging, hammering. Edwin and William and a few other lads watched them from the road, but weren't game to venture any closer. A tent near the main line became known as a place a man could buy a gill or two of gin. William said he'd heard if you smiled kindly at the girl who poured it, you could buy a bit more than gin.

One afternoon, as they made their way to the tent, a skinny man in a smart serge jacket pushed past them, his chin in the air as if he was somebody important.

'Jesus. Isn't that Jack Bullock?' William said.

'Look at him swagger like lord of the manor.' Edwin stared, disbelieving. Last time he'd seen him, Jack was bloodied and bandaged after an accident in the fields during harvest. 'Let's see what he's got to say for himself.'

They had to duck their heads under the sagging canvas roof. William bought a couple of gills of gin from a girl who called him 'sir' readily enough, but curled her lip into a smirk when she said it.

'To your good health,' Edwin said. He downed his drink in one go and wiped the back of his hand across his mouth. 'Christ.'

'Christ indeed.' William coughed.

'Let me buy you another.' Jack nodded to the girl and held up three fingers. 'How's the tailoring business, Salt? Still scraping by?'

'Couldn't be better.' Edwin looked Bullock up and down. His uniform jacket was too big. 'You dressing formal for ploughing fields now?'

'I've gone up in the world, Salt. Once the railway's finished, who knows where I'll go.'

'You working for the railways?'

29

'The Excise.'

'You're an excise man?' Edwin shook his head. 'So you're still digging dirt, but for Her Majesty instead of your father.'

'Whatever you say, Salt.' Jack handed the girl some money and winked at her. 'Keep the change.'

'Thank you, sir.' The girl smiled at Jack. Edwin felt a stab of envy.

Jack grinned at Edwin and William. 'I can afford it.'

If Jack Bullock was happy to buy gin, Edwin was happy to drink it. The gin made his eyes sharper and the shabby tent seem brightly lit. He and William stood with other lads he recognised as the sons of millers and farmers, but who now wore the jackets and smug expressions of railway clerks and excise men.

Before sunrise, his head gin-foggy and his mouth sour, he continued to stitch collars, cut arms and torsos out of serge and fix Mary's botched buttons and cuffs.

The railway will wait for no man.

Work with your mind instead of your hands.

Keep the change.

* * *

One cold Tuesday morning in 1848, when fog draped over Stowe Pool, Samuel Salt climbed a ladder, took down the sign above his shop and sent Edwin to the merchant for paint. It was late afternoon before Edwin returned.

'In the name of all that's holy, what took you so long?' Samuel said.

Edwin looked directly into Da's rheumy eyes. 'I went to the Excise Office. I'm sitting the entrance exam on Tuesday.'

Mum kissed Edwin's cheek and watched her husband carefully.

'Well, well. My eldest son is destined for greatness.' Samuel stood back and sneered at Edwin, then clapped slowly. 'Congratulations, son. But before then, you've got work to do. Those buttons won't stitch themselves.'

★ ★ ★

'For the right man,' Mr Brown emphasised, 'Her Majesty's Excise represents an opportunity. Young men with a certain . . . tenacity will find rewarding employment in the collection of Her Majesty's government revenue.'

Edwin paid close attention as Mr Brown talked. Taxes paid on tobacco, sugar, tea, whisky — even paper and soap — enabled Her Majesty's government to provide important services for its soldiers and fine citizens.

'Makes it sound not so bad,' William Neville whispered. 'Taxes, I mean.'

'The salary is adequate for a single man otherwise destined for the fields or the factories.' Mr Brown stalked between the desks, peering at each young man in turn, noting who flinched and who looked him in the eye.

'Or a tailor's shop,' Edwin said to himself, but in the small room, his voice echoed. Mr Brown looked at the list of names he carried with him, then back at Edwin.

'If I may continue, Mr Salt, any one of you could find yourself in London or beyond at a moment's

31

notice. There are many opportunities. For the *right* man.'

Mr Brown returned to the front of the room. 'Most of you will be particularly grateful to know that the uniform includes a brand-new winter coat and a sturdy pair of boots.' Mumbles of approval rippled through the room.

'So ask yourself,' Mr Brown's voice boomed. '*Are you the right man?*'

Edwin leapt to his feet. 'Yes, Mr Brown, I believe I am.'

The others began to fidget in their seats. William mouthed *Sit down, you fool*, and sliced his finger across his throat. Edwin remained on his feet, his arms straight by his sides as if this were the army.

'Sir, you said you wanted tenacity,' Edwin gulped. 'If I'm not brave enough to speak up in a room like this, how can I hope to do the job Her Majesty requires of me?'

Mr Brown walked slowly up to Edwin and stood so close Edwin could smell sweat on his shirt.

'Congratulations, Mr Salt.' Mr Brown offered his hand. 'You are precisely the kind of man Her Majesty is looking for.'

* * *

A week later, he joked with Mary, James and Sam Junior about visiting him in the big city. Mum hugged him goodbye and held on until the coach driver insisted they had no more time. Eliza rode with him to the railway station.

'Don't worry about Da,' Eliza said as they reached the end of the road. 'He'll calm down.'

32

'Too late now. He's got James, and Sam Junior.'

Eliza rolled her eyes. 'Sam Junior. Really, Edwin.'

'Well, you and Mary, at least.'

'Samuel Salt and Daughters,' Eliza grinned. 'Careful. He's having enough trouble coming to terms with the railway.'

People were already boarding the train. Young girls shrieked at the steam sputtering from the funnel, and young boys ran up and down the platform slamming doors and opening them again.

'My goodness,' Eliza said. 'It's like a living creature.'

'Look after Mum.' Edwin kissed the top of Eliza's head and opened the nearest carriage door. He squashed into a seat and pressed his boots hard into the boards until the train had gathered speed and Eliza's cry of 'Good luck, old man!' melted into the shrill hiss of steam and the high-pitched grinding of metal.

Edwin pushed through the crowd of families to the opposite window, or at least the place the window glass would have been, had his ticket cost more than the cheapest penny fare. He leaned out as far as he dared.

Dry, coaly air and specks of soot blasted Edwin's face. Past the canal, past the postage stamp–sized patch of land that was all that remained of Parkin's field, past the place where the gin tent used to be.

'There it goes.' A young lad pointed towards the cathedral spires growing smaller, smaller, smaller.

Agnes

East Perth, 1875

Mam scooped little Walter up into her arms and took Agnes's hand. Da held her other hand and they walked in a gang, Da whistling. It was such a comical noise, high-pitched above the thrum of crickets hissing in the heat of the morning. If Da was whistling, it meant he was in a better mood. He winked at Agnes. She squeezed his hand tighter, and hoped this would make his cheerfulness last.

'Thank the Lord for whatever's got into you, Edwin,' Mam said. They passed through a thicket of trees and reached the shaded riverbank. The hot air burned Agnes's throat. Figures seemed to move in the trees, then disappear. Mam sat Walter down under a tree and plonked herself down beside him. Da pulled his boots off and sighed so loudly it was if his liberated feet were doing the sighing.

Rosie, the black woman who lived with Da's mate Mick McCarthy, said that the river was alive; a creature that had been here since before the world was born. This riverbank — their riverbank, as Agnes had come to think of it — was a branch apart from the main stretch of river, protected from the mess and stinks from the tannery and the slaughterhouse and deep enough for men and women to wade into. Rosie got tears in her eyes when she talked about bad stuff going into the river but she said they didn't have to worry about the water down here — it was as fresh as

34

the day it first tumbled as rain over rocks high up on the scarp.

Their little stretch of river certainly seemed alive today, swarming with the Smiths and their daughter Daisy, a clutch of whooping black children and a fluid group of others whose mams and dads all seemed to know Da from the hotels on Howick Street, or some place called Before. Mr Molloy sat under a tree, smoking and staring at nothing, ignoring Mrs Molloy, who talked constantly. Agnes sat down next to Walter and Mam. Mam wiped her forehead and brushed ants off Walter's legs.

Da rolled his trousers up to his knees. 'Time for a dip.' He roared silly animal noises and ran in up to his waist, splashing Mam, who pretended to tell him off, while Walter waved his pudgy arms around. A bird with a red beak peered at him. Maybe the bird thought Da was mad, too.

'Da's happy,' Agnes said to Mam.

'It's a good day when your father's happy.' Mam said it to Agnes but she kept her eyes on Da.

Suddenly Da lost his footing, stumbling and thrashing.

'Cath! Help!' he called to Mam.

Smith looked up and smirked. 'Keep the noise down, Salt, you madman.'

'Mam, help him!' Agnes jumped to her feet.

'You going in to save your prize-idiot father, Agnes?'

'Help! Smith, Molloy!' Da's arms hit the water, making it bubble and surge.

'Get on with it, Salt! Make it quick, it'll save us having to throw you overboard,' Molloy shouted, and Smith roared his mirth.

At the sound of the word 'overboard', Mam leapt

35

up. 'That's enough!'

She ran to the edge of the riverbank, pulled off her boots and her stockings and strode in. Da thrashed around. As Mam reached him, Da beamed and he suddenly made a miraculous recovery, standing steady and opening his arms to receive Mam. She took hold of Da's hands, and her skirt billowed up. Mam's laughter, it sounded like bells.

Agnes watched Mam and Da sway in the water, their hands clasped, Da humming a cheery tune. Mam leaned her head on his chest as they moved, and the river held them. Agnes watched them and her racing heart calmed down. Nobody was drowning. Smith knew it, Molloy knew it, Mam knew it, Da knew it. He had been pretending to struggle all along, Agnes realised, just to get Mam to dance in the water with him.

★ ★ ★

Mam dozed on the bank with Walter. The sun dried her clothes and her hair. Da lazed under a tree, smoking and chatting with Smith and Molloy. The water looked golden and inviting. Agnes pulled her shoes off the same way as Mam and Da had done and walked to the edge. The river smelled of weeds and salt. She knew it was shallow enough in the middle for Da and Mam to stand up, but she couldn't see the bottom from where she stood. When he saw her take off her shoes, Da stopped talking and jumped up, holding out his hand.

'Let's go for a dip, Agnes girl.'

'Dunno, Da.'

'Are you scared?'

Agnes shook her head but didn't move.

'Hold tight!'

She gasped as the riverbank seemed to tilt and she felt herself fly up towards the sky. It was Da, lifting her up so she could sit on his shoulders. She shouted in surprise and clasped her hands tight under his stubbly chin.

Da held her up high and walked into the water. The sun bled through the treetops. The water was clear enough to see Da's white, lumpy feet lumbering around on the riverbed. He walked her into the middle of the river and then kneeled down carefully so she could kick her feet in the water. It was surprisingly cold. From here, Mam and Walter looked smaller. A thin curl of smoke escaped from Smith's pipe. The Molloys took no notice of them.

'What d'you think?'

'It's good.' She swished her feet and made waves.

Da let go of her with one hand and splashed water on his face. He stood up and Agnes hurtled through the blue sky again. She panicked and grabbed onto Da's hair to stop herself from falling. He swore and Agnes giggled.

'I've got you, Agnes girl,' Da said quietly. They walked around in the water like this for what seemed like hours. Da's shoulders were strong and he seemed much taller than he did at home in the yard or sitting on the back step with a drink. He told Agnes about the first time he'd seen this river, so long ago it was even before he started working in that mongrel Henry Wood's tailor shop. Agnes didn't pay much attention to what he was saying but his voice was so soothing and calm he sounded like a different Da to the one who shouted about money, or the confounded heat.

The sun lost some of its sting and the shadows of trees lengthened over the water. The Molloys and the Smiths waved their goodbyes. Agnes forgot to be scared, she held onto Da's shoulder with one hand, let go with the other, and waved back.

★ ★ ★

It was a week later when Mam very near flew down the track to the road, Walter bouncing in her arms, and Agnes had to run her hardest to keep up. When they reached the river, Mam put Walter on the ground under a tree, ran over to the shallow bank and jumped in.

'Come and have a dip with your mammy.' Mam waded in until the water was up to her waist. It gave her dress a floaty life of its own. She unpinned her black hair and it uncurled past her shoulders.

'Mam, what are you doing?'

'Come on, love!' There was music in Mam's voice. That jingly lilt could make anything sound like a good idea. Da called it her Old Country accent, how she lingered in the middle of words, teased them out. Even 'leeches' and 'cod liver oil' and 'a good hiding' sounded like something you'd want, coming out of Mam's mouth.

Agnes took her shoes off and walked in slowly up to her knees. Mam's hair glowed blue-black in the sun.

'What's wrong with Da? He looked mad.'

'Your father's got' — she paused — 'company this afternoon. Family.' Mam said 'family' like it tasted bitter. 'You know how he gets sometimes.'

Agnes had never heard of Da having any family. The only people who came to the house were the Molloys,

38

the Smiths and Henry Wood. When Da had got back from town today he'd been on his own except for some letters he'd thrown on the table. That had been when Mam grabbed her and Walter and said brightly, 'Well then, Edwin, we'll leave you to it!' Mam was like a weathervane for Da's moods — she sensed them before anybody else knew they were coming.

The water tickled Agnes above her knees and she hesitated. 'I can't.'

'Don't be a big baby. I'll catch you.' Mam opened her arms wide.

'You better.' Agnes held her breath, shut her eyes and jumped. She hit the water hard and paddled for all she was worth. Water went up her nose and for a moment there was only her blood throbbing in her ears, nothing to hold onto, nothing under her feet.

Mam's rough hands on her bare arms, Mam's heart beating against her ears.

'My goodness, you made a meal of that!' Mam kissed Agnes's wet hair. 'See? Not so hard for my brave girl.'

Mam led Agnes back to the riverbank and waded back in. Agnes pushed her hair out of her eyes and coughed. Her wet dress was plastered to her legs.

'Again,' Mam commanded.

'I can't.'

'Yes, you can.' Mam's voice could also be like thunder, depending on her mood.

Agnes leapt. She stretched her arms out in front of her and kicked her legs as if she were fending off a wild animal. This time the river didn't fight. Mam caught her again and this time, she clambered up to the riverbank by herself.

'That's the way, my love, you're nearly there. And

39

again!'

Agnes leapt. Her bottom hit the soft riverbed. She spluttered and reached for the sky. Agnes swallowed air into her middle, her ribs rising and falling like gills. She threw her arms around Mam's neck.

The river tasted of salt and stones. Mam's face was pink and shiny.

'You look like an apple,' Agnes grinned.

'Cheeky.' Mam wiped hair out of her eyes. 'By Jesus, it's hot.'

'Lucky we're in the water.'

'One more try.' Mam let Agnes go, the river held her and Agnes was finally swimming on her own. Brown weed tickled her ankles. Mam clapped and whooped. Agnes floated on her back and stared at the endless blue sky. Weightless, no sense of where she began or ended.

Agnes swam. Mam climbed out and played with Walter. Mam climbed back in again and brought Walter with her. Agnes held Mam's hands and they made a circle in the shallows. Walter splashed between them, beaming as he floated in his illusion of freedom.

'Now you can swim and you'll always be safe,' Mam said. 'Even if you were being chased by a fire, you'd be able to get away.' Mam's voice rang in the hot blur of afternoon. Even the crickets stopped to listen.

★ ★ ★

The house smelled of rum. Da was asleep in his chair.

'Da, Da, guess what I did today!' Agnes's voice was bright and loud in the quiet house. 'I can swim now, Da, I can swim.' She jabbed at his arm.

Da woke, startled, and slapped his hand at where

40

the noise was coming from. He caught Agnes's cheek and she yelped like a dog.

'What the feckin' hell you doing, Edwin?' Mam pushed Agnes behind her.

'Stop shouting, woman.' He rubbed his eyes and said with care, 'I didn't mean to, Agnes girl. I was half-asleep, you gave me a fright.'

Agnes's face stung and she blinked hard. 'Sorry, Da.'

'All caught up on your news from home?' Mam's voice could sometimes be like sharp bits of glass. She nodded towards the letters on the table. 'How is your dear Eliza?'

Da scowled at Mam. 'Get out, both of you.'

★ ★ ★

Agnes used the mangle to wring the river out of her dress, her underthings. Mam sat on the back step and let the hot twilight dry her off while Da smoked. She could hear Mam talking to Da in that breezy tone she used if he was ranting about Henry Wood's laziness or if he'd had too much rum. When Agnes had done her clothes, she twisted the river out of her hair. Her fingers were wrinkled, her skin felt stretched on her bones. She rubbed her cheek where Da's hand had caught her. It was sore. All the mangling made her tired and when she cleared her throat, up the river came.

The next day everyone pretended nothing had happened. Agnes blamed her sore cheek on river stones. Mam didn't ask about dear Eliza. Da barely spoke and the air grew heavy with his not talking. Agnes hated the silences more than his ranting and she thought Ma probably did too, the way she talked in that singsong voice she used when she was trying to get Walter to go to sleep. Agnes thought about the river. The smell of it lingered on her and she wondered if some part of it ran inside her now. She wondered if Mam and Da could see it behind her eyes, how she was changed.

Fan

Adelaide, November 1906

The days before they left slipped through Fan's fingers quicker than normal days. She made herself wake up early in the hope she could sneak out for a swim, but the wind and rain lashed all the doors shut. Sarah and Aunty Florence and Ma went through every room and stood with their hands on their hips and somehow agreed on what could be taken and what could be left behind. All of a sudden Ma's talk was full of 'your grandfather' this and 'your grandfather' that. 'You'd better pull your socks up, Fan, because your grandfather won't stand for your insolence.' Fan had never heard of insolence or known that she had it. It had turned up the same time as her grandfather, who now filled up their lives as if he'd already moved in.

When they got to one box of old things, Aunty Florence and Sarah huddled and closed up around Ma like a clamshell. Ma clutched something and started to cry. It looked like an old blanket that might once have been white. It seemed to Fan like a big fuss over nothing. The three women stood together. Nobody noticed Fan and nobody noticed her leave.

The clouds were dark, even though it was daytime. The rain pelted. Fan was barefoot and in her swimming costume and she didn't care who saw her and who was scandalised. She ran past the same old shops and the houses that got bigger. When she reached the spot where the road dropped away towards the sea,

43

she opened her arms as wide as she could to take every last thing in, to leap over the dunes, to allow for the possibility of flight.

The tide was high. She plunged into the sea, which was oddly warm. It swelled and gently pulled her under. Fan put all her anger into her swimming, but the current was too hard to swim against. She slapped at the rain-puckered sea. Weed slithered against her legs.

Coughing and crying, she waded out of the water. She grabbed handfuls of sand, shells, whatever the tide had thrown up, as much as she could carry.

Ma would rage at the sight of her dripping and shivering in the rain. She'd just have to hang on until Ma's anger passed. She didn't dare guess at what Dad would say. He didn't get mad often, but when he did, he talked real quiet and somehow made you feel like he'd torn a layer of your skin off.

Pools of rain and sea water collected at her feet. Fan opened the door and prepared for the worst. But Ma's face was all waxy and bluish under the eyes and she opened her arms and held Fan so tight she wriggled and almost said, 'See, Ma, I'm still here.' But for once in her life, Fan kept her mouth shut and just rested against the familiar, bready scent of Ma's hair.

Fan had been expecting a siren, a bell, a man blowing a whistle, some noisy signal. But, without warning, the queue of passengers heaved forward and carried her along like a rolling wave.

The press of Sarah's skin against her cheek. Aunty Florence's arm strong around her waist. Uncle Ernest's big hug, his wide-open smile. Ma resting her head in the warm hollow where Uncle Ernest's shoulder curved into his chest.

44

Then the sound of her own shoes hurrying across the gangplank. Dad gently pulling Ma away from Uncle Ernest.

'Come on, love. It's time.'

The hiss of steam and the smell of coal. The sparkle of sunlight on flat water before the darkness below deck. The letting go.

Edwin

Birmingham, 1848

Birmingham turned his snot black. It gave his skin the translucent, grey pallor of a man who was constantly being woken up by shouting whores or whinnying horses in the alley below his lodging house. But he didn't care. He loved the square-windowed factories, the hissing of machines he couldn't see, the stench of rotting rubbish and the high-pitched hammering from the shopfronts in the Jewellery Quarter. He loved the stink of horse shit in his nostrils and too many people crowding him at his elbows, even in the few minutes it took to walk from his mouldy room in a house near the Bull Ring to the Excise Office in New Street.

His tailor's eyes were quick to spot patterns in figures, to notice columns crossed out and rewritten and too neatly finished. The merchants turned up their noses and called him 'that pompous excise man'. It wasn't that Edwin Salt was cleverer than his fellows, although he held more in his memory than most. It was, as Matthew Sharpe the tobacconist put it, that he took such a bright-eyed pleasure in watching a merchant squirm.

At night, Edwin and his colleagues drank at the Anvil, a low-roofed tavern that backed onto the narrowest part of the Gas Street canal. In the smoky air of the Anvil he could say, 'I am an excise man. The Queen relies on me to fill her coffers,' and a girl would touch her hair and adjust her dress and giggle,

46

'With a uniform like that, you can fill my glass with a gill, lovely boy.' At first, he'd been suspicious; most of the Lichfield girls he knew rationed their affections with the ruthlessness of an army on a long march. But here, a certain type of girl was clear-eyed about what she wanted. After closing time, down nameless alleys or on mouldy mattresses and sometimes his own bed, he took advantage of Alice or Amelia or Sally or any other girl the ale or gin had made willing. Sometimes a girl rummaged through his pockets with one hand while she fumbled in his trousers with the other, and that's when he took more liberties than the girl had strictly agreed to. If she whimpered or hissed obscenities, he felt a stab of guilt, but it always left him by the time he stumbled back to his room. Birmingham was a city built on transactions. He was an excise man, and everyone from the richest merchants to the lowest girl knew exactly what they owed.

★ ★ ★

Matthew Sharpe lit a fresh pipe and the room filled with the smell of wood and oranges.

'Your arithmetic is faultless, Mr Salt.' Sharpe smiled through stubby yellow teeth. 'Where are you from?'

Edwin closed the ledger. 'Near the Bull Ring, sir.'

'Ha ha. Very good. I mean, of course, before you landed in our fair city.' Mr Sharpe blew smoke from his pursed lips. He reminded Edwin of those cartoon pictures of the north wind. 'You are uncommonly smart. I wondered about your background.'

'Smart isn't uncommon, where I'm from, sir.' Edwin held Sharpe's gaze. 'Lichfield. Home of the great writer Dr Johnson, among others.'

'A fine town. Fine cathedral. And some of the finest minds of our time.' Mr Sharpe smiled even more broadly and pushed a small pouch across the desk. 'Please accept a token of my appreciation for your work these past few weeks.'

Sharpe took a long puff on his pipe. Edwin stared at the pouch.

'Oh, come on, Mr Salt. Don't be so . . . provincial. Your supervisor tells me he's tasted no finer blend.'

'And what would you be expecting from me?' Edwin picked up the pouch. It was about the size of his hand. Easily a fortnight's worth of tobacco. He took some out and pressed it between his fingers.

'Let me tell you how it works in the city, Mr Salt. Show your supervisors that you have a good relationship with the merchants and you'll go far. Get promoted. Have you spent a winter living in Birmingham yet? Miserable.'

★ ★ ★

The tobacco pouch made barely a bump in Edwin's jacket pocket, but he was convinced it was making him itch. He downed a gill, and another, and ordered a third. His mind remained stubbornly clear. He slammed the glass on the table and left.

Around the back of the Anvil, he peered out across the canal. The air stank of dead fish and rubbish. Lanterns swung on barges. He filled his pipe with Matthew Sharpe's tobacco and took a long, slow draw. It was sweet, rich. He took a few more puffs but he couldn't get beyond the bitter taste in his mouth.

'For Heaven's sake, throw 'em in.'

Edwin spun around. A young woman was staring

into the water. She wore a plain blue dress and a shawl.

'Throw your wishes in.' She turned to him. 'Quick, name one.'

'What?'

'You heard me.' Now she grinned. 'Name one wish.'

His mind was blank. He shook his head.

'A man with no wishes. Never met one of them before.' The woman had pale skin and silvery blue eyes. A strand of hair, the dark yellow of burnt straw, had escaped her bonnet.

'Sorry to disturb you, Mr Wishless. Just that you look like you got the weight of the world on your shoulders.' She nodded her goodbye and, as she hurried down the canal road, Edwin noticed her round hips, her chin tilted in the air as if she was much more interested in where she was going than in the stupid, wishless man she had just encountered.

'Wait, miss.'

He ran after her, dodging two braying horses and a whip-cracking carriage driver. By the time he caught up, they'd reached a bridge. The sky was the colour of gunmetal and there were dark spots of rain on his jacket.

'Wait, miss! Please wait.'

'Are you following me?'

Up close, her eyes were the palest blue he'd ever seen, but there was a steeliness about her gaze that unnerved him.

'No. Yes. I wanted to talk to you.'

'Me? Why me?' Her accent was corn-rough and suddenly he was in his mother's village, the place of summer and fields he could only remember visiting once, but the buttery smell was in his nostrils now.

'You were mistaken,' he said, 'about me being

49

wishless.'

'Was I indeed?' She tilted her head back and laughed hard. *Ha-ha-haaaaah*. He caught the sweet whiff of gin.

'Yes. I have plenty of wishes. Dreams, too — big ones. Some so big they'd make your lovely hair turn white.'

She stared at him. His face flamed.

'I could tell you about them, one afternoon.' His voice was quiet in the cold air. 'We could go for a walk.'

'What work do you do?' she said. 'I've my respectability to think of.'

'I am an excise man.' He waited for something about this woman to open itself up a little more. 'Paper, spirits, tobacco. Other things from the new world.'

'I know what excise is. You collect taxes that nobody wants to pay.' She turned to leave. 'Even the Bible don't like tax collectors.'

'Wait.' He reached for her arm.

'What do you think you're doing?'

'Sorry.' He let go of her. 'Some of us are honourable men.'

'I suppose there must be honourable men in even the lowest professions.'

They stood a body's width away from each other.

'Today a merchant gave me this.' Edwin took the pouch out of his pocket. 'I think it means I took a bribe. I'll show you an honourable man.' He tried to throw it into the canal, but she grabbed it from him just in time.

'You're quick,' he said.

'I've had to be.' She opened the pouch and sniffed. 'That's fine stuff. Shame to waste it.'

'I'd have stayed in my father's tailor shop if I wanted to be pissed on by the likes of Matthew Sharpe.'

'You took what he was offering. Looks to me like you're already stinkin' and wet.' She wiped her hair from her eyes. She looked like she was waving away a butterfly. 'Tell you what.' She rolled a pinch of tobacco between her fingers. 'You give this to me. I'll make good use of it.'

'And in return?' He moved a little closer. 'How about that walk?'

'I suppose that would be fine, sir. That would be acceptable.' She said acceptable carefully, as if she had learned the word a long time ago but hadn't had any use for it until now.

'My name is Edwin Salt.'

'Mary Ann Hall.'

'Delighted.' Edwin took her hand gently, touched his lips to her knuckles.

Her cheeks coloured. 'Goodness, aren't you the gentleman.'

Agnes

East Perth, 1875

Some days Mam shooed Agnes and Walter out of the house and said she'd be along much later once she'd tended the vegetables, and taken care of Da. Some days Mam worked at the governor's laundry and they didn't see her at all, so Agnes and Walter amused themselves. On these days, Agnes swam and floated on her back and watched the flat blue sky for hours.

Agnes loved it best on the hot, still days when Mam put Walter to sleep under a tree and they had the whole river to themselves. That year, Mam's belly got fatter. She waddled in the water and made Agnes giggle, but Mam swore it was the only thing that helped her swollen legs feel better.

Agnes and Mam held hands. Their clothes floated; their hair wisped around their shiny faces.

'Agnes, love, this heat could melt us to nothing!' Mam kissed the cross she wore around her neck.

So what if Da was asleep from rum on more days than he wasn't? So what if Da was at home more than he was at work? So what if Mam was so tired from being a laundress and watching the beets and beans grow that she often fell asleep whenever she sat down? Mam came alive in the water. The blacks said the river had been there at the beginning of all creation, but Agnes knew different. With her feet so sure of the riverbed, with her arms wide open, it was Mam who invented it, Mam who mapped it, Mam who sang it into being, fresh and new for her squealing, grinning fish of a daughter, every single day.

★ ★ ★

They called the baby Cath, after her mother. She screamed all day and all night. Da screamed at Mam and slammed the door when he left for the Western Hotel. Mam screamed at the closed door about rum and laziness and the bloody luck of the Irish. If Da got home full of grog he screamed at Agnes. Where was her mother and why was there no confounded dinner on the table? Agnes put her knuckles in her mouth to stop herself from crying. She prayed to God that everybody would stop being angry. You could see it on Da's reddening face and that ropey muscle twitching in his neck, and the way he clenched his hands together, over and over. It looked to Agnes like it took Da more effort to keep his fists by his side than it would have to hit something. Mam shouted that if she'd known she'd had to work this hard to coax anything out of this blasted soil, she'd never have left Ireland.

The shouting followed Agnes to bed and into her dreams. Mam said not to worry but Agnes developed a sick feeling in her stomach. The only time she didn't feel sick or think about the shouting was when she was swimming. Jumping off the sheltered bank, lying on the bottom of the riverbed and drowning in quiet, Agnes wished she could stay there for another thousand years.

Days rippled into weeks. Agnes swam, dived, floated. No sound but the birds high up, the distant buzz of a sawmill. Underwater, nothing but the gentle

53

pulsing of her own blood against her eardrums.

Until one afternoon, a cry cut through: not a saw-mill, not a bird. A familiar rhythm throbbing in her skull. Agnes swam to the surface. It was Daisy Smith, standing on the riverbank, shouting her name.

54

Arrival

Arrival

Fan

Fremantle, November 1906

Dad made a big fuss of how lucky he'd been to get the house. One of his old Sunderland shipyard mates had left to try his luck on the goldfields and put in a good word with the landlord. Theirs was the end house of three joined together on Ellen Street: the closest to the fancy house perched at the street's highest point. Dad said Fan should be grateful they'd landed on their feet, but Fan wasn't grateful.

Of course, Ma insisted 'your grandfather' would have the front room to himself. It would get the best morning sun and the afternoon breezes. It was only a few paces wide — his feet might touch the opposite wall when he was in bed — but it had its own fireplace. Dad and Ma put a big chair with a cushion near the window, and another chair next to a little round table. They shouted at each other while they were doing it, Ma yelling, 'Bugger him! If he wants to get here on his own, then let him. As long as he pays his board and lodgings, he can turn up on a bloody flying machine for all I care.'

Ma never said 'bugger him' or 'bloody' anything, let alone flying machines.

Fan would have to share the sleep-out with Tom and Ned to make room for him. 'Your grandfather' wasn't here yet and already he was making them crowd up closer so they could fit him in.

'Fan, get me a knife,' Ma shouted. 'A sharp one.'

57

The kitchen smelled vaguely of fish. Fan slammed the drawer and the window rattled.

In the front room, Agnes stood on a chair in front of the window.

'They're all blunt.' Fan held the yellow handle and pointed with the blade.

'It's proper to hold the blade and offer the handle — you know that about knives,' Ma said.

'Sorry, but without Aunty Florence to remind me what's proper, I clean forgot.' Fan's voice was the sharpest thing in the room.

'Perhaps if you look at this window with that miserable face, you'll crack it open.'

'P'raps if you didn't have to look after *whatsisname* we wouldn't be in this stinking place.'

'He's your grandfather. Have some respect.' Ma took the knife and hacked at the layers of white paint that had glued the window shut.

'You can talk,' Fan said. 'So, Mother, what would you like me to call him?'

'Call him whatever you like. Call him Grandpa, Granddad, Sir. Call him Father Christmas or the Devil, for all I care.'

Ma shoved the weight of her body against the sash. The window screeched open. Flakes of white paint fell to the floor.

'Maybe if you'd said a word about him sometime in my whole entire life, I'd know what his name is.'

Fan's limbs ached from being folded up for days in the steamer. Her feet craved the scratch of sand. Maybe she'd go take a look at Fremantle. She went into the yard where Tom was sorting through timber planks that were piled up by the fence. Ned was chasing a couple of chooks the other family had left behind.

'They need names, Ned. They need to learn their names so they'll come to you.' Fan made clucking noises with her tongue. 'I know. Let's call them Mother and Grandfather.'

Ned snorted.

'Don't leave the house, young lady,' Ma shouted from inside. 'Fremantle's not a very nice town.'

'Bugger you, Ma,' Fan whispered. She shut the gate behind her so Mother and Grandfather couldn't escape.

Fan wandered past houses with washing fluttering out the front, a bakery, a butcher's, a hotel, another hotel, yet another hotel, houses with sleepy verandas. That limestone wall that encircled the gaol, the highest wall she'd ever seen. The closer she went to the dock, the more the air stank of grog and fish. Men with inked-up arms followed her with their eyes. Fremantle looked shabby, like it had just woken up from a hard night on the rum. Fan stopped outside a laundry. A Chinese man stood on the step, smoking.

'You lost?' he said.

'No,' Fan mumbled.

'You know how to get home from here?'

'Think so. Thanks, mister,' Fan said.

'You better go before your mum come looking, yes?'

Fan nodded. She traced her steps carefully back to Ellen Street and let herself in the back door.

Ma glared with her thunder-eyes. 'Your grandfather arrives tomorrow, and I've got so much to do. For once in your life, Fan, can you just be good?'

Fan left Ma to it and went back into the yard. The chooks scratched the dirt and peered at her. What did it mean, really — be good? Specially in a town with a walled gaol on the hill behind them. From the outside, its gates looked like a storybook castle, but what on earth needed a wall that big? Fan shivered at the thought of it. She cooed and clucked and chased Mother and Grandfather to the gate, threw it open and set them free onto the street.

Edwin

Birmingham, 1848

Mostly, they walked: the length and curve of the canals, the tree-lined streets of Edgbaston where every house had picture-book gardens and six windows for only one family. Edwin was surprised at her briskness. He found it hard to keep up with her. She wriggled her hand into his and it shocked him, the raw intimacy of her rough, nail-bitten fingers. With other girls, he'd never once held their hands. Sometimes Mary Ann leaned against him, her head resting in the dip between his neck and his shoulder, and he enjoyed the slight but unmistakeable weight of her body against his — her trust, he would recognise it as, much later.

After a gill or two at the Anvil, Mary Ann grew glitter-eyed, scarlet-mouthed. The more Edwin drank the more he pushed his luck: a hand on her belly, a stroke of her thigh. She always firmly put his hand back on his own knee. But outside the Anvil, or in the spidery shadows of the bridge, they kissed and let their hands read something of each other's clothed bodies. Eventually, after many minutes, she sighed and pressed her palm to his chest, easing him away, and he held himself within the boundaries of his own skin.

Mary Ann wasn't like the others. He could be sitting at the Anvil, doing vicious mimicry of fat merchants and myopic account-keepers and his excise brothers would slap him on the back and buy him more gin. But Mary Ann's silver-blue eyes stared right through his snivelling inadequacies.

'Honest to God, Edwin, I never seen anybody carry on like such a bloody lunatic,' she said one night. 'I need to find myself a new sweetheart.'

When he left her at the door of the brass founder whose house she cleaned in return for board and lodgings, she turned her cheek to him and closed her eyes. He brushed his lips to her skin, her hair. He marvelled that despite the dust and grime of Birmingham, her hair still smelled sweet, a fragrance he remembered from childhood but could not quite identify: perhaps the warmth of sunlight, the sweetness of a yellow crop.

'All these years in Birmingham and you still smell of home.' He pressed his face to her straw-gold hair.

'Don't be daft.' She slid her hand into his. 'Scrubbing floors has wore that place clean off me.'

'Your hair is so beautiful.'

'My hair!' She pretended to push him away. 'Edwin Salt, you got a lot to learn about wooing a lady.'

The next evening as they kissed goodnight, she rummaged in his jacket pocket.

'Not there.' He grabbed her hand, moved it. 'Here's more like it.'

'Don't push your luck.'

Later, when he lay clammy and sleepless in his bed, even in his imagination there were things he could not make her do. Mary Ann stirred in him a longing he hadn't felt in months. Suddenly his head ached from the noise of the Bull Ring, and his skin itched in the coal-thick air. He got up and walked along the canals, sniffing the air like an animal, thirsty for the clean smell of an open field. Instead, he found a nameless woman, compliant with gin, who knew where to put her hands.

Afterwards, he shoved her away and felt in his jacket pocket for a coin. He found one — and something else. In the foggy lamplight Edwin recognised it immediately. He paid the woman and hurried back to his room, where he wasted no time in opening Matthew Sharpe's tobacco pouch. Inside was a lock of Mary Ann's straw-gold hair, no wider than a finger, tied in the middle with twine.

★ ★ ★

They were married on a freezing November day in the small church of Saint Peter in Birmingham. Mary Ann wore a once-white, loose-fitting dress, not really a dress for weddings — or for winters — but Mrs Blunt hadn't minded giving it away. Eliza had taken in the waist, taken up the hem.

'See? Custom-made for you,' Eliza said.

'You should open your own tailor's shop,' Mary Ann said, and both women guffawed at such an absurdity.

Eliza stitched a yellow silk rose to Mary Ann's waist. 'It almost matches your hair.' Eliza pushed a strand of Mary Ann's hair away from her face. 'You look perfect.'

There was nobody at Saint Peter's when they arrived.

'It's bad luck to be early,' Mary Ann said.

'Rubbish. Stupid superstition.' Eliza said. 'Besides, I want to draw you. Goodness knows when there'll ever be another proper bride in the family.'

Eliza positioned Mary Ann in the doorway. The crisp early-morning sun made her hair shine.

'I never been drawn before,' Mary Ann said. 'How long's this going to take? It's freezing in this damned dress.'

'Serves you right for getting married in November.'

'Edwin got his first transfer. A promotion, he says. He don't want to leave me behind.'

'Of course he doesn't. Now smile, please.'

Mary Ann grimaced.

'I mean smile properly,' Eliza said.

'I'm trying to stop my teeth from chattering.'

Eliza drew big, sweeping charcoal strokes over the paper. Mary Ann shuffled and sighed, but didn't complain again.

'Here you go. See, I missed my calling.' Eliza gave Mary Ann the picture. 'Call it a wedding present.'

Mary Ann smiled at the sight of herself as a bride, a long train tangling with her hair. In the picture, her husband stood by her in a smart suit with his arm around her waist.

'You got Edwin perfect, and he's not even here.'

'He's always the same,' Eliza said. 'I've been looking at him all my life.'

'Thanks for standing up with me,' Mary Ann said. 'I got nobody else.'

'You're not on your own.' Eliza touched Mary Ann's hand. 'Do you know what to expect, you know . . . tonight?'

'I been in Birmingham for a long time.' Mary Ann coloured. 'It pays to know enough to keep out of trouble.'

* * *

64

Edwin could see the fine hair on Mary Ann's bare forearms bristle with cold. She looked ghost-like: white, shimmery, the sunlight bouncing off her dress. He wanted to get the wedding part over and take her to his room. He wanted to touch her bare shoulders, scoop his hands into the absence of flesh that was the curve from her ribs to her hips.

On Edwin's side of the church: Da in his best suit, Mum in her good hat, Mary eyeing off Edwin's old friend William Neville, the dozen or so excise men who came to cheer him along. His two brothers were at the front, standing up with him. Sam Junior, James and Edwin, the three Salt boys, identical brown eyes, identical brown hair. Small, medium and large. 'Cut from the same cloth,' Da trotted out his tired old joke, and everyone except Edwin smiled.

On Mary Ann's side: Mr Blunt, the brass founder, and Mrs Blunt.

The minister nodded. Mary Ann held her head high and began her long walk into the sea of his witnesses.

★ ★ ★

In his bed that night, she cried, but not with fear. She opened herself eagerly to Edwin and afterwards he watched her as she slept. Her lips were plump and blood-red from all the kissing. He stroked her breast and she quivered, her eyes still shut while the feeling awoke her. He took another swig from the gin bottle and buried his face in her beautiful hair. She moved her hand underneath him. His last thought before the tide of feeling overtook them both: *You are my wish.*

Agnes

East Perth, 1875

The curtains were pulled across the window.

'Too much sun.' Mrs Molloy dabbed a wet cloth on Mam's face. 'We found her down the yard, asleep near the vegetable patch.'

'For the love of God, Cath, wake up.' Da laid another wet cloth on Mam's hair.

Agnes squeezed Mam's hand, but Mam didn't squeeze back. Instead, she groaned. Her head lolled over the side of the bed and she vomited.

'We've got to get her cooled down.' Mrs Molloy grabbed a bucket. 'Where's the tub?'

'She can hardly sit up in it, it's too small,' Da said.

'The river, then.'

'For God's sake, woman, it's too far.'

Mam groaned again.

'Wake up, Mam, wake up,' Agnes pleaded, but Mam wouldn't open her eyes.

'Wake up, Mam.' Walter's face was deathly white. He gripped Agnes's hand.

Da lifted Mam up and she flopped like a ragdoll.

'Agnes, stay here with Walter and the infant,' Mrs Molloy said. 'We'll look after your mam.'

The baby wailed. Agnes picked her up. She smelled of milk and it comforted Agnes. Walter cuddled up next to her and she put her other arm around him.

Agnes prayed. She prayed to God, she prayed to the river that might be alive, she prayed to Mick

66

McCarthy's woman, Rosie. She held tight to Walter and Baby Cath and prayed to anyone who might know how to fix such a terrible thing.

★ ★ ★

It was dark when Mam and Da came home. Mrs Molloy wasn't with them. Walter was asleep next to Agnes. She'd put Baby Cath to sleep in the little wooden cot. Agnes was rigid with wakefulness.

Mam seemed to loop her thin arms around Da's neck. Her hair was matted. Da carried her to the bed and laid her down. He opened his mouth to speak but no words came out.

'Mam?' Agnes whispered. She looked like she was asleep.

Da's face was all shadows and hollows and there was a blackness in his eyes. Agnes didn't know a name for a look like that.

'Mam?' Agnes spoke louder. Walter woke up and began to tremble. Da shook his head. In the wooden cot, Baby Cath wailed. Agnes waited for Da to do something.

Da buckled in the middle. He lay down next to Mam and lifted her arm over him. The baby's crying grew harsher and deeper and louder until Agnes realised this new noise was coming out of Da.

Agnes grabbed Walter's hand and they waited.

★ ★ ★

Da got up and mumbled something about 'the arrangements'. He said he'd fetch Mrs Molloy who had offered to help with 'all of that'. He slurred his words like he did when he'd been at the Western.

Agnes curled herself up next to Mam just like Da had done. She pulled her knees up to her chest and held Mam's hand and pretended she could feel Mam's body rattling with snores as it sometimes did when she slept. The blanket was damp and the smell of the river was everywhere. Agnes shut her eyes and sank deep under it, deep enough to reach the place where Mam laughed and sang and called Agnes 'love'. She watched Mam brush her hair and talk about something called snow that dropped from the sky in winter and was so cold it could make your toes drop off. She felt Mam kiss her goodnight.

'Come back,' Agnes said, in case Mam was only sleeping, after all.

Da said Mam's blood had boiled over because she'd fallen asleep down the yard and nobody knew. If Agnes hadn't stayed in that water so long . . .

Agnes held Mam's hand tighter. It was limp and cold. She curled up as close as she could to her mother's body. Come back. Come back. Come back.

★ ★ ★

Something inside Da unhinged. Most nights, Smith brought him back from the Western full of grog and muttering terrible blasphemy and things that didn't make sense, like 'Is this your doing, Mary Ann?'

Walter ran around the yard calling for Mam. Agnes tried to tell him Mam had died. Dead like the roos Molloy shot, dead like the snake Da killed last week, dead like leaves that fall off trees. But none of these kinds of dead explained it well enough for Walter. He bawled and pummelled his little fists into the ground.

Da couldn't stand to hear Mrs Molloy use the infant's name. 'Baby Cath needs a bath. Baby Cath won't settle.' It sent Da into a rage.

'Go home and look after your own husband, or did his real wife finally arrive from England?' he shouted. The baby cried all the time, no matter what Agnes did. It was like she cried for all of them. Agnes took to sleeping with the poor little thing next to her. Cath settled easily next to her sister, and everyone slept better.

One morning a letter came for Da. It was sealed with red wax. For the first time since Mam died, Da smiled.

'Agnes, Walter, get dressed and bring the infant.' Da put his good hat on. 'It's to be done today.'

They made a motley procession. Mrs Molloy carried Baby Cath. Walter wandered ahead and complained it was too hot to be out. Da walked ahead of them.

Agnes wondered if Da wanted them all to go to church, to say some prayers for Mam. But he walked past the church and up to the small door that led to the convent. The sound of children's chatter wafted over the walls. Da took off his hat and knocked. A nun with a pale face and stark blue eyes opened the door. Da handed her the letter he'd received this morning.

'The governor has been very understanding about the terrible situation I find myself burdened with since the death of my wife.' Da spoke in the starched-up voice he kept for best.

'Oh, yes. Such a tragedy.' The nun took Da's hand.

'I do not have the means to provide for all my children.'

'We would be pleased to take her in.' The nun

69

turned to Agnes and smiled. 'Most of our girls eventually find positions in service here or in the country.'

The sun blasted the convent's shadeless entrance. Baby Cath mewled.

'I am Sister Joseph. What's your name?' The nun's voice lilted like Mam's.

'Agnes.'

'Like the saint,' the nun smiled. 'Your mam must have loved you a great deal to give you such a beautiful name.'

Agnes blinked hard to stop herself from crying. The nun wiped a tear from under Agnes's eye with her finger.

'And the infant? What's your sister's name?'

'Catherine. We call her Cath. After my mam.'

'Another lovely saintly name. Are you ready, Agnes?'

'What for?' Agnes turned to Da again.

'Will you give little Catherine to the Sisters of Mercy so the good Lord himself can take care of her?'

'Da?' Agnes said dumbly.

'Thank you, Sister,' Mrs Molloy whispered.

It happened like a dream. The nun's fingernails scratched Agnes's arm as she took Baby Cath away from Mrs Molloy. Agnes tried to kiss her sister's milk-smelling head, but she was gone — there was nothing but air. Agnes waited for Da to take Baby Cath back from the nun and explain it was all a silly mistake, that Mam would never have wanted this, that orphanages were for orphans. She and Walter and Baby Cath weren't orphans. They still had Da.

But Da was already halfway down the road towards home.

★ ★ ★

70

If Da had done a long day at Henry Wood's, it was best to keep out of his way. If Da wasn't back from the Western by sundown, it was best to keep out of his way. If Da came back with Mick McCarthy and a bottle of rum, it was best to keep out of his way.

Agnes helped Mrs Molloy with what she could of the women's work, but Walter seemed to do nothing except make Da angry. He cried and shouted in the middle of the night. He kicked Da in the shins when Da came back from the Western. Walter got a belting, more often than not, even if he was quiet.

Da barely spoke more than a grunt to anyone. But oh, his voice at night. Low, guttural howling worse than a dying animal. The first time, Agnes was terrified Da was being attacked by a snake, or a black. When the wails subsided, she tiptoed to Da's bed and whispered, 'Da? What's wrong?' But he didn't seem to hear her. His eyes were closed, and Agnes realised he was asleep.

Even though she'd been ignored by God before, Agnes found herself praying again. She prayed something good would happen. Prayed no more bad things would happen. Prayed that Da wouldn't get up one morning, put on his good hat and give her and Walter away to the nuns.

Agnes wasn't sure if it was good or bad, but something did happen after all the praying: a letter from England arrived. Agnes put the letter on the table with Da's rum. She looked under the bed for that old tin where she knew Da kept his other letters and things, and put the tin next to the rum. She waited and waited, but by sundown, Da still hadn't come home, so she left the tin and the letter and the rum on the table and went to bed.

Next morning, she woke in shock. It took her a moment to realise it was Da, shaking her awake.

'Da, what are you doing?'

'Get up.' She stumbled out of bed, half-asleep, and he shoved her into the kitchen. The rum bottle was almost empty and there were some letters scattered on the table.

'What do you think you're doing with my possessions?' He picked up the metal tin. His voice was deadly quiet.

'I know where you keep it, Da. I just put it on the table for you. I didn't do anything with it.' Agnes started to cry.

He pulled her hair. Agnes felt sick from the smell of rum.

'Don't you ever go near this again. You hear me?'

'I promise, I promise.'

He let go and Agnes felt like she was on fire. She ran from the house and down the track towards the river. Ran and ran and ran.

The sheltered wedge of riverbank was almost deserted except for a couple of black children and they waved to her. Agnes waded in and slid under the water. She swam out to the edge of the cove. It was cool and still. The water took her in. Mam's laughter like bells. Mam's shiny face, smiling. The wiry certainty of Mam's arms. Agnes sank into Mam's absence like it was water so deep she'd never touch the bottom. It was Mam and Agnes together again on one of their river days and Da somewhere else, his mouth all slack and wide with his shouting, but too far away to be heard.

Brown jellyfish brushed past and suddenly it was Mam with matted hair, Mam slung over Da's shoulder,

72

Mam who wouldn't wake up. Mam's beautiful black eyes, opaque and expressionless. In the river, Mam was so close, and yet so completely gone.

Agnes climbed out of the water and started to run. One of the black girls called out to her but she didn't turn around. The river poured from her eyes. At home she sneaked into the washhouse and filled the tub with as much water as she dared. She scrubbed until her skin was red and she could smell only soap. Afterwards she took her sodden clothes outside and shoved them underneath the pile of rubbish for burning.

The scratching sounded like a possum or a rat. The lamp was still on. Maybe Da had fallen asleep in the chair again. Agnes got up to investigate. The metal tin was on the table and Da was writing on letter paper. Writing and talking to himself. Or maybe he was talking to the person he was writing to. Who was it? Why did receiving and writing letters make Da carry on like he did? Plenty of people they knew got letters when the ships came in. She had seen people in the street on mail day, some hugging each other, some crying. Agnes went back to bed. So many questions. All she knew for certain was that it was better not to ask.

★ ★ ★

Mrs Molloy came in to cook, then after one of Da's shouting rages, she stopped coming. Mrs Smith came to cook and brought another woman with her, a woman called Annie who had wispy grey hair and bird-like eyes. Mrs Smith stopped coming but the bird-eyed woman continued to visit. Annie was there when Agnes and Walter went to bed and sometimes she was still there, fussing in the kitchen, in the morning. When Annie was around, Da's rages stayed away. Da let Annie rub his horrible feet with eucalypt ointment. What a sight it was. Annie winked at Agnes. Annie didn't seem bothered by those lumps around Da's ankles. In fact, it was as if she expected all ankles to have lumps like that. Annie knitted socks for Walter and mended the holes in Agnes's clothes.

'Why don't you give me a hand with the mending?' Annie asked one evening.

'Edwin Salt and Son, tailors of the Swan River.' Da lifted up Walter's hand and examined it. Walter wriggled free.

'I meant Agnes.' Annie handed her a needle and thread. In the dim light it was almost impossible to see properly. Da took the needle from Agnes and threaded it for her, and from then on, every night Da threaded up Agnes's first needle. Annie started her off with hems, and praised her as she got the hang of it. As the months passed, Agnes repaired moth-eaten blankets and the worn knees on Walter's trousers. She took up the hem on Annie's good dress so it no longer trailed unevenly across the dirt floor. She held the finished dress under the lamp for Da to inspect. He turned the fabric over and back again and smiled.

'Well done, Agnes girl,' he said, and got back to his reading.

So much got mended that year.

★ ★ ★

Da married Annie in September 1877. After they got home, his new bride cleaned every window, swept

74

cobwebs from the ceiling and dirt from the floor. She moved things around. She saved some things and not others. She hung a pretty pink curtain over the door to stop the flies coming in on warm days. Even the copper looked like it'd been scrubbed shiny. Annie was so houseproud she must have washed Mam's dresses because they weren't where they'd always been, behind the door in the washhouse.

Agnes ran down to the back of the block to where the washing line was strung up. Perhaps Annie had already folded them up and put them somewhere special, because Mam's dresses weren't there, either.

'Where's my mam's things?' Agnes said to Annie that night.

'They were mouldy and smelly and full of holes,' Annie frowned. 'They wouldn't even do for rags.'

'You witch.'

'I'm your father's wife.' Annie slapped her hard across the face. 'Don't ever call me that again.'

'I don't care what you are,' Agnes screamed. 'You'll never be my mam.'

Agnes

Fremantle, November 1906

Agnes made them line up, eldest to youngest. She hushed them for good measure. Fan, Tom, Ned. Fan was tall and starting to fill out. Fan, whose real name, Frances, nobody ever used. Tom, eleven, named for George's father and his face beginning to lose the roundness of a child's. And Ned, eight 'and a bit' as he always pointed out, only a few milk teeth left and his eyes permanently fixed on his older brother. Ned, named for her own father at George's insistence. He'd said a proper family name gave a boy somewhere to belong. Agnes went along with it, but she vowed never to say her son's christened name out loud. He'd been Ned from the minute he'd opened his eyes.

'How long do I have to stand here?' Fan fiddled with her plait.

'Be quiet, Fan.' Agnes poked her daughter in the back of her ribs. Fan wriggled.

There was a knock. Agnes felt light-headed. She inhaled: in, two three. Out, two three. She opened the door.

The man standing on the step was much older and thinner than the father she remembered. His hand was papery when she shook it. Agnes had to blink a couple of times to be sure it was him.

'Father. Da. Welcome,' she said with false brightness. 'Come in.'

He took off his hat and tucked it under his arm.

76

Her father's face was red and shiny, and there were deep lines around his eyes and mouth. His waistcoat puckered where the buttons stretched too tight over his sagging middle.

'We would've come for you,' Agnes said.

'I am still capable of making my own way.' He moved like his feet hurt.

'These are my sons. Tom and Ned.' Agnes pushed the boys in front of her. 'Your grandsons.'

Da peered closely at Tom. 'You look like your Uncle Walter.'

Tom's cheeks reddened and Ned burst into fits of giggles.

'We've got an Uncle Walter?' Fan's eyes widened. 'Ma never said. You'll have to tell me all about him.'

'Excuse my daughter's rudeness.' Agnes glared at Fan, who grinned back.

'Hello. I'm Fan. Your granddaughter.' Fan stepped forward and extended her hand regally. 'Ma says you might be the Devil, but I think I'll call you Grandpa.'

All the colour drained from his face.

'Ma, what's happening?' Fan shouted.

Agnes caught him before he hit the floor. 'Fan, get him some water.'

★ ★ ★

Agnes and Fan helped him to his room. He tried to shove them away and stumbled heavily into the chair.

'Fan, get out,' Agnes said.

Fan didn't need to be told twice.

Agnes helped her father out of his jacket. He grumbled and resisted, but Agnes was persistent. In the end, he slackened like a ragdoll.

77

'For Christ's sake, woman. I'm not an invalid.'

'You collapsed, Da. Are you ill?' She was shocked that his suit was so big on him. His eyes were yellowed, and, without his hat, it was clear he needed a haircut. Not to mention a bath. He could be any of the men who slept outside the Jetty Hotel.

'Of course I'm not ill. Annie exaggerates, you remember how she is.' He sounded stronger but his face looked waxy and pale. 'Your daughter is the image of your mother,' Edwin said. 'It gave me a shock. Her hair. So much like Cath's.'

'Fan's hair is like the rest of her. Unruly and difficult to manage.' Agnes touched his forehead. It was still clammy.

Tom and Ned carried in an old wooden trunk and dropped it under the window.

'This was on the front step. You got much stuff in here, Grandpa?' Tom asked shyly.

'Leave your grandfather alone.' Agnes shooed the boys out.

'They seem like fine boys,' Edwin said.

'They are fine boys.'

'Tom has the look of your brother about him.'

'I wouldn't know. I haven't seen Walter for years.' The smell of stale tobacco and rum made Agnes feel queasy. She opened the window up further. 'And, before you ask, Ned is named after you, but I hope that's where the similarity ends.' Agnes pointed at the bed. 'That's where you'll be sleeping.' The breeze wafted the drape.

Edwin coughed violently. 'Will you shut the damned window?'

'You aren't well. You need fresh air.'

'Nothing fresh about the stink of that sea.' Edwin

78

tried to get up out of the chair but winced and slipped back down. Agnes tried to help him, but again he pushed her away.

'I need a rum.' Edwin wiped his forehead with his shirtsleeve. 'Would you please just get me a drink? That's all I ask.'

'A drink? Nothing's changed, then.' George always kept a bottle in the kitchen. Agnes fetched it, and a glass, and put them on the table. He scowled at her and poured one. Drank it straight down, and the colour returned to his face. He poured another.

'There'll be three meals a day. Use the washhouse whenever you like. I do the washing on Wednesdays. I'd appreciate you paying your board and lodgings on a Thursday.'

'Thank you,' he said stiffly. 'I won't bother you unless I need to.'

'Well, then. I'll leave you to settle in.'

The breeze whipped in through the window she'd gone to such trouble to open. Her father wheezed.

'If that irritates you so much,' Agnes said, 'shut it yourself.'

★ ★ ★

To the rhythms of the wharf bell and the salty wind that blew in from the ocean every afternoon, they lived their lives. George left every morning before dawn. He got shifts every day and started walking taller, making jokes again. Ned and Tom settled into the boys' school and new names peopled their conversations: Charlie, who was Italian, and Simon, who was from Fremantle, and a Chinese boy, whose proper name nobody could pronounce so everyone called him Lee.

Fan complained she was one of the oldest at the girls' school, but Agnes insisted she went, because with Grandpa's board and lodgings, Fan wouldn't need to start at the brush factory for another year.

Despite Agnes's knocks on his door every morning, her father refused to leave his room except to use the washhouse. He didn't seem to want to talk to anyone, so she instructed Fan to leave his meals by the door and collect the plates in the morning.

Agnes told herself it was the same life, a life that ran to the timetable of the wharf bell and the tides and the weather. It was more or less the same house. But there was also the lemony smell of her father's soap, the cinnamon tang of his tobacco, his wheezing and snoring and outhouse noises. At night she heard him padding about the house and sometimes in the morning there'd be a glass on the table that smelled of rum. All the signs were there, but Agnes couldn't be sure if she'd recognise him in the street, her invisible father who made the house heavy with the blank presence of himself.

'You and Grandpa never talk to each other,' Fan said, one morning before school.

'Don't be ridiculous,' Agnes said.

'It's true. Honest to God, he can't be that bad. I feel sorry for him, shut in like that day and night.'

'No need to feel sorry for him. We put a roof over his head and food on his plate. It's more than he deserves.'

'I never seen you so mean. What did he do that was so horrible?'

'Fan. Listen to me.' Agnes gripped Fan's shoulders and looked her directly in the eyes. 'He is an old man whose mind and heart are failing, and we are giving him a bed because he is my father and that is what you do. You are to focus on school or else we'll put you in service, or factory work. Do you understand?'

'Service never did you any harm.' Fan rolled her eyes.

'I want better for my daughter,' Agnes said. 'He's paying us some money and it helps.'

'All right, all right.' Fan wriggled loose from Agnes's hands. 'But you still never said what's so bad about him.'

81

Agnes

East Perth, 1886

By the time he was thirteen, Walter was already a head taller than Agnes. Annie could rest her head in his armpit and reach up and pinch his cheek, which always made Walter swear. He sprouted downy hair on his arms and a lopsided smile that showed where he'd lost a tooth so long ago that nobody, not even Walter, remembered the incident. His voice sometimes cracked into the sound of a man's, echoing Da's gruffness so perfectly that it made Annie snap at him for no reason. Walter's hair darkened and grew curlier. Da began taking Walter to Henry Wood's to teach him tailoring because a boy Walter's age should be earning his keep. In the evenings, Agnes bathed Walter's calloused hands in salt water while Walter winced in pain. Da swigged rum and unpicked his son's failings. Walter was slow, Walter was sloppy, Walter was lazy, Walter couldn't hold a needle properly.

'I'd rather take my chances with the Noongar than work for my old man,' Walter said, after a long day at Henry's.

'The who?'

'The Aborigines. They've got their own names, y'know.' Walter put a smoke to his lips and blew three heart-shaped smoke rings into the sky. 'You're a saint, Ag.'

'I'm not a saint.' Agnes snapped the thread off with her teeth and handed the finished shirt to Walter. 'You

82

should learn properly. It's not that hard.'

'Saint Agnes of the Blessed Seamstresses.'

'Shut up, Walter.'

'*Shut-up-Walter.*' He mimicked her in a high voice.

It was too hot, really, to be outside, although the back step was already in shade.

'Bloody hell, Ag, you should hear them.' Walter's eyes were shadowed. 'Him and Henry Wood going on about the promise of the new country, land, sons to carry on the name.'

'Maybe the drink's made them see visions,' Agnes said. Henry Wood had bought the only patch of East Perth scrub he could afford, too close to the tannery, but it meant his children could run as wild as they wanted. Henry always talked business up, but many times Da complained about late wages or no wages at all, and Mrs Wood had gone back into service for a solicitor whose name graced a new Perth road.

'You should do what he wants, stay in his good books.' Agnes started on another shirt.

'I don't care about being in his good books. Soon as I can, I'm off up north. Or east. Or to the moon. Anywhere.' Walter spat out what was left of the smoke. 'Look at Da, McCarthy, Mad Molloy or even Smith. Stay in this place too long and it makes a man rotten. You can see it in their eyes.'

Agnes folded up the shirts. 'Put them back so he'll think you've done them.'

'Thanks, Ag. I could nail 'em to the door and he wouldn't notice, he'll be so full of grog when he gets home.'

'Don't thank me. How about giving me half your wages?'

'Now you're imagining things,' Walter said. 'Ask

83

Annie for half her wages — it's you that does all the cooking and cleaning.'

'You know what she's like with me.'

'You dunno how to handle her, Ag, that's all. She's bone-tired. She works day and night cleaning up after lunatics and then has to come home to the old man. You'd be grumpy too.' Walter ran his fingers around one of the collars. 'Perfect work, sis, as usual. You're a saint. I mean it.'

★ ★ ★

The shouting jolted Agnes awake. She got up and followed the noise through the back door into the yard.

In the moonlight, the white shirts she'd finished for Walter had been strewn on the ground. They looked like ghosts. Someone had torn the sleeves out of the shoulders. The collars had been ripped clean off and tossed near the chook run.

'Go back inside, Agnes.' Da slurred his words.

'What are you, one of Annie's lunatics?' Walter said. 'Edwin Salt and Son? There is no family business, Da, and there never will be. The only family you keep in business is the one who owns the bloody Western Hotel.'

'Your brother thinks I am easily fooled.' The muscles in Da's face twitched. 'I suppose you thought it a good idea to do his work for him.'

'What difference does it make who does the work as long as it gets done?' Agnes's mouth was gluey with nerves. 'It's not Walter's fault he's no good with a needle and thread.'

'Stay out of it, Ag,' Walter said, his face twisted with contempt. 'If it weren't for Annie we'd starve half the

84

time. What kind of man lets his woman do the earning?'

Da swung his fist and hit Walter's jaw. Walter howled and put his hand to his face.

'Stop!' Agnes shoved past Da and put her arm around Walter. She thought her knees would give way, she was so scared.

Da's flat hand cut through the air and stopped dead, inches from her face. The cold air he had disturbed made her shiver.

'For God's sake, Edwin.' Annie stood behind them. Her voice was shaking. 'Leave your good-for-nothing children alone and get me a rum. I've just done twelve hours straight and we lost a poor young girl tonight.'

Da threw the dismembered sleeves and collars at Walter. 'Finish those shirts by morning.'

'Bastard,' Walter said after Da had gone. His bottom lip was fat and bleeding.

'Don't worry,' Agnes said. 'I'll finish the damn shirts.'

Walter winced and touched his face. Agnes gave him a big hug, just like she used to when he was little. After a while, he rested his head on her shoulder.

★ ★ ★

Walter stopped going to Henry Wood's. He stopped coming home before nightfall and some nights he didn't come home at all. If Walter came home smelling of fire smoke, his pale arms dotted with mosquito bites, he'd been down at the river with the blacks. If Walter came home blotchy-faced and unsteady on his feet, he'd been sneaking into the Western. Da crowed that Henry Wood was taking in more work than he had in years. Things were picking up. Da left shirt collars, sometimes a waistcoat, for Walter to finish. Agnes always did the work, even if it took her most of the night. In the morning Da picked them up without a word.

Walter said sneaking into the Western Hotel had taught him a thing or two about what kind of man Da made clothes for.

'You'd be surprised who drinks in the Western,' Walter said. 'You'd be surprised what they'll tell you about your old man, when they're so full of grog they don't know their arse from their elbow.'

Fan

Fremantle, November 1906

This time Fan waited until he opened the door.

'I got tired of leaving food for you like you're a stray dog.' Fan marched in before he could protest. She put the bowl on the table next to a bottle of tea-coloured liquid. His room smelled of the same malty sweetness outside the Commercial Hotel on High Street. That and stale tobacco. 'It smells funny in here. You want me to open the window?'

'Certainly not. Nothing worse than the smell of the sea.'

'I love the sea. Reckon I was born in it.' Fan pointed at the bowl. 'Good luck. It's Ma's horrible soup.'

'How does your mother make that? Is it the fruit of the horrible tree?'

'Yes. It's from the horrible bush in the yard. It's a speciality of hers.' He squinted at her like he'd forgotten her name.

'Why don't you and Ma talk to each other?' Fan asked.

Grandpa opened the bottle and poured some of its contents into a glass.

'Is that whisky?' Fan asked.

'Rum.'

'Ma said you came to Western Australia to seek your fortune. My Uncle Ernest did that, sort of. He's not really my uncle, though. He's some other thing.'

Grandpa drank and poured himself another.

87

'Who's my Uncle Walter and why doesn't Ma talk about him like she don't talk about you?'

'You ask a lot of questions.'

'I want to know a lot of things.' Fan looked through the books he'd put on the mantelpiece. 'So, did you find your fortune?'

Grandpa's big, meaty laugh was almost too big for the room and made Fan want to open the window again.

'What's so funny?'

'Nothing.' Grandpa wiped his eyes. 'Shall we say, I await the discovery of my fortune with much hope.'

'D'you mind if I wait while you eat?'

'Suit yourself.' Grandpa gestured to the other chair.

Fan had never seen anyone eat like this, shovelling it in like he'd been hungry for a month. She looked around the room. He'd made himself at home. A couple of waistcoats lay on the bed and that mouldy old trunk was open.

'How do you like Fremantle?' Fan said. 'Not that you seen it much. You're always in here.'

'I've seen enough to know I loathe it. How do you like it?'

'I miss home,' Fan sighed. Saying it out loud made it real. 'My dad reckons anywhere can be home, but I dunno about that.'

'I think it's perfectly acceptable to miss home. I miss my home too, sometimes.'

'Where's your home, Grandpa?'

'On the other side of the world.'

'Really? My dad told me you came from Victoria Park.'

'So, Miss Johnson, we are both living away from home against our will. We are both living in exile.'

88

'No, we're living in Ellen Street.'

Grandpa's face lit right up. 'You are quite a wit, Miss Johnson.'

'You talk funny.' Fan had never heard anybody talk like him. His talking was nearly as old-fashioned as his clothes. 'And you got a lot of books.' Fan picked one up and thumbed through it. 'I don't like reading. I'd rather be in the water.'

'Why ever don't you like reading?' Grandpa wiped bread around the soup bowl. 'A bright girl like you.'

'Won't be much call for reading when I'm doing shifts at the brush factory next year.'

'Perhaps you just never found a story you liked well enough.'

'I bet you know some stories, Grandpa.'

'I do indeed.'

'Ma says I shouldn't bother you on account of your failing health.' Fan picked up the soup bowl. He'd wiped it so clean she could see the cracks on the bottom.

'As you wish.' Grandpa dabbed his mouth with a handkerchief. 'Your mother wasn't much for reading, either. You must get your love of the water from her.'

'What?' Fan stared at him. Maybe he wasn't right in the head after all. 'She hates the water. Mam won't even get her feet wet at Semaphore.'

'When she was little, it was like your mother was born for water, not the earth.'

'I don't believe you.'

'Ask her, Miss Johnson. And as for your Uncle Walter — well, he used to talk to blacks. He lived with them sometimes when they camped at the bottom of our yard.'

'Lived with Aborigines?' Fan's eyes widened. 'In

89

your yard?'

Grandpa leaned closer and whispered, 'Any time you want to hear a good story, Miss Johnson, you come and see me.'

★ ★ ★

It might have been the warm, airless day or the low-level buzz of schoolgirl whispers, but Fan couldn't concentrate on the important dates of history. The windows were open and she could smell the salt and fish and hear the seagulls. A port is a port, Dad always said, but she longed for the familiar sights and smells of Semaphore. She drummed her fingers on the desk. The redheaded girl sitting next to her glared.

'Sorry.' Fan began to copy the important words dutifully into her notebook. Napoleon. Waterloo. The Bore War, she wrote and smirked.

The schoolmistress droned on. Fan drew a picture of herself: tall and gangly with a braid of scribbly hair topped with one of Florence's flowery hats. Then Ma, her stick-arms bent, hands on her hips. Dad with a flat cap and a pipe. Then Tom and Ned, and finally a big circle around Uncle Ernest, Aunty Florence, their two children, and Sarah.

On the next page she drew a stick figure in a chair and labelled it *Grandpa*. Next to him another figure for Uncle Walter.

They'd barely been in Fremantle for a month and suddenly her life was crowded with strangers she was related to. If there was Grandpa and Ma and Uncle Walter, then where was Ma's mother? Funny how Ma had never, ever mentioned her. Fan drew another stick figure wearing a long dress.

90

On a page by itself she wrote what Grandpa had said about Ma, and underlined it: *Born for water, not the earth.*

Agnes

East Perth, 1886

Nobody ever knocked. But somebody was knocking.

'Maybe it's Mad Molloy coming for Da with his rifle,' Walter said.

'Mad Molloy wouldn't be so polite.' Annie got up to answer the door. They heard a man's voice, musical, rich. The thud of a bag. Annie spoke in the pained tone she used with strangers.

When Annie came back, her face was strained with shock. 'Edwin, dear. There is a man at the door who says he is your nephew from England.'

'Jesus.' Da stood up so fast he almost fell over. 'Jesus Christ.'

'No, father, although the Almighty would have his work cut out for him here,' Walter said. 'It's a relative from England.'

Annie forced a smile. 'I'll leave you to deal with him, shall I? I've got an early shift tomorrow. I'm going to bed.'

Da went to the door. From the muffled voices and Da's overblown cheeriness, Agnes could tell her father was nervous. After a while the two men emerged.

'Ernest, these are my children, Agnes and Walter.' Da waved his hand through the air as if he were a magician showing a trick. 'My dear children, Ernest is your cousin from England. He appears to have turned up before the letter announcing his arrival.'

At the sound of 'dear children', Walter coughed.

Agnes raised her eyebrows at him.

'I've told him he is welcome to stay for a couple of nights, sleep on the veranda. Then he'll be off,' Da said.

'Off where?' Agnes blurted. She couldn't stop looking at Ernest. He was taller than Da, with pale blue eyes and dark brown hair cut army-short.

'Don't know yet,' Ernest grinned. 'You hear about opportunities. Gold. Land. Work. After the army it'll be paradise.'

'If you're looking for paradise, you're in the wrong place.' Walter tipped his imaginary hat at Ernest. 'Good evening, cousin. Welcome to the land of tanneries, sawmills and slaughterhouses.' Walter smiled beatifically at Da. 'And delightful local villagers.'

'Pleased to meet you.' Ernest shook Walter's hand vigorously, then turned to Agnes, lifted her hand to his lips and kissed it. Her cheeks flamed.

'Hello, Cousin Agnes. Delighted to make your acquaintance.' He smiled again. Agnes had never seen a man smile so much and he'd only been here a minute.

Da poured himself a rum. He didn't offer Ernest one. Ernest took off his jacket and sat down. Da didn't take his eyes off him.

Ernest looked younger than his twenty-one years and more innocent than his army service must have left him. His face was pale like a child's, but his hands were strong and sun-browned. When he smiled, Agnes's cheeks flushed pink under the force of his gaze. He explained he was the son of her father's brother, Samuel — 'Sam Salt Junior,' he said — so Da was his uncle. Ernest rattled off names of places in India and the subcontinent that didn't even sound like real words to Agnes. There didn't seem a place in

93

the world Ernest hadn't been.

'So, tell me about your world, my antipodean cousin.'

'I don't have one.' Agnes twisted the corner of her dress into knots so he wouldn't see her shaking with nerves. 'I've never been anywhere.'

'I bet your life here is much more interesting than my dull army existence,' Ernest said. 'Go on. I dare you.'

It didn't sound like much of a world when she said it out loud. The stink of the slaughter yards that was always worse on a breezeless day. The summer so hot and dry she had to carry buckets of water down to the vegetable plot twice a day to keep their food from wilting. The rain that could come down in spring hard enough to knock trees over and bring the river out of the ground. Ernest leaned forward and paid attention like she was the Queen of England. Agnes wanted to poke him in the ribs to see if he flinched, to check if he was real.

Da had begun to nod off.

'What about our family? Da never talks about them.' She shifted closer. 'He sometimes gets letters, but he never says who they're from.'

'Oh, goodness, there are dozens of us!' Ernest said. 'My Hannah, of course; my mother Sarah, my brothers, and a host of aunties and —'

'I warn you, don't go filling her head with stories, Ernest.' Da yawned and shook his head to rouse himself. 'Not much use for family here in the colony.'

Ernest nodded slowly at Edwin. 'Of course, uncle.' He moved closer to Agnes. 'Nothing much to tell. All very dull. So, what about your family? You've got one too, you know.'

'Well, you've met my Da.' Agnes turned around. Da had fallen asleep again. Ernest winked and put his finger over his lips.

'Then there's Annie.' Agnes lowered her voice. 'Da married her after our mam died. It's best not to get on the wrong side of her. And Walter, my brother. I worry about him.'

Ernest yawned, then apologised.

'You must be sleepy after a long day.' Agnes stared into her mug of tea. 'I'm not.'

'Unlike your father.' Ernest pointed at Da, snoring in the chair. 'He looks like a sack of flour.' Agnes giggled.

'Watch this.' Ernest tiptoed towards Da's chair. Agnes shook her head and gestured furiously. Ernest stood behind Da, pulled a bug-eyed face and pretended to stick his fingers in Da's ears. Tears of mirth streamed from Agnes's eyes. It was no good. She ran out the back into the dark.

'What's all this merriment, young Agnes?' a stern voice hissed.

'Oh, Jesus,' she said, expecting Da with the strap in one hand and a face like thunder. But it was Ernest, his pale blue eyes almost ghostly in the night, laughing with her.

★ ★ ★

The following day, in bright sunshine, Agnes showed Ernest the uneven fence that had been there ever since anyone could remember. It was old now, and mended in places with wire and wood and piles of stones. Fixing that fence was the only work Da ever did on the property. While everything else rotted and

95

faded and sprang loose, Da checked that fence once a week, rain or shine.

She pointed up to the tall trees that Walter said were hundreds of years old and showed him where the magpies made their nests every year. They peered into the well that was famous among the Molloys and the Smiths for never running dry. She took him to the spot where the Aborigines used to live, under the river gums on the edge of what used to be the river. She poked a stick into the ashes of a long-dead fire and sent tiny lizards scattering. The same group used to stay here all the time, she told him, but nobody, not even Walter, had seen them for a couple of years.

'Maybe they come and go like the swallows,' Ernest said.

'No.' Agnes pointed in the direction of a tin roof glinting through trees. 'It's because they're smart enough to keep away from Mad Molloy and his gun.'

'It's beautiful here, Agnes. You must love it.'

'I'd rather live in one of those fancy houses on the Terrace.'

'Rubbish,' Ernest said, smiling again. 'You have your own palace and grounds right here.'

She showed him where Mam had died. It seemed such a short distance to the house. The sun blazed overhead. She told him how Mam sat down and went to sleep and died of too much sun. How Da and Mrs Molloy found her. How Agnes had been swimming in the river for what felt like hours and didn't know how ill Mam was until it was too late.

'I don't know if Walter remembers.' Agnes's chest felt heavy. She didn't want to cry in front of Ernest. 'Walter never says anything. Da never talks about her. Sometimes I wonder if I made her up.'

'I lost my father a couple of years ago. My mother sits in our house back home and says nothing, goes nowhere. That's why I wanted to leave, see the world, make my fortune. I didn't want to feel like I'd died before I'd lived.'

'I didn't know about your father. Da never talks about brothers or sisters or anything about England.'

'Maybe forgetting is easier on the heart.'

'I'm not sure he's got a heart,' Agnes said, attempting a smile.

'So, we're both orphans. Sort of.' Ernest patted her hand. 'We'd better stick together, cousin.'

The crickets sang. The sun flared white above Mad Molloy's roof. Nobody called her cousin or looked her in the eye or touched her hand. Nobody stood behind Da and pulled faces. Agnes never lived in a palace or said Jesus or talked about Mam. Not until now. Not until Ernest.

★ ★ ★

When the sun had set completely and Da still wasn't home, Agnes asked Ernest to write down the names of their English family.

'I don't know, Agnes,' Ernest said. 'You've got to promise not to tell your father, all right?'

'Of course, Ernest, of course.'

'Don't worry about the old man,' Walter said. 'In a week's time he won't even remember you were here.'

'I want to know,' Agnes said. She put a pencil and paper in front of him.

'Very well.' Ernest started drawing. 'Our family is from Lichfield, in the middle of England. Our grandfather Samuel was a tailor, the old-fashioned kind.

Our grandmother — well, nobody talks much about her. She died years ago. Samuel married again.'

'So, where's our Da?' Agnes pulled her chair up so close she could smell his apple-scented hair oil.

'Probably at the Western.' Walter blew a curl of smoke into the air.

Ernest drew a circle around Samuel, then three lines coming from its centre. 'Your father's the eldest, then James, then my father, Sam Junior.'

'Draw them,' Agnes said.

Ernest drew three circles. 'Large, medium, small,' he joked.

'You missed something.' Walter leaned over Ernest's shoulder and took the pencil. 'D'you mind?'

Walter drew two enormous ears on the biggest circle. He'd captured the round shape of Da's ears perfectly.

'My father was called Sam Junior after his father, but he was no tailor. He was all thumbs.'

'Runs in the family,' Walter said, holding up his own thumbs.

'No daughters?' Agnes said.

'On the contrary. Our family is full of useless daughters.'

Agnes punched him in the arm.

'This' — Ernest drew a figure so shapely that Agnes blushed — 'this is your Aunty Eliza.'

Dear Eliza. 'I've heard that name before.' A memory stirred in Agnes. 'I think she used to write to Da.'

'There haven't been letters from England in years,' Walter said.

'You'd have liked her. By all accounts she was a fiery sort. The best tailor of all of them, but she was a girl.' He drew a sad face on Eliza. 'It's said she spent her Sundays trudging around the Birmingham canals trying to save women of ill repute.' Ernest lowered his voice. 'Word was her own reputation wasn't the purest.'

'A scandal?' Walter asked. 'Now I'm interested.'

'Eliza's charms were as ample as her generosity to certain gentlemen. Or so said the priest who buried her.'

'Certain gentlemen?' Agnes's eyes widened.

'There may have been a child,' Ernest whispered behind his hand. 'Eliza may have lived with a man without being married.'

Walter let out a long, slow whistle.

'And let me introduce you to your father's other sister: your Aunty Mary.' Ernest drew another line. 'Mary had to get married.' Ernest mimed a big curve around his belly. Agnes blushed.

'Mary's baby and her husband both died.'

'Poor Aunty Mary,' Agnes said.

'Some said it was punishment. For —' Ernest mimed his pregnant middle again.

'Sounds more like dreadful luck,' Agnes said.

'What do they say about our esteemed father, back in Lichfield?' Walter asked.

'My mother and father told me he went to the colonies to seek his fortune,' Ernest said. 'A good enough story on its own, don't you think?'

Ernest's little piece was so neatly drawn. Grandfather Samuel, the tailor. Da, James and Sam Junior in three fat circles: large, medium, small. Luckless Mary dressed in black, shapely Eliza with her ample charms. Their names written in neat little oblongs. Like coffins, Agnes thought.

'You tell a good story. Not sure I believe it, though.'

Walter finished his smoke and began rifling through the pockets of Da's old jacket.

'Jesus, Walter, you know Da never leaves tobacco behind,' Agnes said. 'Ernest, do they know about Walter and me, in Lichfield?'

'Why don't you introduce them to the antipodean branch of the family?' Ernest drew a line out from Da and handed Agnes the pencil. His fingers lightly brushed her hand.

Agnes wrote carefully and slowly: C A T H. She trapped Mam and Da in a big square of land and separated it from the rest of the page with a stick fence. Then she drew two lines radiating into the blankness: Agnes and Walter. She imagined a third line growing through the uncharted page, curling around the whole family, protecting them from too much sun and the long fingers of a nun.

Agnes gave the pencil back to Ernest. 'There you go. The family of the brother who went to the colonies to seek his fortune.'

'You've got such a lost look about you, poor little bird.' Ernest rested his hand over hers. 'Now you know where you fit.'

'D'you think they'd like me?' Agnes felt dizzy from the hand-holding.

Ernest scribbled half a dozen more circles and more names-in-coffins. 'At grandfather Samuel's funeral, my mother told me Saint Mary's was full to the gunnels. Brothers, sisters, aunties, uncles, rows and rows of cousins just like you and me, and all those screaming brats that our grandfather's second wife kept popping out every year like Christmas puddings.' Ernest drew an enormous circle around the entire family. 'The point is, all those people in the church that day were

100

your people, Agnes. Every single one.'

Agnes stared at Ernest's drawing. So many names, she could hardly take it in.

'Thank you,' she said. She rested her hand on his. Ernest gave her a kind look.

'Of course, there'll be another branch of the family here one day.' Ernest looked her right in the eye again. He drew a big heart around his own name with space for another right next to his.

'What do you mean?' Agnes's mouth was so dry she could barely get a sound out.

'Hannah and me.'

'Hannah?' Agnes was confused. Wasn't she one of the sisters, or an aunty, or a third cousin twice removed?

'Hannah is my wife, Agnes.'

'Oh.' Agnes stared at the drawing, the scattered confetti of names.

'She got the soonest passage out after I took up my last posting. She's due here in February, depending on the tides and the prevailing winds.' Ernest wrote Hannah's name inside the heart next to his. 'You'll like her. She's so lovely. Auburn hair and green eyes.'

Ernest made a curly flourish on the bottom part of the H of Hannah's name and trailed it along the paper like the train on a fancy wedding dress.

Agnes tried not to think about Hannah or February or prevailing winds. It was only October and there was no breeze coming through the open doorway.

★ ★ ★

Work was easy to find for a carpenter with determination and a wife on the way. Every day Agnes expected

101

to come home and find Ernest's swag gone from the front veranda, but Ernest's two-night stay stretched into a week, two weeks, a month, and Da didn't say anything about it.

'Your cousin has made a deal with the Devil.' Walter rolled a wad of tobacco into a tight little ball and threw it across the yard. 'Cheaper to stay here.'

Ernest charmed Annie with flattery and saucy stories he said he'd heard in the army. He sat on the back porch and smoked tobacco with Walter. Soon it felt to Agnes that Ernest had always lived with them. Da must have been happy about Ernest staying on and paying board and lodgings because he started buying more expensive rum. He bought himself a new pair of boots. He even bought new hats for Annie and Agnes. The only one who got nothing new was Walter, but Walter said he wanted nothing from the old man, anyway.

Hannah would like the trees. Hannah would find the hot nights difficult. Hannah would be able to persuade Mad Molloy to put his rifle away. Ernest wrote on a piece of paper the number of days until the *Kapunda* was due to arrive in Fremantle and every evening he crossed a day off, grinning, as if he was glad to see the back of it.

Edwin

Gloucestershire, September 1849

From early autumn in Lydney, Gloucestershire, the midwife's cottage disappeared into the long shadows of the Forest of Dean and could not be seen from the road. Edwin found it eventually and bashed on the door.

Elizabeth Dalton had packed her father's old leather bag with small bottles, boiled rags and some instrument in the use of which old Dr Dalton had instructed his spinster daughter before his death five years ago. Her face was all angles and red, broken veins, and her hands were cold, or so the wife of Edwin's supervisor had told him, but he would have to trust this woman to guide the baby from Mary Ann's hard and swollen body.

Hours later, Elizabeth Dalton emerged from behind the closed door and handed Edwin a bottle.

'This will help her sleep. Give her as much as she wants.'

'What is it? Gin? I've plenty of that.'

'A tincture.' Sarah wagged her finger at him. 'It weren't easy for Mary Ann or the poor child. Keep yourself away from her for a good three months.'

★ ★ ★

Edwin tickled his boy's arm and the baby sleepily grabbed at Edwin's finger. His son's fingers were long,

103

already an old man's. Tailor's fingers. The baby's face rippled, and Edwin saw his own mother's firm mouth, Eliza's wide smile, Da's squat nose.

Cut from the same cloth.

We have a son. We named him Albert, after the prince, he wrote to Eliza, and the lamplight flickered like applause.

At night Edwin kissed his wife gently, chastely.

'Not yet,' she whispered. 'I'm still not right.'

'It's been so long, my mistress. You're tired, that's all. Our boy keeps you awake.'

'Albert sleeps all the time. It's me, master. I'm not right.'

He nestled his chin into the curve of her neck, his desire blunted by the cotton of her nightdress.

One night, stumbling in late from drinking with his excise brothers, he tickled her waist. Pinched her hard breasts. She tried to roll over. His hand clamped around her wrist. His other hand tugged her under-clothes.

'Be my wife, Mary Ann.' His urgent, malty mouth. 'I promise I won't hurt you.'

She gripped the blanket while he moaned and shuddered.

★ ★ ★

Lydney, Bath, Battle, Belfast. Years passed. The divine powers of Her Majesty's Excise had invented their own language for towns — they were dubbed 'collections', administrative divisions drawn on the map to indicate where Her Majesty's wealth collected in pools like rainwater. These colonies of wealth were peopled by uniformed young men otherwise destined

104

for the trades or the factories. For the right man, it represented an opportunity.

Dublin, Galway, Coleraine. Every place was different. Every place was the same. Edwin used to feel more solid and upright in the excise uniform but now it was tight, it made him itch, there were holes in the elbows. Worse, the distinctive shape and colour telegraphed to influential men of business that he might be clever, but he would never be one of them: he wasn't to be trusted; he was the enemy standing between honest, hardworking men and their money.

For every new posting, the same tired story. A night journey on a train or a coach, or a ferry crossing that made Mary Ann vomit until her skin turned grey. A winding turnpike road in a bitter gale. A cottage filled with the stains and stinks of other people. At least three taverns on the walk home from the Excise Office and at least a dozen men willing to drink until closing. All for a wage that never seemed to go up and always ran out a day or two before the next one came in.

The boy born in Belfast lived one night. Mary Ann's breasts overflowed with milky grief. The midwife explained as much as was possible to tell a man. Everything about Mary Ann's baby was in the wrong place. The cord was wound around his neck instead of sticking out ropey from his middle, his bottom was ready first instead of his head, his lips were blue instead of pink. His death before his life.

'Make sure she has another baby quick smart,' another excise man told him. 'It cured my wife.'

Every night he pushed himself furiously into Mary Ann. She did not refuse him and he took no joy from it. Afterwards he gave her a gill or two of gin and poured one for himself.

Their next child was born in Battle. As if he knew the bloodied history of the Sussex town he'd landed in, not to mention something of his own conception, little Edwin Stewart fought his way out of his mother's heaving womb. He fought the midwife with feet and hands that looked too big for his puny body; he fought Mary Ann with tiny fists that pummelled her chest when she fed him; he fought Edwin's sleep with screams that lasted for hours. Edwin Stewart's eyes began blue like Albert's, but unlike his elder brother's they remained so. His hair was the colour of wet sand and his face looked just like Mary Ann's. At first, Mary Ann held Edwin Stewart like she'd never let go, but as it had after Albert, a blackness came into her eyes and she stared at her son as if he were a stranger.

'Be his mother,' Edwin said, thrusting the child into her arms. He gave her a shove to wake her up.

'Don't touch me.' Mary Ann took the infant and held him close, tight enough, but from the look on her face anyone could see there was no warmth in it.

By the time the leaves on the oak trees turned amber, another red-sealed letter had arrived. Edwin left it on the table.

Mary Ann picked it up and ran her fingers over the wax seal.

'Is it more money this time?'

'Next time it will be. I'm sure of that.'

Mary Ann began throwing things in Edwin's old carpet bag. Edwin Stewart screamed and cried. He spoke for all of them.

★ ★ ★

106

Trains used to be what he dreamed of. Now they smelled of piss and failure. He wondered if that schoolmistress — what was her name? — had ever experienced what she talked about with such earnestness that day. Or if she'd ever been on a dark, rolling sea at night when the sky and sea soaked into each other and the sound of strangers retching rattled in her ears.

Another baby was born in Dublin. They called him Matthew. She loved him well enough at the start, but after a few days Mary Ann became grim-lipped once again. Sometimes there was no tea on the table when Edwin came home at night. Sometimes Mary Ann cried for no reason and screamed at him until a clip around the ear was called for. He recognised a pattern. He poured Mary Ann a drink and pulled on his coat. Every place different, every place the same. Whatever town this was, there would always be a tavern.

* * *

'What do they do, cover their eyes and stick pins on a map?' Mary Ann stood with her hands on her hips. 'Half the men they got in Ireland are English and all the English officers are Irish. Now they're shipping us to bloody Edinburgh.'

'You hate Dublin. You say the people smell of peat.' Edwin downed his drink.

'At least the whisky's cheap.' Mary Ann raised her glass and drank it down. 'Happy travels.' She hurled a couple of his books into a bag. 'Another bloody house too small for the five of us and other people's shit still warm in the privy,' she said.

'Be careful of my things.' Edwin downed another

whisky.

'You be careful of my things.' Mary Ann pointed to the closed door that led to the other room where the boys slept. 'They'll wake up wondering where on earth we're pitchin' up next.'

'Don't be a fool. They're children — they'll do as they are told.'

'Will you earn more money in the next place, master?'

'A man died.' He grabbed her arm. 'They have to do the best they can with the available men.'

'So, the answer is no.' Mary Ann scowled at his fingers gripping her arm, then back to his reddening face. 'After all these years, when's a promotion coming? God knows we could use the money.'

'Show some respect. I'm your confounded husband.' He poured and drank another, slamming the mug on the table.

'Husband? I wonder. All that drink, you're not even half the man I married.'

He slapped her cheek.

Mary Ann cupped her face with her hands, the whites of her eyes moist and bright.

'That's the way.' Her lip trembled. She moved close enough for him to kiss her, if that's what he wanted. 'Ten years, no promotion, and now they're making you fill a dead man's boots.'

'I said, show some respect.' He slapped her face harder. Mary Ann whimpered and fell to the floor.

The sight of her on the floor infuriated him. He kicked her middle. 'Get up.'

Mary Ann pulled her knees up to her chest, protected her face with her hands.

'Please stop.'

His eyes were hot. Her pleading made him angrier.

'Anything else you'd like to say?' He grabbed her arm and pulled her up from the floor.

On the table, their empty mugs sat mutely next to each other. Edwin filled them both.

'Drink up,' he said, before downing his and slamming the mug on the table.

Mary Ann rested one arm over her stomach, and picked up the mug with her other hand.

'To your good health,' Mary Ann muttered.

Edwin tipped the bottle upside down, throttled it, but it was empty. The whisky hadn't helped. His hands hurt and there was nothing in his veins but the nauseating sense of his own smallness.

In the doorway, a small shadow: Edwin Stewart, his namesake, sniffing, staring. His eyes so blue, like Mary Ann's.

'Go back to bed.' Edwin drummed the table with his fingers. 'Your mother isn't well.'

Agnes

East Perth, 1887

As is the way with bad news, it spread quickly.

The *Kapunda* collided with another ship and sank so quickly that the passengers never stood a chance. A few men survived, but all the women and children drowned. The waters off Brazil were warm, some people reasoned as they read the newspaper, so perhaps there wasn't much suffering.

Ernest read the telegram and the softness in his face disappeared. He became hard-edged, angular. This would be his face now, Agnes knew.

'You ever been on a ship, Ag?'

'You know I've never been anywhere.'

'All that water. Some days you don't think you've moved because it looks exactly the same as it did the day before, and the day before that. You look for anything to tell you you're getting somewhere. A bird. Something on the horizon. Anything.'

'Oh, Ernest.' Agnes rested her hand on his.

'I think I told her I loved her when we said goodbye. I'm sure I did. I used to tell her all the time.'

'She would've known. She would've been thinking about you. At the end.'

'You sure?' Ernest filled up his glass with rum. 'I told her it'd be an easy passage. "Trust me," I said. Perhaps at the end she was thinking, "Bugger you, Ernest! Wrong again!"'

'That's the rum talking.' Agnes moved the bottle

110

away from him. 'Any wife would've been thinking about how much she loved her husband. I would've.'

'You're much too kind, Ag. Maybe I'll turn into a lonely old drunk. That'll be my punishment for telling her she'd be safe.'

'Don't be daft.'

'Ha. Daft. You say it flat and short, the Lichfield way. And I thought you were a real colonial girl.'

'Your head's going to ache tomorrow.'

'Sweet Agnes, always concerned for me.' Ernest kissed her cheek. He smelled of rum and cologne. 'You are by far the prettiest thing in all this exotic land.'

⋆ ⋆ ⋆

The newspaper listed the names of the *Kapunda*'s lost passengers in alphabetical order, huddled together in a single, narrow column of print.

'This is all I've got left of her now.' Ernest held the newspaper so tight his knuckles turned white. 'Hannah Salt. No body, no coffin, no bloody church full of people offering me their damned sympathy.'

'I've got an idea.' Agnes grabbed his hand. 'Come with me.'

The water was wide and brown, and the tide was up high. Grey birds swooped and crickets hummed. Agnes wondered if she'd have forgotten how to get there but the smoky smell in the air brought everything swimming back. She led Ernest through the shin-high scrub along the edge of the river until they reached a tall river gum.

'This is where I used to come with my mam.' She led him to where a deep pool of river cut into the

111

bank. 'I don't think of her as being in that church-yard. This is where she is, I know it.'

'Oh, Ag.' Ernest watched his footing. 'You're such a sweet little thing.'

'I'll leave you here for a while. You could tell Hannah you love her. All the things you would've said if — you know — if you'd known.'

'Is this an exotic colonial custom? Most people would do that in a church.'

'Da always says people like us were done with church years ago,' Agnes said.

'Since you put it like that, I'd be a fool to ignore you,' Ernest said. 'Don't leave me alone too long now.'

'Don't worry.' Agnes smiled shyly. 'I won't.'

Agnes walked as far as she could around the edge of the river to the point just before Ernest disappeared from view. Ernest stretched his arms out wide and called her name in a booming voice. *Aaaaggggnessss!*

'Don't make fun of me.' Agnes walked further up the bank.

Ernest leaned against a tree. Agnes thought she heard him talking in a low voice, but she couldn't be sure if it was him or the crickets. He slouched forward, his head in his hands. And then, there was no mistaking it: his dead wife's name mingling with the river noises and the magpies and the one lone kooka-burra. Hannah. Hannah. Hannah.

Agnes pulled off her shoes and walked to the edge of the water. She closed her eyes and hitched up her skirt. Her feet sank into the river sand.

It was as if no time had passed. It could almost be one of their river days: the thrum of crickets, the rustle of leaves in the trees, the cool water on her feet. Fragments of Mam glinted through shadows. A

112

dark eyebrow. A pink cheek. Her red washerwoman's hands. Agnes shut her eyes tighter and wished hard, like she did when she was small: Come back. Come back. Come back.

★ ★ ★

Ernest was already up and about. That halting way he whistled, starting off loud then stopping abruptly and almost whispering, pierced the other sounds of the morning: the wind rustling the tops of the river gums, the distant crunch of jarrahs falling in scrub. You'd think there'd be no trees left, the way the men with axes were at it day and night.

Agnes put on her good dress. Instead of putting her hair up as she usually did, she brushed it until it was glossy and hung in a gentle wave past her shoulders.

In the kitchen, Ernest looked at her and smiled. She blushed.

'I've got something important to say, Ag.'

Agnes leaned on the table to keep herself steady.

'There's nothing here for me now. Thought I'd try my luck in South Australia.'

'What do you mean, nothing?'

'I feel like I've lost it all. Can't lose much more, eh?'

'I don't understand.'

'Everything here's been about waiting for Hannah. I can't look at the damn sky without thinking of her.'

'Oh.'

'Come and see me in Adelaide sometime. You're almost old enough to travel alone. It's about time you went somewhere. I'll miss our chats.'

'Me too, Ernest. I'll miss them too.'

113

The evening before Ernest left, Annie had taken an extra shift and, as usual, Walter was nowhere to be seen. Da put on his hat and said he couldn't stay, but he made a big show of shaking Ernest's hand.

'Thank you, uncle,' Ernest said.

'No, Ernest, I should thank you.' He tipped his hat and bowed his head before leaving.

It was unusual, Da saying thank you to anyone, much less tip his hat in gratitude. He didn't talk to Ernest much but whenever he did, it was always 'thank you'.

Agnes had no appetite but ate anyway. The noise of forks scraping against plates was unbearably loud.

'Dear Ag, wipe that glum look off your face, I have good news.' Ernest leapt out of his chair and made one of his grand bowing gestures. 'It's good manners for the guest to leave a gift.'

'A gift?' Agnes couldn't help smiling. 'You're as poor as a church mouse.'

'And a widower to boot.' Ernest pulled both his pockets inside out. 'So, I've decided on something so special, no amount of money could buy it.'

'I don't need a gift. You've brought me so much.' Was it love or pain? Whatever it was, it swelled in her chest and made it hard to breathe. Agnes took inventory. His hair had grown out of its army cut and was curlier. His face had browned in the sun. He'd put on weight around his middle since he'd been here. Then there was his nose: flat and round, a bit like Walter's and a bit like Da's. She wondered what it would look like to see Da, his brothers, his sisters, their sons and daughters, all lined up together.

114

'I've decided to leave you with our family story, told so you won't ever forget it,' he bowed again.

Agnes's eyes shone. 'You come to visit all the way from England and all you have to offer is a story.'

'Ouch! Mortally wounded.' Ernest slapped his hand to his heart, then stood army-straight and began. 'Ladies and gentlemen, I present to you, *The Tailor's Tale* by Ernest Salt:

Grandfather Samuel, the tailor from Lichfield,
He was the old-fashioned kind.
Used needle and thread, 'til he dropped down
   half-dead,
And his eyes were all yellow and blind.

Sons, three in all: large, medium, small.
And daughters, useless, but fair.
Sam Junior the small, no tailor at all,
Ten thumbs and he just didn't care.

James was the medium, found tailoring tedium,
He spent all the profits on gin.
Eliza, Eliza, oh pretty Eliza,
To love her, some said, was a sin —'

'What does tedium mean?' Agnes asked.

'Boredom, Agnes. Boredom.' Ernest cleared his throat and continued.

'Poor Mary, so sad, lost her son, and his dad
And died broken-hearted one day.
This — *earnest* tale —'

115

He rolled his eyes and Agnes groaned.

'— is be-yond the pale,
But it's true, every word that I say.'

He recited it again, stuck his thumbs in the air for
Sam Junior, mimed a bulging belly for poor Mary.

Agnes clapped. 'It's perfect.'

Ernest took another bow. 'In the army, we turned
everything into a silly rhyme or a song. It broke the
tedium.'

'James was the medium. Found tailoring tee-dee-
yum.'

'Good work, Ag.'

'Eliza, Eliza, oh pretty Eliza!' Agnes repeated in a
high-pitched voice, clasped her hands to her chest
and fluttered her eyelashes.

'Brava!'

'Put me and Walter in the story.'

Ernest furrowed his brow. 'I know. How about this:
Agnes and Walter live on a faraway river where it's
freezing in June and hot in December.'

She shook her head. 'It doesn't fit with the rest of
it.'

'I'm a carpenter, Ag, not a poet.'

'Agnes and Walter live near the Swan River, as far as
an ocean away,' Agnes sang, to the rhythm of Ernest's
tale.

'Oh, well done! You're the family's first colonial
poet,' Ernest clapped.

Agnes kissed his cheek.

Ernest drew back a little. 'Come on, Ag, don't go
getting sentimental on me.'

'Don't leave. Why can't you go up the Murchison

116

or right up north, even? Come back every Christmas once you've made your fortune? Jesus, Ernest.'

'Language, my dear Ag.' Ernest fished a handkerchief out of his pocket and dabbed it under her eyes.

★ ★ ★

Agnes said it in the washhouse. She said it in the kitchen. She said it when she woke up and before she went to sleep. She said it to Walter, who said, 'Don't be a damned fool', and skulked off before she'd got to poor Mary. She said it like a prayer with her hands together and her eyes shut and in the hope that, when she opened them, Ernest would walk in. She shouted it to the magpies and the river gums. She muttered it when she picked Da up off the floor after he'd had a big night at the Western. She called it down the well that never seemed to run dry and the ghost names floated back up to her, distorted and hollow.

She whispered it into the fire when everyone was out. She said the names of her family to the chooks, and they scratched and squawked and ignored her.

She tried to write it down. Agnes had never liked writing — the words always limped along too far behind her thoughts — but she whispered Ernest's rhyme over and over until she'd copied the whole thing as best she could.

'Reckon you've gone mad.' Walter looked over her shoulder. He smelled of Da's tobacco. 'Might have to talk to Annie about carting you off to the asylum.'

'Jesus, Walter, shut up.'

'There's something missing.' Walter pointed to the paper. 'He's left Da out.'

'No he hasn't. Three sons: large, medium and

117

small,' Agnes said. 'We see Da every day. Ernest probably didn't think there was any point in putting him in a story.'

'You want to know about Da, you go have a chat with Mick McCarthy.' Walter's eyes were dark underneath with tiredness or bruises: it was hard to know which.

'Don't be daft. McCarthy's just an old drunk. I heard he'd left Rosie and gone bush.'

'He's sleeping rough in Howick Street,' Walter said. 'I been taking him and Rosie some tea and bread. He reckons the law's after him for some evil thing.'

'You can't hang around Mick McCarthy,' Agnes said. 'Da'll go off his head.'

'Da can go to blazes.' Walter lit up a smoke. With his mouth all grim and pursed up, he looked even more like Da than usual. 'Like I said, you want a true story about the old man, go talk to Mick.'

That night Agnes blew on the window and wrote names in the condensation: Edwin, Cath, Agnes, Walter. They evaporated before she'd finished, leaving only a smear of fingerprints. Da came to the colony to seek his fortune, Ernest said, and that's where the story ended. So where did that leave her? Agnes exhaled on the glass again, wrote her name again and watched herself disappear.

★ ★ ★

Reading Ernest's letters was like listening to him talk. The noise of the rail yards in Port Adelaide, the five pubs on the way home. The letters came every fortnight in his scrawly writing until one fortnight a letter in different handwriting arrived. *Dear Agnes*, Ernest's mother, Sarah, wrote. *If I can survive the voyage from England, I'm sure you would find the trip to Adelaide very easy. You're welcome any time, if things at home ever become difficult.*

And just like that, Agnes began: a coin here, a banknote there. Small change from the tin on the mantelpiece that she was sure Annie would never miss. Coins out of Da's pockets after his blind afternoons at the Western. Jesus, Agnes, she sometimes said to herself. You've turned into a common criminal.

mother,' Sarah, wrote. 'If I can survive the voyage from England, I'm sure you could.' 'But the trip to Adelaide very easy. You're welcome any time, if things at home ever become difficult.'

And just like that, Agnes began a con here, a banknote there. Small change from the tin on the mantelpiece that she was sure Annie would never miss. Coins out of Da's pockets after his blind afternoons at the Western. Jesus, Agnes, she sometimes said to herself. You've turned into a common criminal.

Miss Salt of the Sea

Fan

Fremantle, November 1906

'Miss Johnson.' Grandpa put down the papers he was reading. 'What a lovely surprise.'

'I was wondering about my ma's mother. My grandma.' Fan stretched her mouth around the words. They felt like a foreign language.

Grandpa beckoned for Fan to come in. She sat down on the other chair.

'What would you like to know?'

'I dunno. Everything, I suppose,' Fan said. 'What was her name, what did she look like?'

'Ah, well, Miss Johnson.' Grandpa stuffed his pipe with tobacco. 'Her name was Cath. She looked an awful lot like you. Her hair was dark — even darker than yours. Skin pale as cream. Cath was from Ireland.'

'I look like my grandma?'

'Yes, Miss Johnson. There is a strong resemblance.' He puffed on his pipe and the room filled with sweet smoke.

'Some of the kids at school have got Irish mums and dads,' Fan said. That faraway look on his face made her think he liked talking about Cath. 'What was she like? Was she like Ma?'

'You mean, was she bad-tempered and a poor cook?' His eyes twinkled.

'Grandpa, shhh!' Fan giggled. 'Ma's got eyes in the back of her head, she's probably got another set of ears somewhere, too.'

'Cath had a good heart. Her temper sometimes got her into trouble.' He stared at the window even though there was nothing to see. 'She had the sweetest singing voice you ever heard.'

Fan had never heard Ma sing. Maybe singing wasn't the kind of thing that got handed down, like good hearts and bad tempers. 'I never think of Ma as having her own ma.'

'Has Agnes never told you about her mother?'

'Sorry.' Fan shrugged. 'Ma's not big on family. She never told us about you neither and you're not even dead.'

'Not yet. Not today, at least.'

'We've got Uncle Ernest and Aunty Florence and Sarah, Uncle Ernest's mum. They're back home in Adelaide. Ma reckons they're all the family we need.'

'Perhaps she's right, Miss Johnson.'

'Maybe. But we've moved our whole lives thousands of miles to look after you, so now you can't be completely useless — isn't that right, Grandpa?' she grinned.

'Cath would've liked you,' he said. 'A mind of your own.'

'I bet I'd like her, too.' Fan paused. 'Grandpa, when Ma was a girl, did she answer back to Cath like I do — I mean, like Ma reckons I do with her?'

'Miss Johnson, your grandmother died when your mother and your Uncle Walter were very young.' His voice was suddenly quiet. 'Much younger than you are now. It was a very long time ago.'

Fan felt herself get teary, as if she had gained and lost a grandma in the space of one evening. 'How did she die?'

124

'She was working in the yard.' Edwin spoke with effort. 'She was outside too long in the heat, and she died from it.'

'Poor Ma,' Fan said. 'Poor Uncle Walter.' For all Ma drove her mad sometimes with her fussing and telling off, Fan couldn't imagine never seeing her mother again. Never hearing her voice or seeing her smile. Imagine having to dress Ma for the grave and shut her away in a coffin. Fan felt tight in the throat just thinking about it.

'Did you love her more than your other wife?' Fan asked.

'I beg your pardon? My other wife?' Grandpa's face seemed to freeze.

'Sorry, Grandpa. I mean Annie. Did you love Cath more than Annie?' Fan's cheeks burned scarlet. 'I mean, oh goodness, I should be less imper . . . imper . . .'

'Impertinent, I believe, Miss Johnson.' Grandpa had stopped smiling.

'Yes, like Ma says. I didn't mean to upset you.' Fan jumped up. 'Let's talk about something else.' She pointed to the brown leather bag at his feet. There were a lot of papers spilling out. 'What you got in there?'

'My possessions are none of your concern, Miss Johnson.' For the first time, his voice had an edge. It pushed Fan towards the door. 'I am tired. Thank you for your company. Perhaps you might leave me to myself for the rest of the evening.'

Later in her room, Fan made a page in her notebook for Grandma. She drew a square house with a triangle roof and trees and a fierce, blazing sun in the sky. She gave the sun an angry frown. Fan wasn't great with words, but she wrote as best she could of what she remembered: *My grandma Cath. My ma's mother. Died from the heat. Irish. Hair and eyes like mine and a temper that got her in strife.*

Poor Ma, to lose her own ma so young. Fan had known girls whose mothers had died. Sometimes their fathers got new wives, but you could tell by the shadows under those girls' eyes, their lives were never the same. She drew a little stick-figure girl next to a grave with a single flower growing from it.

$$\star \quad \star \quad \star$$

With a belly full of food washed down with grog, Grandpa became expansive and theatrical, leaning back in his chair, his voice booming as if he had an audience of a dozen. Fan always egged him on, even if she wasn't sure what he was talking about. Sometimes he got sleepy from the talking and the grog and he mixed names up. He called Fan Cath, and sometimes he called her Agnes, and a few times he called Uncle Walter some other names she'd never heard before. If she asked too many questions he snapped or swore or just plain stopped talking, but Fan took to filling up his glass and, after a couple of swigs, he forgot he'd got mad and carried on talking. Fan listened very carefully because she needed to remember as much as possible to put in her notebook later.

'Your mother took to the water like nobody ever did. All the children used to swim there. If you couldn't find Agnes and the weather was even a little bit warm, you knew where to look first.' He leaned back in the chair, hands behind his head, holding court.

'I thought, well, if I had to go back to tailoring work, I might as well set up a shop. Edwin Salt and Son. I

126

was in demand! But Walter had other ideas. Walter was a bad sort. He went off the rails. Made friends with the wrong sort of people. Took to drink. I told him to smarten up. He disappeared one night, and I never saw him again. Good riddance, I say.'

Fan's eyes widened. She couldn't imagine Dad ever telling Tom or Ned good riddance. Dad was forever mucking about with the boys and ruffling their hair and calling them 'my bonny lads' and, even when he shouted at them, there was never any heat in it.

'You told me Walter used to hang around with the Aborigines,' Fan said. 'Was that why he went off the rails?'

Grandpa's neck twitched. 'There was a group that came back every year. Their women would have children, and in a few years, you'd see them grown into lads. They seemed to think they had a right to it, the way they'd break the fence and set up camp for weeks on end. Walter took blankets and food out to them. Food meant for our mouths. He stole from his own flesh and blood and told the kind of lies a man should go to Hell for. Walter was a bad sort, a bad sort.'

★　★　★

Fan drew some squiggles for the river and a figure swimming: Ma in the river at the place everyone knew where to find her. On her page for Uncle Walter, she drew a pile of blankets and some squares and squiggles for food. She wrote carefully: *Off the rails. Took to grog. Liar and a thief. Lies he should go to Hell for.*

What kind of lies would someone go to Hell for? Ma always said all lies were bad, but Fan had seen Dad tell Ma she didn't look tired when her eyes were so baggy she looked a hundred years old. Fan was pretty sure Dad wouldn't go to Hell for that.

Tom wandered in, carrying a rusty can and a hammer.

'What you doing with that rubbish?' Fan said.

'Nothin' much.' Tom shrugged. 'Never mind me, what are you doing? World must be about to end. You with a pencil in your hand and you ain't even in school.'

128

Edwin

Fremantle, November 1906

Edwin woke, slumped in the chair, cold and unsure of where he was. The night outside was black and quiet, except for the distant rumble of sea. He stood up and the room seemed to lurch sideways. For a moment, he felt his legs wobble and he wondered if he would throw up overboard. He pressed himself to the deck until it steadied and then he reached up to try and find the rail. It was a wall. As his eyes adjusted to the darkness, he remembered where he was. He took off his jacket and clambered into the makeshift bed. He stretched out and his head touched one wall and his feet almost touched the other. At least there were three meals a day and he didn't have to bathe with a dozen other stinking men.

He'd outlived all his fine, upstanding shipmates, only to find himself thrown out of his own house by his wife, serving a life sentence at the mercy of his daughter and suffocated by the ever-present stink of the sea in his nostrils.

The window was open. He struck the wall with his hand again, again, again. The force of it made the window rattle and it slid shut with a loud bang.

Edwin reached for the bottle, poured a glass of rum and lit his pipe. His evening ritual. In his old place at East Perth, he would do this at the bottom of the yard among the river gums. He liked the feeling of space when he walked from the house to the trees. He'd

129

never tired of it. It wasn't the same in Victoria Park, where even outside he'd felt strangled and fenced in, but he drank anyway, if only for the satisfaction of seeing how it got Annie riled up.

He unpacked the bundle of Eliza's letters from his leather bag. Edwin wondered what Eliza would have made of Fan, the girl with a head full of questions and her cheeky wit. He suspected Eliza would have liked his granddaughter immediately, and that Fan would have admired her great-aunty in return. Edwin's room still hummed. He felt warm in the heart but this time he knew it wasn't the grog. Fan seemed to like him, and he had begun to look forward to her visits. He peered at his reflection in the small mirror Agnes had hung near the bed. What would you say, Eliza? he thought. Could the tailor ever make his threadbare self anew?

130

Agnes

East Perth, 1889

The point about bushrangers, Da said, was that you never saw them in Perth. Or Fremantle. You never saw one galloping down Barrack Street past the bootmakers or the tobacconists. The man looking through the window at Henry Wood's shop might be a vagrant or a sailor or a black, but he would most certainly never be a bushranger. The point about bushrangers, Da continued, was that you only ever read about them in the newspaper, in far-off places like York or Toodyay — or even further, in the wilds along the Blackwood, or on the south coast near the Sound.

'You talk some rubbish, Edwin.' Annie didn't look up from her knitting. 'Everybody knows bushrangers are out there. You've got to be careful.'

'That's precisely what I mean.' He downed his rum and slammed the glass on the table. He was settling in for the night. 'Everybody thinks bushrangers are out there. Everybody knows somebody else who's seen a bushranger. But nobody in his right mind has ever seen one. Not you. Not me. Not Agnes.' He turned to Agnes and raised his glass. 'And wherever your lazy lout of a brother is, I'm damned sure he's never seen one, either.'

'What's it to you?'

The sound of Walter's voice made them all turn around.

'You'd better come quick, Da. It's Mick McCarthy.

131

He's been shot and he's asking for you.'

The wild look in Walter's eye made Agnes follow Da and Annie out the door.

The narrow alley that ran down the back of Howick Street stank of rum and piss. Mick McCarthy lay on the ground. Rosie cradled his head on her lap. Someone had covered Mick's legs with a blanket. The smell of blood was everywhere.

Walter sat down next to Mick.

'How's he doing, Rosie?'

Rosie shook her head. Mick's face was grey.

Walter whispered something in Mick's ear. Mick tried to lift his head but couldn't. Rosie and Walter slid their hands underneath Mick's head to help him sit up. Rosie beckoned to Da. He seemed to be the only man in the small crowd who didn't understand what Rosie meant because he just stood there. Agnes pushed him forward.

Mick mumbled and coughed. The smell of blood made Agnes want to run but Annie had hold of her hand so tightly she couldn't pull loose.

'It was the policeman,' Walter said. 'Swore Mick broke in and took his rifle. Said if Mick didn't have a rifle, he'd bloody well give him a rifle.'

'He never did it, he didn't steal any rifle,' Rosie said, tears starting. 'They said he probably done it and if he didn't do it today he'd likely do it tomorrow.'

Da kneeled down. Mick struggled to raise his arm and groaned, as if it were heavy, but it was as thin as a stick.

'I gave 'em a good run, Salt.' Mick spat blood. 'To the end of the earth, ain't that what we used to call this godforsaken place?'

'Damn right. Now we call it home,' Da said. 'Do

132

you want me to take you back to your house?'

'Not sure I'll make it. I'm pretty banged up.' Mick lifted the blanket.

Da winced. 'Walter, go find a doctor. Or an apothecary. Now!'

'Too late for me,' Mick said.

'McCarthy. Fight, man,' Da said. 'You're our best fighter, remember?'

'Looks like there's a vacancy opening up, Salt.' Mick smiled weakly. His mouth was dark with blood. He tried to turn his head. 'Walter, make sure Rosie's looked after, will you?'

'Of course, Mick,' Walter said.

'Salt, your boy's a saint.' Mick coughed again. 'Couldn't have got through these past few weeks without him keeping us fed.'

Rosie stroked Mick's forehead.

'Your secret's safe with Walter. No need to worry about him.' Mick's voice was faint.

An odd look crossed Da's face. 'Don't talk, Mick. Save your words for Rosie.'

Mick mumbled something hard to understand through the coughing. Da stood up and herded everyone except Rosie away.

Freedom. That's what Mick had said, Agnes would realise, weeks later. Freedom.

★ ★ ★

Walter was drunk and unprepared for the first blow, which landed smack in his gut. The second split his lip. The third. The fourth. Again. Losing count. He spat blood on his shirt.

'Da, stop! You're hurting him,' Agnes screamed.

133

Da ignored her and hit Walter again. Walter stumbled and fell.

'What has Mick McCarthy been telling you?'

'What do you think?' Walter swung his fist and hit Da's upper arm. Da was incendiary, wide awake, eyes cat-like, alert. He hit Walter again. Again. Again. Annie tried to stand between them, but Walter shoved her away.

'Stop him!' Agnes shouted to Annie.

'God help you, Edwin.' Annie's voice was heavy. She shook her head and hurried back into the house.

'McCarthy called you a saint,' Da sneered. 'This is what you get for listening to the confession of a lying drunkard.'

Walter crumpled to the ground.

'Stop, for the love of God.' Agnes crouched next to her brother and lifted his head. His eye was swollen and bleeding.

'You're a damned coward, Da.' Agnes's voice was oily with hate. 'You touch Walter again and I swear I'll get Mad Molloy's gun and shoot you myself.'

'Who the blazes do you think you are?' Da was ruddy-faced, slurring. 'Speaking to your father like that. I'll take the strap to you.'

'Do what you like,' Agnes said, but her mouth was dry with fear. 'Look at you, drunk, and turning on your own son. And for what? The likes of Mick McCarthy? Poor Mam would be turning in her grave.'

'You leave her out of this.' Da's eyes looked small in his ruddy face.

'You came to the colony to seek your fortune? Well you've pissed it away and your own children hate the sight of you. How fortunate are you feeling?'

'Agnes, stop,' Walter said.

'No.' Agnes stood up. She was shaking. 'What could be so bad that you have to hurt Walter like this? What was so bad about letters and home and Walter not being cut out for tailoring? The only thing you've never got mad about was that you didn't save our mam. Were you asleep and full of grog when she was out there on a stinking hot day burning to death? Look at you. No wonder they don't talk about you in Lichfield.'

'I warn you, Agnes.' His hands twitched.

'No, Da. I warn you.' Agnes kneeled back down next to Walter, still shaking. She looked up at her father again. 'Leave us alone.'

The door to the house slammed shut behind him.

★ ★ ★

Da's rum bottle was empty. The front door was open, and the stench of blood and skin wafted in from the drying sheds at the slaughter yard. Normally, Agnes didn't notice it, but this morning her senses were tuned to the smell of injury. Da's boots were missing from the front step. He must have left early, perhaps to wait outside the Western until opening time.

The rags she'd held to Walter's face were in a pile on the floor. He'd always seemed so brave and mouthy but underneath, Walter was fragile. Always those narrowed, darting eyes. Agnes picked up the empty bottle and threw it as far as she could. It shattered unseen and sent a bird screeching into the clouds.

In the sleep-out, Walter snored. The cut on his face had bled onto the blanket. Agnes shook him gently. He coughed and winced.

'How's that eye?' Agnes asked.

135

'I'll live.' Walter touched his cheek. 'How's the old man? Worse off than me, I hope.'

'He and Annie are out,' Agnes said. 'Come on, Walter. We're leaving.'

'You running away, sis?'

'I thought we'd go to Adelaide. Stay with Ernest and his mother.'

'I can't.' Walter's eyes were black in his sallow face. He suddenly looked a lot older than his sixteen years. 'The old man owes me. There's stuff you don't know and it's better you don't, but trust me: he owes me.'

'Jesus, Walter, what is it?' Agnes picked up another rag and wiped his cheek. Walter flinched. 'Is it money? You can get work in Adelaide, Ernest will help.'

'I told you. It's better that you don't know.'

'Please, Walter, do it for my sake. I don't want to go on my own.'

'Go.' Walter put his arm around her. 'He's bad news. Get out while you can.'

Agnes burst into tears.

'Don't cry, you sook,' Walter said. 'How d'you expect to charm those Adelaide gents with your face all puffed up?'

Agnes went inside and threw a few things into Mam's old button-up bag. A hairbrush, her good dress, Ernest's letters. Even after all these years, the bag still smelled of Mam. Agnes's heart swelled with aching. What would Mam say if she could see them all this morning?

She took Annie's tin off the mantelpiece and emptied the contents. Something kept her staring at the shelf. It was one of Walter's sketches that had been squashed behind the tin. Annie had declared that it was good enough for the newspapers. He'd drawn them all: Annie with a long nose and a hairy wart, and a face shaped like a lemon. Agnes, tall and bony, with her long brown hair like a nest on her head. Walter had taken the mickey out of himself as well, drawing his crooked front tooth protruding over his fat bottom lip. Da was in the background slouched in a chair, a bottle nearby, a pipe in his mouth. He looked like a madman — spots on his face and wisps of flyaway hair. Da the tailor who boasted he could make any man more than he was and Walter, his son, the expert in reducing everyone to an outline of their flaws.

Agnes put the drawing in the bag and went back to the sleep-out. Walter had gone back to sleep. She drew the blanket over his bony shoulders and kissed his forehead. He rolled over and pulled the blanket up over his head. She left the bag on the back step, because there was one more thing she needed to do.

Agnes ran until she reached the sheltered curve of riverbank. The sun was high in the sky and the wood-cutting noises had already begun. A magpie warbled in a tree. The water was clear and still.

Mam's laughter like bells. Mam's smile shining like glass beads on the surface of the water. Agnes scooped her hands in and drank greedy mouthfuls. The river behind her, the river in front of her and now the river, so obviously alive like Rosie always said, pouring Mam into her heart.

★ ★ ★

Annie stood on the back step holding Mam's bag. 'They're saying Mick McCarthy died a hero.'

'Mick McCarthy died because he was hungry and drunk and he was an easy target for a policeman with a gun,' Agnes said.

'Were you leaving without saying goodbye?' Annie put Mam's bag down between them. 'I credited you with more guts.'

'I thought you'd gone to work.'

'I went to the apothecary to get ointment for Walter.'

'Da's really hurt him.' Agnes's eyes stung. 'You should have done something.'

'What do you think I could have done?' Annie said. Her hair seemed greyer and thinner than usual and there were smudgy shadows under her eyes. 'For the love of God, Agnes. What could I have done? You saw the mood he was in.'

'I wish my father was dead instead of my mam.' Agnes picked up the bag. 'Tell Walter to come to Adelaide. His family will be waiting. I hope I never have to see you or my father, ever again.'

On board the steamer, the hold was crowded and sour with the smell of wet hessian and unwashed skin. Children snivelled. The sea moaned constantly. Agnes pushed her way up onto the deck until she was pressed against the rail and staring down at the water. Her clammy hands clung to the rail as the boat cut the water into an ever-widening V and she watched her old life disappear.

★ ★ ★

'Brown eyes, brown hair. The nose.' Sarah embraced Agnes as if she'd known her all her life, then they both sat down. 'You have the Salt family colouring, my dear.'

Sarah had a wide, warm face like Ernest's, and her

hair was almost completely grey. She had pale brown eyes and smooth English skin. Agnes focused her attention on the curtains, the rug on the floor, the noise of chooks squawking outside. Anything to stop herself from crying. Ernest brought tea on a tray.

'Have you survived my mother's inquisition?' He ruffled Agnes's hair and the unexpected touch made her cheeks redden.

'That's enough, Ernest.' Sarah poured three cups. 'I was going to ask Agnes about home, about Walter.' She exchanged a look with Ernest. 'And her father.'

'I haven't come all this way to talk about home.' Agnes sipped her tea. 'I've travelled the high seas to seek my fortune in a new land, just like you all did.'

'Then we'll talk only of the future.' Ernest raised his cup to Agnes. 'To your brave new adventure.'

Ernest's four-roomed cottage backed onto the railway line, a decent walk from the Port Adelaide rail yards where Ernest worked six days out of seven. He joked that the walk to the yards took him past two hotels in the morning, but four on the way home. Sarah worked on the women's ward at the Adelaide Hospital, sometimes at night, and after her night shifts, she slept all day with a blanket hung at the window to keep out the light. Agnes cooked and cleaned and washed Ernest's shirts and sometimes did nothing but listen to the distant sounds of shunting rail engines. Before dawn, the whistling trains scared the chooks and they screeched and flung themselves at the chook-house walls, *thud-thud-thud*, waking Agnes with a jolt. On these mornings, she lay in bed and listened to Ernest padding quietly about the house, then she inhaled the faint smell of laundry soap that drifted from his shirt as he closed the door.

Ernest had outgrown his boyishness. His hands were stained brown with the paint the carpenters used on the railway carriages and his walk had relaxed into a slouch. But Agnes too was older, and rounder where it counted for a girl. She knew how to pinch her cheeks pinker and bite her lips redder. She knew how to brush her hair out so it hung in gentle waves, its plain brownness glowing richer in yellow lamplight. Agnes did this on the evenings when Sarah had a night shift. She turned the lamps down from blazing to muted and waited for Ernest to come home.

But Ernest didn't seem to want to talk to her all that much. He was frequently at the Exeter until closing, and garrulous but sleepy when he got home. Or he was tired and quiet after a day cutting railway sleepers in the hot sun. Every Sunday morning Ernest took extra time in the washhouse and emerged freshly shaved. He put on a hat and his good jacket and kissed the top of Agnes's head before he left. 'Not church, Ag. You showed me something better. On Sundays I walk along the jetty at Semaphore right to the end. It feels like the middle of the ocean out there.'

He didn't ask her to join him, but it was early days yet.

Fan

Fremantle, November 1906

At the beach, there was a feeble warmth and the breeze was fierce. Agnes hurried them along the sand. Ned and Tom ran along the water's edge. Fan sat on the sand and stared at the horizon.

'Not going in, Fan? That's not like you,' Agnes said.

'Are you mad, Mother? It's too windy.'

Ma rummaged around in her bag and pulled out a sandwich.

'Marmalade,' she said.

'No, thank you.' Fan stared out to sea. 'I don't want a mouthful of sand. Where's Uncle Ernest to build a windbreak when you need him?'

'You'll love a swim once you're in.'

'What about you? Why don't you go in? That's right. You don't even own a costume. Grandpa told me you used to swim in the river. What was it he said?' Fan pursed her lips, put her hands on her hips and stuck out her middle in the best imitation of the old man she could muster. 'Your mother was born for water, not the earth!'

'Don't be ridiculous.'

'Born for water. You, Ma.' Fan looked her mother up and down. 'In fact, apparently you loved swimming so much that if people couldn't find you, they always knew to look by the river.'

'For goodness sake,' Ma said. 'I told you, his mind is going. If you're going to repeat everything he says like it's gospel truth, you can stop taking meals to him and he can come out of that room and damn well eat with the rest of the family.'

'Language, Ma,' Fan sighed. The water did look inviting. She stood up and stripped down to her costume. 'Maybe I'll give it a try.'

The sand under her feet was biscuit-coloured and grainy like sugar. She hated the way she sank into it as she ran. Fan dived in. The ocean began to pull on her arms and legs. She swam underwater and slithered along the seabed as far as she could before the water pressed too firmly on her lungs.

The salt on her lips, the stiff breeze making her shiver, the brown weed tangled in her sea-heavy hair. She should have felt right at home. She turned away from the sun, half-expecting to see Semaphore Jetty. Instead, she saw small wooden sailboats cutting across the waves. Fan waded out of the water and sat down with a thud next to her mother.

'He told me about your ma.' Fan wrung her hair out on the sand. 'My grandma.'

Fan could have sworn she felt the temperature of the air change. Or was it just the look on Ma's face?

'What did he say?' Ma asked.

'He said I look like her. And she died.'

'Yes, Fan, she did.'

'It must have been horrible.'

'It was.'

'I couldn't imagine not having you. I mean, apart from when you annoy me.'

'Charming!' She elbowed Fan in the ribs.

'Grandpa told me about my Uncle Walter, too. What happened to him?'

'It was all so long ago, Fan.' Ma pointed out to sea,

her mouth set firm. 'Can you see Tom and Ned? It looks like they're swimming out to those sailboats. Poor Ned's little legs. Tom had better look after him or I'll give him a good hiding.'

★ ★ ★

Fan liked it best when Grandpa talked about the place where he was born. Lichfield, it was called — as in 'witch-field', as she reminded herself, because she wasn't sure what the word would look like. The stories tumbled out of him. His father — 'Your great-grandfather, Samuel' — and 'my dear, dear mother.' His brothers, and a school friend called William Neville. His sister Eliza, whose name he sighed out so quietly she almost didn't hear it.

'Eliza's a lovely name,' Fan said. 'You must miss her. I'd miss Tom and Ned, even though they make me mad as a snake half the time.'

They sat in his room without talking for a while and Fan wondered if he was tired. She stood up to leave, but he waved her back.

'Eliza was my greatest blessing,' Grandpa said. 'She saved my life.'

'What do you mean?' Fan said. 'Did you have an accident?'

'Eliza was the smartest person I knew.' His voice was very low. 'Much smarter than me.' He took another drink. 'And on no account tell her I said this, but she was without question the finest seamstress in the family.'

'Don't worry, Grandpa,' Fan grinned. 'Your secret's safe with me.'

Grandpa leaned towards her and Fan hoped there

was something scandalous he was about to whisper. But Grandpa clasped her hands in his.

'Thank you.' His eyes were cloudy. 'Thank you with all my heart, Miss Johnson.'

Fan shrugged. 'I'd better get a move on. Ma'll be on the warpath if I don't get back soon.'

Halfway down the hall she realised she'd left his empty plates behind. Ma would be furious. She knocked as she pushed his door open. Grandpa was staring out of the shut window again, his arms folded across his middle.

'Sorry Grandpa, I forgot your plates.'

Fan picked up the crockery and saw it was that old leather bag he was holding onto, and there was a pile of letters on the table.

'I'm surprised you find your grandfather so interesting,' Ma said when she returned.

'Nah. Not really. He mostly rambles a bunch of nonsense.' Fan hoped her voice wasn't shaking, because Ma always said she could spot a lie before Fan had even thought it up. 'Like you said, his mind is going. I reckon he just likes the sound of his own voice.'

Edwin

Fremantle, November 1906

Edwin didn't know how many letters his sister had written over the years, or how many letters he had written home. But the only two from Eliza he had managed to keep were wrapped safely in his leather bag. He felt grounded somehow, tethered to a place of certainty, knowing that the remembered rhythm of his sister's voice was always there if he needed to hear it.

Talking to Fan about Eliza had stirred her to life again. He opened both her letters and put them on the table, lingering over his favourite lines, even though he knew them by heart.

My dear Edwin. Da says you are as good as dead to the family but, like progress, I choose to pass him by!

Even so many years later, her wit made him warm with pride.

Albert and Edwin Stewart are settling in with Da, although it is very cramped. They go to the church school and learn writing and arithmetic. Matthew is living with me. He is a sickly boy with a constant cough.

I took them to the cathedral last Sunday and showed them our childish old games. You will be glad to know that I outran them, and that Saint Chad is still dead.

There is some sad news. Our mother died soon after you left for the colony. She didn't suffer. Da gets some help from young Amy Bullock next door.

I hope you are doing well. There are always stories of men out there making good, even men with your unfortunate start.

Next to Eliza's letters were two others he couldn't bring himself to throw away. He opened one of them now. Still, when he read the sentence that began I regret to inform you, his throat closed up with emotion and he felt Eliza's death as keenly as if the news had been delivered ten minutes ago. The pompous tone of his father's haughty young wife — *Mrs Samuel Salt (Amy Bullock)* — was enough to give any man heartburn decades after the event. But it always gave him comfort to bear witness to his sister's passing.

I regret to inform you Eliza died in her confinement this July past. The child a girl died with her. My husband your father Samuel asked me to inform you of this sad news as a duty nothing more as she confessed she were writing to you.

It were a great turnout to see her laid to rest, Eliza were much loved even with her odd ways.

Amy had a lot more to say, but tonight he didn't have the stomach for it. The fourth letter in the bundle was from New South Wales. He never read this one, but he liked to know it was there. Keeping it felt like he could keep that no-good swindler where he could see him.

Edwin took the lock of hair out of its resting place and held it to his face. He wished he could remember Mary Ann alive and beautiful, but there were traces of her other self everywhere. She was in the smell of whisky, in the fraying threads of his waistcoats, in the restless dreams that left a gloom clinging to him.

He looked at the letters again. So many versions of himself contained in a few faded lines. If he squinted at them all together, could he make some parts disappear? He stared at the names. Eliza. Albert. Your father Samuel. Saint bloody Chad. Mary Ann. Mary Ann. Mary Ann. He stared unblinking until the pages blurred. A few pages of handwriting were his only proof that these people had existed, that he himself had existed before this barely lived life.

He drank more rum.

Agnes

Adelaide, 1889

Dear Walter, there's loads of work at the port. You'd soon be swimming in money. Loads of work at the rail yards for hardworking men.

Agnes was a slow and clumsy writer, but every week she sent her brother a piece of Adelaide: the noise of the engines that made the windows rattle; the faint smell of sea in the air; the paint peeling off the Jetty Hotel's sagging veranda. Sometimes she drew a little sketch and made fun of herself:

You'd draw this so much better than I could, Walter. Adelaide needs you to draw it. There is a newspaper that prints sketches, just like in Perth. I know you're not much for writing, so I don't mind that you don't reply.

She always sealed the letters up tightly and put a cross on the seal so Walter would know if Da had tampered with it. She wrote Walter's name very clearly so there could be no mistaking. Agnes printed her new address in neat, readable capitals. Months went by, but no word came from Walter. Agnes's heart grew heavier with every letter she posted, and every week of silence.

★ ★ ★

Ernest wasn't usually home on a week day, and nor had she ever seen him dab a handkerchief to his mother's eyes because Sarah never, ever cried. In the time it had taken Agnes to walk to the port and back, something cold and sad had come among them.

'It's the anniversary of my father's death,' Ernest whispered. 'She feels it even worse now she's so far away.'

'Poor Sarah. I can make myself scarce,' Agnes said.

'No need to scurry off, Agnes,' Sarah said. This wasn't the Sarah that Agnes had come to know, the woman with the steel spine who tended to newborns and the dying and many of the living people in between. She looked so frail.

'My Sam would've liked you, Agnes.'

'She nursed him for months, didn't you, Mother?' Ernest held Sarah's hand.

'I couldn't make him well,' Sarah said.

'Not for want of trying. Personally, I can't believe he had the gall to disobey your orders by dying.'

'My Sam always had a mind of his own,' Sarah said.

Agnes sat down. The table was covered in papers, pictures, newspaper clippings and a couple of notebooks. Sarah showed Agnes an old photograph. A man in a well-tailored suit stood in front of a backdrop of classical pillars. His foot rested on a stool and he leaned towards the camera thoughtfully. He had carefully tended whiskers and a round nose. Familiar eyes.

'Isn't he handsome?' Sarah said. 'Always the handsomest man in the room.'

Sam had all the same features as Da, but he was a much finer-looking man. He was slimmer and his face more relaxed.

149

'Sam Junior the small, no tailor at all,' Agnes murmured.

'I beg your pardon?' Sarah said.

'It's nothing. Just a little rhyme Ernest used to tell me.'

'I wonder if it was the right thing to do. Leaving him in England.' Sarah's eyes misted over.

'Why would you stay in England to tend to a grave?' Ernest sifted through the papers on the table. 'You'll always have your memories and your lovely keepsakes.'

Sarah picked up a notebook. The faint smell of lavender escaped. Something familiar about one of the pictures, half-buried underneath a book of flower pressings, caught Agnes's eye. She picked it up. It was a sketch on paper, faded and yellow with age.

For a moment she thought it was one of Walter's drawings: some of the flourishes could so easily have been his. But this picture was beautiful, not drawn to poke fun. Two people stood in an arched doorway. The man looked like her father, only younger, cleaned up. A big, wide smile. The woman's dress had a long train that swept gently upwards. It tangled with her long hair and framed the couple. The man had his arm around her and he wore a smart suit. It was only a sketch, but still Agnes recognised the formality, the church setting. She turned the drawing over.

Edwin and Mary Ann. Love from Eliza.

'What's this?' Agnes showed the drawing to Ernest.

'Goodness!' He leaned closer. 'I haven't a clue.'

'Sarah, is that my father? Who's Mary Ann?' Agnes traced her finger over the woman's face. The picture had faded but there was no denying the wide-eyed stare, the stubborn curve of this woman's chin.

'Can this wait until another day, Agnes dear?'

'Not really, if you don't mind.'

'Ag, how about you go and make Mother a cup of tea?' Ernest said.

'I believe Mary Ann was your father's wife in England.' Sarah was her brisk self again.

'What happened to her?'

'I'm not sure. I think she died.'

'Did you know about her, Ernest?' Agnes asked. 'Have you seen this picture before?'

'Agnes, today is a difficult day,' Sarah said. She began packing everything up into the hatbox. 'You know how it is with family keepsakes. People end up with all kinds of things. Ask me anything you like tomorrow, the day after or even next month, but please, not today.'

'No, Sarah, I don't know how it is with family keepsakes.' Agnes fled to the washhouse.

★ ★ ★

Agnes looked at Eliza's drawing and then at Walter's — the one she'd taken from their mantelpiece. She traced her finger around the outlines of Annie, herself, Walter, Da, following the trail of spots down Da's cheeks.

She wondered why she'd never noticed it before. They weren't spots. They were tears. Da was slouched over the bottle, collapsed, crying. Walter had seen something about Da and drawn it here, plain as day for everyone to see.

It was Mary Ann's face that Agnes saw when she closed her eyes.

The next afternoon, Agnes was outside throwing scraps to the chooks when Sarah appeared at her side.

'My dear Agnes.' She touched Agnes's arm gently. 'You've brought such joy to our home. Ernest and I wouldn't be without you.'

'I hardly see Ernest anymore.'

'He's been grieving for Hannah,' Sarah said. 'It's helped him to be here. Sometimes people travel great distances because it helps them forget.' Sarah put her arm around Agnes's waist. 'They leave their old life behind and start afresh somewhere new. I did that after my Sam died. Perhaps your father did that. And now you, is that right?'

'I suppose.' Agnes's voice trembled.

'Does it really matter anymore, who that woman in the picture was? Keep the silly drawing. But for all our sakes, let the dead rest in peace.'

My dear Walter, Agnes began. *I found something out about Da.* She crossed it out.

Dear Walter. Did you know that Da had a wife?

She crossed this out too.

Dear Walter. What do you think of this news? Da had a wife who died.

Cross out. Throw away. Start again.

Dear Walter. Nothing new to tell you this week. There are so many hotels in Port Adelaide I swear when the wind blows it smells of grog. There's so much work at the port. Get on the next steamer and in a month you'll be rich.

Agnes had hoped it was only a matter of time before he asked her, but when the invitation came it still took her by surprise. Something special, he'd said. She brushed her hair into a smooth coil and dabbed rosewater behind her ears. Ernest wore his hat and a smart jacket. They walked arm in arm down the wide road that led to Semaphore Beach. Agnes turned her face up to the sun and allowed Ernest to steer her through a group of shrieking children.

Semaphore Jetty seemed to stretch from the shore to the horizon. It cut the sea in half down the middle. Families sat in colourful chairs along the sands. Children paddled about in the shallows, and at the end of the jetty, far enough away to look like dots, people squealed and swam in the fenced-off sea baths.

Ernest took her arm. 'Come on, let's walk.'

'All the way to Brazil?'

'Something like that.'

The water was so clear Agnes could see the ridged seabed. Men slouched on the rail and tipped their hats at her. The rail wobbled and rattled in the strengthening breeze and Agnes lost her footing.

'You're safe with me.' Ernest tightened his grip on her arm. 'I won't let you fall.'

At the end of the jetty the breeze was fierce and cold. Young men slid their arms around the waists of their sweethearts, and the sweethearts held onto their hats and leaned closer to their young men. The swimmers were a squealing mass of arms and legs and colourful costumes. Agnes hoped Ernest might take her hand

153

or something, but he let go of her arm and turned to face the horizon.

'The day we found out about Hannah felt like the day my life ended,' he said into the air. 'Before then, I used to go to bed every night and plan what we'd do. Children. A house.'

Agnes touched his arm.

'When I first came to Adelaide I didn't care much about anything. I didn't know how to live, I suppose.' Ernest faced her. He blotted his eye with his sleeve. 'I'm not crying. It's the wind.'

She suppressed a smile. 'All right, I believe you.'

'I started coming to the jetty to talk to Hannah. It's odd, but with her being' — he pointed to the horizon — 'out there somewhere, when I stand here, it's like she's not gone. I feel close to her.' He rubbed between his eyes. 'You showed me the river and told me about your mother, so I started coming here in case it helped. And it did.'

Now it was Agnes's turn to wipe her eyes, but it wasn't the wind.

'Hannah told me it's time to start living again.' He took both her hands and spoke more slowly. 'Whatever else happens, always remember, you saved me.' He nodded to emphasise the point. 'You, Ag. My antipodean cousin. I owe you everything and I'll never be able to thank you enough.'

'No. You saved me.' His confession had made her feel bold. 'Can I ask you something?'

'Anything.' Ernest let go of her hands and stared back up the jetty to the seafront.

'The song you sang about our Lichfield family, was it really true? I mean, since my Da and that woman — Mary Ann —' the wind whipped her words away.

154

Ernest didn't seem to have heard her. Agnes took another deep lungful of air.

'Grandfather Samuel, the tailor from Lichfield,
He was the old-fashioned kind.
Used needle and thread, 'til he dropped down
    half-dead,
And his eyes were all yellow and blind.

Sons, three in all: large, medium, small.
And daughters, useless, but fair.
Sam Junior the small, no tailor at all,
Ten thumbs and he just didn't care.

James was the medium, found tailoring tedium,
He spent all the profits on gin.
Eliza, Eliza, oh pretty Eliza,
To love her, some said, was a sin.

Poor Mary, so sad, lost her son, and his dad
And died broken-hearted one day.'

Ernest applauded. 'That's priceless. I'd forgotten all about that silly rhyme.'

His words stung. 'It wasn't silly to me. I wrote it down so I wouldn't forget where I fit in.' She stood up straighter.

'Agnes and Walter live near the Swan River,
As far as an ocean away.'

'My dear Ag,' Ernest said. 'You fit in here with Sarah and me. We'll always be your family. You were so sad back then, I wanted to cheer you up.'

'Was it a lie?' The wind bit her face.

'I didn't get back to Lichfield very often.' Ernest checked his pocket watch. 'Even my mother only visited our family for funerals. Some things you really know, some things you hear and other things, well, you just fill in.' He turned away and began walking back along the jetty.

It took a moment for Agnes to realise that Ernest wasn't walking away from her. He was walking towards someone: a woman. A smiling woman running down the jetty towards him. She was taller and more filled out than Agnes and she wore a coral-coloured dress and large hat. The woman kissed Ernest's cheek.

Ernest's face was flushed, his eyes sparkling. 'Agnes, may I present Miss Florence Turner.'

'So pleased to meet you, Agnes. I've heard all about you.' The woman offered her hand. 'We got chatting one Sunday afternoon and now I'm afraid he's stuck with me.'

'That's right. Poor me.' Ernest slid his hand around Florence's waist.

Agnes had never seen Ernest smile like this. It was as if some exotic flower had burst open inside him and here it was on his face. Is this what he meant — 'whatever else happens'? She shook Florence's hand and let go just as soon as was polite.

* * *

Ernest married Florence at the parson's house in Port Adelaide. The bride wore a pale dress and carried a spray of daisies, and her honey-coloured hair wisped around her face. The way they held hands and hurried through their vows, it was obvious their attention

156

was on what would come later. Agnes tied a blue ribbon around her hat and made herself smile.

Florence moved in and the house began to smell of Florence's rose perfume. Ernest no longer stayed out late at the Exeter. He came home on time every day, and they all ate together, but as soon as they'd finished, Ernest and Florence disappeared into their room and shut the door until morning.

★ ★ ★

Agnes began to go to the jetty in the afternoons and watched the fishermen, the lovers, the vagrants, the children, the men smoking pipes. She watched the vast ocean that divided one side of her life from the other. Perhaps Walter hadn't written because he had no money for stamps. Perhaps, if she sent him some money, he'd at least send her a thank you letter, and she'd know he was all right.

Perhaps she'd held onto Ernest's rhyme, and the idea of him as a fairytale prince, far too long. It was as hopeless as trying to keep a hat on in a breeze.

One particularly windy day, she walked back up to the road to the row of pretty houses on the beachfront. She knocked on the first door, then the second door. She knocked on every single door and thanked them politely when they shook their heads. Until she knocked on the door of a tall mansion that cast a shadow on the smaller houses next to it. Mrs Jensen asked her in and showed her into a small, sunny room. Agnes took off her gloves and the woman inspected her hands, looked her up and down.

'Where is your family from?' Mrs Jensen asked.

'My father is long gone,' Agnes said. 'And my

mother is long dead. I live with my family up the road. My aunt is a ward matron at the Adelaide Hospital.'

'That's good enough for me.' Mrs Jensen gave Agnes an apron. 'I shall call you Agnes. I don't much care for formality, except of course if I have guests, in which case I shall call you Miss Salt.' Mrs Jensen chuckled. 'Miss Salt of the Sea.'

Edwin

Edinburgh, 1859

Juniper Green was one of several villages knotted along the thin thread of river known as the Water of Leith, a few miles from the middle of Edinburgh. It was a village of paper mills, snuff mills, windowless cottages and gin shops, home to farmers, fleshers, mill workers and excise men. Day and night the air stank of cotton rags being boiled for paper pulp.

Soon after their arrival, Mary Ann had another baby, this one eased out of her by a doctor, a man with pale hands and a college diploma. Edwin was comforted by Dr Michael's book knowledge, his sleek black case of glass bottles, his suit. Mary Ann said it was her gentlest confinement of all, but weeks later she insisted there was still something wrong. Dr Michael applied mustard poultices to coax out the illness she claimed was inside her and for which the doctor had no explanation.

'Drink will not make her better.' Dr Michael stared at a chair by the fireplace. Its leg was broken. 'You must insist your wife develops sober habits.'

* * *

Mary Ann swathed herself in the dark-blue fabric. It was heavy enough to fall in gentle folds. The faintest chain of silver flowers trailed diagonally from her breast to her hip.

159

'Silver daisies to match your eyes,' Edwin said. 'But first I want you to do something.'

'Anything, my master, for this.'

He whispered in her ear. 'Give up the gin. Doctor's orders.'

'I told you, I'm not right after the infant. It's the only thing that helps.'

'The doctor says it's all in your head.' His voice was harsh. 'Please, Mary Ann. For the children.'

'All right. I'll try.'

Edwin took her drink from her and gulped it down. Mary Ann trembled ever so gently, like a feather falling against him.

Later, she stood as still as she could manage, arms outstretched. Edwin pulled the tape around her back, under her arms and pulled it snugly over her breasts. Mary Ann wriggled.

'Hold still.' He adjusted the tape and his fingers brushed the side of her breast.

Mary Ann stifled a giggle. 'Careful. My husband might get jealous.'

'Madam, your husband is an extremely fortunate man.'

Mary Ann's cheeks flushed.

Edwin finished scribbling measurements. They didn't make sense. He looked at the numbers again, then at his wife. Her shoulders were rounded, her head sagged forward, her breasts were flat, her waist thin.

'Again,' he ordered, and she stretched her arms out. He poked his finger into her armpit and she laughed, loud and hearty and generous. He let the tape drop to the floor and she pulled his face to her breasts. He grabbed the gin bottle and swigged. She reached for the bottle but he held it away from her and reminded her how beautiful she would look in the new dress, just like the doctor had said. She nodded, and kissed him hungrily, and afterwards in their bed when it was still daylight he wondered, was it the taste of the gin on his tongue she had wanted?

★ ★ ★

He hadn't meant to stay so late at Wallace's gin shop, but the Edinburgh excise brothers had welcomed him warmly and he didn't like to leave until he'd drunk more than every last one of them. Now it was dark and his head was foggy. Mary Ann would have to wait one more day for him to finish the dress. He tripped over a sack of potatoes near the door, cursed Mary Ann for leaving it there, cursed the potatoes and cursed God himself.

Inside, Mary Ann sat at the table with a woman he didn't know. A bottle, two mugs.

'Edwin, this is Jane McKenzie. She's going to help me with the bairns.'

Jane ignored him. 'Are you sure you'll be all right, love?'

Mary Ann nodded.

'I'll come by in the morning,' Jane said. She glanced at Edwin, then rested her hand over Mary Ann's. 'If you need me, you know where I am. Don't wait a minute longer than you have to.'

The almost-made dress lay crumpled on a chair. After Jane had gone, Edwin pointed to the bottle, the mugs.

'What's this?'

'Not as much as you've had, I'll wager.' Mary Ann

161

stood, lifted her arms and opened her palms. 'See? I'm fine.'

'You promised.' His head throbbed.

In the doorway, Edwin Stewart appeared, half-undressed and rubbing his eyes.

'Get back to bed!' Edwin shouted, and the boy fled.

'Leave him alone,' Mary Ann said through gritted teeth. 'The bairns have done nothing to you except be born.'

'And what a price I've paid for that.' Edwin swigged from the gin bottle. The sweet liquid warmed his throat. 'Four sons and no wife to speak of.'

'Five sons.'

'Four sons living and no wife or mother to speak of.' The back of Edwin's hand caught Mary Ann's face.

She shouted in pain, and rubbed her cheek. 'Bastard.'

He hit her again, and she fell, coughing. 'Bitch.' And again. 'Drunkard. Madwoman.' Again. Again. Again. 'What kind of mother.'

Edwin took the almost-finished dress and pulled hard at the arms. One arm dislocated from the dress and this burned in his chest worse than gin. When he was a boy, he could stitch things up so they never came apart. Now his hands were stiff and he couldn't stare at small stitches without getting spots before his eyes. He ripped off the other arm, then the dainty collar, then tore the bodice from the skirt. In the firelight he saw his father mocking the slackness of his work. 'It isn't nearly good enough. Not nearly good enough, Edwin.'

That cotton had cost almost a week's wages. He threw the ragged pieces onto the fire, where they burned acrid, worthless.

162

★ ★ ★

Edwin drank every lunchtime at Wallace's gin shop until he couldn't read the columns in the ledgers in the afternoons. He drank every night at Wallace's gin shop until his voice grew too loud and Wallace refused him any more credit. Tracks of broken red veins spread across his nose, his cheeks. He woke in the mornings with his forehead tight and his mouth dry and his guts ready to heave. When he left home most mornings, Mary Ann was still asleep on the bed she'd made on the floor. Two, three, four kicks to wake her up. The same if she was still there when he got home.

A clip around the ear for snivelling little Edwin Stewart if he tried to push in between his father's boot and his whimpering mother.

Come November, it was dark when he left the house and dark when he returned. The walk along the steep edge of the Water of Leith took him past a dozen mills and the relentless creaking of water on wood, the rush and screech of water and air tumbling down the rocky embankment. The vicious wind hurt his face on the way to Edinburgh and slapped the back of his head on the way home to Juniper Green. The flask kept him company on both journeys. The gin fired him up. The gin calmed him down. The gin fed that other man, the man with the fighting fists, who now walked and slept in Edwin's house.

163

Agnes

Adelaide, 1891

The work at the Jensens' house was hard. There were so many rooms that by the time she'd cleaned the whole house, the room she'd started with was dusty and grubby all over again. After she'd finished for the day, Miss Salt of the Sea watched the water. Before sunset, the tide was always up high and the breeze whipped in from the south, tearing the sea into thin white strips and making women grab their hats. If it was too windy, she stood underneath the jetty, where seagulls made arrows in the sand with their feet, and children splashed fearlessly in ankle-deep water. If she felt like it, she took off her boots and paddled in the sand at the edge or walked in up to her knees. She was Miss Salt of the Sea, who lived with an aunt in Exeter, with a mother long dead and a father long gone. Perhaps Ernest could put that in his stupid little rhyme. It was all Mrs Jensen had needed.

After a few months, Mrs Jensen had given her a small wage rise and asked her to stay longer a couple of days a week to help in the kitchen. Agnes had used up ten more stamps on ten more letters to Walter. She had stopped asking Sarah if any letters had come. The walk to Semaphore became windy and cold. The stench of whisky on the men outside the Jetty Hotel smelled sour and she'd stopped feeling sorry for them and their haunted faces.

On the day of Mrs Jensen's annual afternoon tea

party, Miss Salt of the Sea made a decision about what to keep and what to let go. At Mrs Jensen's she put on a special apron, served delicious sandwiches and earned high praise from all Mrs Jensen's friends. The sky began to turn black over the sea and Mrs Jensen sent her home at five to avoid the rain.

The wind blew like it must be coming straight off the South Pole and the sea bubbled up high on the sand. She knew she'd have to run the last hundred yards home if it began to pelt. People hurried back along the jetty and pointed at the sky and mouthed, You're going the wrong way. A fisherman packed up his line and shook his head at her. The jetty swayed and creaked and down below the water lapped at the pylons.

Agnes took Eliza's sketch out of her pocket, tore it into pieces and threw them over the rail. Every one of Ernest's old letters, envelopes and all. Her badly written copy of Ernest's rhyme was the last thing she let go of. She screwed it into a ball and hurled it as hard and as far as she could. Bits of paper darkened and sank. Gulls screeched and dived.

She hurried back, but the rain was too strong. The wind howled in her ears and soon her shoes were soaked through. Agnes began to cry.

'Let's get you out of this weather.' A hand gripped her arm. 'We can shelter underneath.'

He hurried her under the jetty and the wind died away. It was almost warm, and still. A couple of gulls rested on barnacled beams. She felt hot with the sudden absence of wind.

'It'll pass right over, miss. You'll be safe here.'

Agnes had trouble deciphering the man's accent. It lilted and dragged, it had currents of its own. He

165

said something about sailors and ships, was she warm enough, and that he reckoned it would last no longer than twenty minutes.

An eerie wail of wind. Agnes clung to the man's sleeve.

'You all right, miss?' he said.

'I am fine.' Agnes's cheeks reddened. 'It's your jacket that got my attention. I'm the daughter of a tailor.'

'An' there I was thinking I'd rescued a maid and she were going to thank me properly.' He raised an eyebrow.

'Best grey serge in its day,' Agnes said. 'Which must have been some years ago.'

'Aye, it was that,' he grinned.

'I'm Agnes Salt.' She held out her hand and smiled. 'Some call me Miss Salt of the Sea.'

★ ★ ★

Like his father and his grandad before him, George Johnson wasn't so much born as hammered together with nails and rivets in the Sunderland shipyards. The teacher at the church school had said he was missing 'aptitude', mostly because of his grubby face and the holes in his trousers, but in truth George was sharp as flint. In summer, or what passed for summer in England's north-east, George and the other lads paddled about on the coarse sands at South Shields and talked about stowing away to the Indies. Or joining the navy. Or crewing a boat to the colonies and taking their chances on the wharves. On his last day at the church school, George had cut his leg with a worn-away stone and asked the teacher if the sea really did run in his veins like his father said.

'I'll show you my scar, if you like,' George said to Agnes over dinner, and bent down to roll up his trouser leg. Agnes blushed.

George had never intended to work on the wharves, but after the work fell away in Sunderland, he crewed a boat to South Australia in return for his passage and found himself washed up in Port Adelaide with idle days, a strong back and a good pair of hands.

The way he said 'a good pair of hands' made Agnes blush again.

At the end of the table, Ernest whispered to Florence, who nudged him to be quiet. Sarah spooned another potato onto George's plate. After dinner Agnes went with George to the door. It was chillier out here away from the fire and with only one small lamp lit.

'Thank you, Miss Salt of the Sea. So kind of you to feed a weary sailor.' George clasped both her hands between both of his. He held on so tight. More like a rescue than a handshake.

★ ★ ★

Agnes polished the Jensens' big upstairs window until the sea seemed so vast and close and blue you'd swear you could jump right in. Mrs Jensen's floors had never been so clean. Agnes put her hands in and out of cold water and warm water and soapy water a dozen times a day but it could never wash away the warm feeling of George's hands around hers. It sneaked up on her without warning, made her look forward to the next time she saw him.

'Agnes, you are the hardest working girl I have ever

employed.' Mrs Jensen gave Agnes her wages and a small jar. 'For your hands, my dear. It has lavender. Very soothing.'

Agnes showed the cream to Florence.

'Lucky girl,' Florence said. 'I've seen this in the shops in Adelaide. They say it's miracle cream.'

It may as well have been called Miracle Cream. By the time Agnes finished the jar, two things appeared: a pale, soft layer of skin on her hands, and George Johnson on the front veranda with a bunch of daisies and a declaration of love.

★ ★ ★

Agnes wore one of Florence's dresses. It was the old-fashioned style but still lovely, a luminous pale silver with pearly beads stitched around the neck. Florence brushed Agnes's hair and pinned it up with a rose-shaped clip. Sarah held up a small mirror and Agnes saw herself: her pretty face, slim waist, shining brown hair.

'I can't believe that's me,' Agnes said.

'You look beautiful,' Florence said. 'He's lucky to have you.'

'George is a decent man. He treats you well.' Sarah pulled Agnes close and whispered in her ear. 'If that ever changes, if he ever treats you . . . disrespectfully or ill-uses you — you come home to us immediately, never mind what people say.'

'You don't have to worry. George is a good man, I know he is.'

Florence arched an eyebrow. 'How much of George Johnson's "goodness" have you become acquainted with, young lady?'

'Don't tease. He's a real gentleman.'

'Nothing but decorum from our George. Where's the fun in that?' Florence fished a pair of gloves out of a box. 'Here. To complete the bride's ensemble.'

Agnes slid them on. They were cream-coloured with tiny beads stitched around the wrists.

'Now, twirl,' Florence commanded, and Agnes stretched out her gloved hand as she imagined a ballerina might. She spun on her heels until light winked and sparkled around her neck, her hands, her hair.

'I have something else for you, Agnes.' Florence beckoned her to move closer. 'Decorum is all very well, but tonight you will be a man's wife. There are some things you need to know.' To Agnes's surprise, Florence began whispering in her ear. The more Florence talked, the more Agnes blushed.

'Oh, darling Ag. You look beautiful.' It was Ernest by the door, offering his arm. 'Let's get you married off, little bird.'

Ernest walked her from the hall to the front room and whistled 'Here Comes the Bride'. George had slicked his hair down with oil and put on a shirt that rustled and smelled strongly of starch.

Man and wife. George brushed his lips to hers. A scratch of stubble, a faint trace of whisky. Florence and Sarah and Mrs Jensen clapped. Ernest and Mr Jensen pushed the furniture back ready for dancing.

Ernest was a competent dancer and Agnes let herself be led. He nodded to where George stood talking to Sarah. 'He hasn't taken his eyes off you all afternoon.'

Agnes twirled with Florence's husband in Florence's dress that still smelled of Florence's perfume. 'You should write to Walter and your father. Tell them

169

you're married now,' he said.

'Don't spoil it. Just let me have today. I told George I don't talk to my father and he doesn't care. He left his own family years ago. You, Florence and Sarah are all the family we need.'

'I think they'd approve of George in Lichfield.' Ernest spun her around. 'I can imagine Eliza, with her ample charms, giving him the glad eye. James drinking all the punch. To relieve the tedium. What d'you think, Ag?'

'That old story? I forgot it ages ago, Ernest.' Agnes closed her eyes and twirled.

Dear Walter.

George found us a little house of our own near the port. It's further away from the rail line but closer to the Exeter Hotel. George has so much work at the wharf, he knows all the foremen. It's hard work and you have to know somebody no matter how long you've been there, but George gets shifts every day. He says he could be your somebody.

Dear Walter.

Semaphore in winter is lovelier than summer. At sunset, the sky goes all sorts of colours. Blue and pink and yellow don't do them justice. The Chinese fishermen haul fish out of the sea when everybody else goes home empty-handed. There's so much work at the port, you could be earning the day you got here.

Dear Da.

I'm sorry I haven't written. I hope you are in good health. I wanted to tell you I am very happy in Adelaide. I am married now and I have a baby on the way. You are going to be a grandfather. Is Annie still working at the asylum? Is Walter still living with you? I would like to know how you are all getting along. I know things were bad when I left. Please tell me where Walter is and what he's doing. That is all I ask.

Your daughter, Agnes.

Births and Deaths

Fan

Fremantle, December 1906

For once, Grandpa wasn't waiting at the door.

'Grandpa,' Fan called. 'Teatime. If you can tell what Ma's dished up this time you got better eyesight than me.'

He didn't answer. She elbowed her way in. Grandpa sat in the armchair, snoring. The trunk was open and the room smelled of rum and camphor. Fan was sure she'd heard it wasn't good to wake up an old man because the shock could kill him. She put his meal down on the table and peered inside the wooden trunk. A few more books. A pair of boots. That old leather bag all stuffed and bloated around the middle.

Grandpa coughed.

'You awake?' Fan asked. 'Better eat your tea before it goes cold.'

Grandpa didn't move.

Fan gently shook his arm. 'Grandpa?'

His head fell back and his mouth dropped open.

'Ma!' Fan screamed.

* * *

Ma helped Dr Archer prop Grandpa up in bed and ordered Fan to fetch more blankets. By the time Fan returned, the doctor had taken a clear liquid out of his bag and was measuring it into a glass. He helped Grandpa to drink a few mouthfuls. Fan put one blanket over Grandpa's knees and the other around

175

his shoulders. She prodded him but he didn't move. Was he dead? Ma just stood there saying 'Right, right, what shall we do?', her lips pressing together with worry. After a few minutes, Grandpa fell asleep.

'Fan.' Ma seemed to jolt like she'd just woken up. 'You can go. Dr Archer and I will take it from here.'

'But I can help with —'

'I said now, Frances.' Ma pointed at the door, her eyes stormy.

'All right, all right,' Fan shrugged.

She stood in the hall and left the door open, just a little. If Ma wanted to slam it in her face, well, she'd take her chances.

'His heart is failing and that is probably affecting his breathing,' Dr Archer said to Ma. 'And his age . . . well, there could be . . . other problems associated with men of his . . . circumstances.' He said 'circumstances' like it was an illness all its own. 'Problems of the mind.'

Fan stood as still as she could manage.

'I am supposing he is about eighty — some of the older men who travelled here from England never quite adjusted to the light or the heat. Their hearts fail them and their minds are sometimes weighed down with . . . thoughts of the past. Make sure he takes some air and some light exercise. Lift his spirits.'

'I understand,' Ma said, calmer now. 'Thank you, doctor.'

Fan heard Dr Archer's bag snap shut. Fan imagined herself as weightless and virtuous as a fairy and glided as fast as she could back to the kitchen. Problems of the mind. Thoughts of the past. If Ma only knew. The past was all Grandpa had talked to Fan about since he got here.

176

Whatever the doctor had given Grandpa had proper knocked him out. His snores were wet, nasal: *uhh-ahh, uhh-ahh, uhh-ahh*. The trunk was open and the leather bag was open on the table.

'Grandpa?'

He didn't answer. His chest rose and fell with his snoring.

Fan tiptoed in and picked up the bag. She opened it and quickly flicked through the bundle of letters. Her heart raced. Different handwriting: some with red stamps and some with blue.

Grandpa fidgeted and sniffed. Fan pushed the letters back. She felt some kind of cloth: a pouch. She took it out and opened it.

Inside the pouch was a lock of hair, the thickness of a finger, a few inches long and tied with string. It was dark yellow, like old straw. Not a colour she knew well. Not Ma's or Tom's or Ned's or Dad's. And from what Grandpa had said about Grandma, not Cath's either. Fan carefully put it back and ran from Grandpa's room, her cheeks burning.

'Just down to High Street and back. It'll do you good. Doctor's orders.' Ma used the same brisk tone she used when she was giving Ned a good telling off. Grandpa had put on his good jacket and his hat and his boots. He'd had a shave and his skin looked pink and fresh. Ma handed him his walking cane and he leaned on it heavily.

'What do you think, Miss Johnson? Should your frail old grandfather risk a walk with your mother in the stinking sea air?'

'Honest to God, I think you should always do what

the doctor tells you,' Fan said earnestly.

Ma hesitated before slipping her arm through his. He attempted to pull away.

'I don't need your help.'

'Just 'til you're steady on your feet. Then you can run Fremantle's first marathon, for all I care.'

Fan was terrified they'd change their minds or have some embarrassing shouting match, so she waited until they'd turned the corner at the bottom of Ellen Street. Tom only had eyes for that pile of wood in the yard. Ned followed his brother around like a puppy, so Fan was sure she wouldn't be disturbed.

She tried to be quiet as a mouse, or even quieter, like a young lady, as Florence would say, but the floor creaked, the door to Grandpa's room squeaked on its hinges, the breeze rattled the window pane.

The sour smell of mould and sweat made Fan squirm as she opened the wooden trunk. This room really did need some air. She opened the window and Grandpa's room flooded with cool breeze and bright sunlight. Fan felt like she was standing ankle-deep in the sea at Semaphore on one of those days when the sun blazed overhead but you knew the water would be so cold it'd thump the air out of you once you jumped in.

'Here goes,' she whispered to herself.

She took out the leather bag and opened it. This time she knew what would be waiting. Even in the bright light, the lock of hair was dull, like brass that needed a good polish, but it was beautiful. Fan held it and imagined it uncurling elegantly down the back of a fine lady after a day of sipping tea and ordering servants about.

'Who are you?' she asked.

Fan put the lock of hair to one side and took everything else out. There was the bundle of letters and a folded-up blue cloth, which she spread out on the floor. It was a sturdy cotton that had been embroidered with a picture of a church. Fan could tell the thread used to be white, but it was yellowed now. The church had three spires and underneath each, a single letter: A, E, M. Fan ran her hand over the stitching. Some had come loose, but it was precise and symmetrical and beautiful.

Some of the envelopes were from England — they had the old red stamps. The sender's name was Miss E. Salt. Fan had to bite her lip to stop herself from shouting out loud. Grandpa's sister Eliza in Lichfield. So that's how you spell it, she thought.

Fan's hands were stiff and she swore at herself to be careful. There was a letter from New South Wales, but this didn't have a sender's name on the envelope, just a few words scrawled on the back in an old-fashioned flourish.

The New South Wales letter was postmarked 1901: not long ago. She opened the letter and ran her finger underneath the stilted, badly written sentences.

Dear Da

I am grateful for your kindness with the land all those years ago or else I could not of bought my land were I now live. I hope my poor mam can rest in peace now. You will always have a place with us but if you cant beg my forgivness this is the last time you shall hear from me.

Your son.

Fan's head hurt. None of it made sense. Grandpa and Ma both said Uncle Walter hadn't been heard from for years. Fan thought about keeping the letter just long enough to copy it into her notebook. But the thought of him or Ma finding it — well, she couldn't imagine how bad a punishment they'd think up.

Your son. Fan thought her heart would jump right out of her chest. Walter. She put the letter back in the envelope and put the letters, the hair pouch and the blue embroidered fabric back in the leather bag.

It was only after the commotion of Ma shouting through the front door, 'Fan, come quick! I took a wrong turn and he wandered off somewhere. I can't find your grandfather,' only after Fan stared at Ma's grey face and told her to calm down, only when Fan was running down High Street shouting 'Grandpa, Grandpa!' that she realised she'd left the door to his room open and the leather bag on the floor and her blue ribbon had fallen out of her hair and she'd forgotten to put the lid back on that stupid wooden trunk full of Grandpa's secrets.

Edwin

Fremantle, December 1906

He hadn't planned to escape from Agnes, but when the opportunity presented itself, he grabbed it. As soon as they'd got to the bottom of Ellen Street she'd unhooked her arm from his and walked a short distance in front, her spine rigid, her eyes focused ahead of her.

'Embarrassed to be seen with your father?' he called.

'I won't have Dr Archer blaming your poor health on me.'

His feet took some time to read the ground and he walked slowly behind her, leaning on his cane. She occasionally shouted 'Hurry up' and 'Be careful!' and 'I haven't got all day!' in that clipped voice of hers. Was that who his daughter had become? No wonder Fan made jokes at her expense. Edwin had forgotten the starkness of the Fremantle sky and his eyes watered with the light. He avoided looking at the building on the hill and instead, took the rest of Fremantle in. It was a real town now, a place with meat on its bones; a town of grocers and bakers and tobacconists and a tramline.

He started to wheeze, so he slowed his pace a little. Agnes walked further and further away. It had been easy to slip into the shadows of the Commercial Hotel's wide verandas.

Edwin inhaled the yeasty richness and followed the low rumble of voices inside.

181

The barmaid had bright red lips and a scowl that'd burn flesh. She looked him up and down. 'You'll find your sort down the back.' She poured him a drink and held out her palm. 'But your money's as good as anybody else's, thanks very much.'

It was gloomier inside and away from the street. Edwin propped his walking cane up against a table and sat down. Most of his fellow drinkers' clothes had seen better days and some of them would do better to spend their few pennies on a square meal instead of grog. A couple of the men nodded, some tipped their invisible hats. There was a time a man could walk from his house in East Perth to the tailor shop on Barrack Street and back to any hotel in the town, and every single man he passed would have that familiar shadow about him: the wary eyes, the worn-out body.

'Doctor's orders.' Edwin raised his glass to the man sitting nearby, who nodded. Then, as he always did, Edwin toasted Mary Ann and Her Majesty Queen Victoria, the two women who had made possible his magnificent life.

Edwin

Edinburgh, 1859

Dr Michael gently covered Mary Ann with a blanket and dimmed the lamp. 'Do you know how your wife came upon these injuries?'

'I don't know what you mean. She was drunk. She's probably passed out again.'

'These injuries are significant,' Dr Michael said. 'Serious enough to kill her.'

'What?' Edwin peered at the doctor. Sanctimonious bloody Scotsman. 'She was always drunk. You've seen her.'

'Come along, Mr Salt,' Dr Michael said. 'Somebody is here to speak with you.'

In the other room, a woman he didn't know bounced Edwin Stewart on her knee. Albert held the hand of Margaret Wallace, who nodded at Edwin as if it were any day in the gin shop. Little Matthew sat quietly in the corner.

Edwin recognised Constable Fry from Colinton village and Wallace's, but the constable wasn't smiling. He took out a notebook. Edwin's mind clouded like a pond hit by a stone. The women exchanged a look and hurried the children into the yard.

* * *

The police wagon left Colinton for Edinburgh before sunrise. Constable Fry gave Edwin a sympathetic

183

pat on the shoulder before slamming the door. The wagon was dark and stank of piss. He reckoned there must have been two or three others in there with him, all Scottish accents he couldn't understand except for the profanity. Every time the tired old horse stumbled, the wagon lurched and Edwin's head slammed against the roof. Rain thrashed the wagon and the wind wailed like grief.

If he could have seen out of the wagon, Edwin would have been unable to meet the clear-eyed gaze of Jane McKenzie, who had walked the two miles from Juniper Green to Colinton specially. She waited outside Colinton Church, where the smell of freshly dug soil was sweet and the rain stuck her hair to her cheeks. Jane watched until the prison wagon limped around the bend and was safely out of sight.

★ ★ ★

He awoke on the freezing stone floor of the cell shivering and sweating. Rats scratched at the high window. His head throbbed and his gullet burned when he swallowed.

Your wife is dead, Mr Salt.

Dead drunk, I'll wager, Constable.

Do you know how your wife came upon these injuries?

Even through his whisky-fog he could still feel his hard boot connect with her body. A couple of little kicks, that's all — just enough to get her up and about.

A child's voice in the yard, getting louder, closer. As close as the door.

'I said I need water!' Edwin kicked the bucket that was there for him to piss in.

The hatch on the doorway opened.

184

'Something bothering you, prisoner?'

'A man could die of thirst in here.'

'Thirst is the last thing you're likely to die of if the charge sheet's anything to go by.'

★ ★ ★

He'd been there about a week when an envelope appeared, along with the usual morning bowl of gluey porridge and a pannikin of water.

Edwin gulped water and read the letter.

Dear brother.

I have packed up your things at the house. The boys have been taken back to Lichfield.

Mary Ann was buried at Colinton this Tuesday past. We thought it best to spare the boys. What a terrible business.

Edwin had never been inside Colinton Church, but he imagined it looked the same as every other blasted church: a spire reaching heavenwards, a rain-bow-coloured saint frozen in the window.

He thought of Mary Ann spending her eternal rest in a churchyard she didn't know, surrounded by the rotting corpses of strangers.

Your wife is dead, Mr Salt.

Dead drunk, I'll wager, Constable.

There he was, trapped in the sealed box of that moment, trying to grab at the instant her chest filled with air for the last time and somehow haul her back.

I am arresting you on suspicion of murder, Mr Salt.

Constable Fry's voice had cracked when he spoke. 'Murder,' he stammered, fumbling with the handcuffs, as if he never thought in his entire policing career he'd be important enough to use that word.

Murder was what you read about in the paper. It didn't barge in and put its feet up in the life of one of Her Majesty's excise men, a tailor's son made good, a man with a good head for arithmetic and a certain tenacity.

'She died of drink, ask anybody!' Edwin slammed the cell wall with his fist — his fighting fist.

★　★　★

Alastair Remy had the smoothest voice Edwin had ever heard, and the smoothest hair and smoothest skin he'd ever seen on a man, buffed pale and shiny, no doubt, by the icy wind Edinburgh was famous for. He explained that 'when you boil it down, Salt', in the end, justice was simply a matter of numbers. There would be fifteen men in the jury and any verdict need only be by a majority. Three verdicts were possible in a Scottish court: guilty, not guilty or not proven.

'Not proven?' Edwin asked.

'Our country's esteemed novelist, Sir Walter Scott, called it the bastard verdict.' Remy fiddled with his shirtsleeve. 'Not enough evidence to prove guilt but enough to taint you for life.'

'A couple of kicks. That's all.' Edwin wiped his clammy forehead.

'A verdict of not proven would save you from the gallows and, based on the witness statements, it seems unlikely that eight men will be convinced beyond doubt that you deserve to hang.'

186

Edwin loosened his collar. His face was sweaty.

Remy picked up a piece of paper. 'You say in your declaration that your wife was insane enough to scream at the doctor in the street after her last confinement, and that you considered having her committed to a house of refuge.'

'She said once, she wanted to die. She was a mad-woman. Mad with drink. The children often went hungry.' Edwin tried to speak with authority but the harder he tried, the smaller he felt.

'Do you think your wife was insane enough to injure herself while under the influence of drink?'

'I don't know. She was always falling.' Light tumbled from the high window, light the colour of straw.

'A woman who could drink her life away, having such little regard for her husband and children, much less herself, would surely be capable of all kinds of evil.' Mr Remy took his watch out of his waistcoat pocket. 'Mr Salt, your wife is already dead. If I am to save you from the gallows, this is the most believable explanation.'

Remy checked his watch again. 'May I suggest you consider what you might like your family to tell your sons, in the unlikely event that the numbers do not fall in your favour.'

★ ★ ★

That night in the cell, he could feel Mary Ann sitting next to him on the stone floor.

'You knew how much I loved you, didn't you, my mistress?' Edwin asked.

Oh yes, my master. I couldn't blame you for being angry with me. I were always in the grip of it, and you a man

187

of such sober habits. How far away is Lichfield from here?
'A day on the train. Perhaps longer.' His mind
blurred. It was the sort of fact he used to know.

*Well, then, I bet my boys forgot about me already! How
lucky they are to have a father like you.*

He asked for paper and ink and wrote long into
the night, even though there was no light except a
weak glow from the moon through the high window.
He never remembered falling asleep. He woke at day-
break, shivering on the floor, sheets of paper crushed
under his arm. He stared at the words and searched
for the floating memories he was sure he'd pinned
down. But most of it didn't make sense and what was
left was crossed out. He screwed up the paper and
threw it into the corner where it rested with the ruined
corpses of yesterday's efforts. There were no words
for this. Pigeons gathered on spires. A flower seller
swigged cheap toddy from a pannikin. The remains
of the weekend's snowfall piled up in drifts all the
way up to Parliament Square, and the newspapermen
up from London wiped their runny noses with their
gloved hands. Somebody led Edwin into the dock.
The Lord Justice Clerk peered down from his high
seat and asked him a question. Edwin became aware
of a heavy silence.

'I said, how do you plead?' The Lord Justice Clerk's
voice echoed.

Edwin looked at Alastair Remy, who was almost
unrecognisable in his gown and wig. Remy nodded
to him.

'Not guilty,' Edwin said.

In his ear, a whisper made him wave his hand about
so violently that some of the jurymen flinched.

Oh, Edwin. I know different, don't I, my master?

188

In the public gallery a man whistled. Edwin looked up. He thought he recognised faces of people from Juniper Green, but he couldn't be sure. A brown-haired woman in a dark coat leaned over the rail. It was Eliza.

The Crown tore Mary Ann's skin off and laid her out, bloodied and bare. His defence held her mouth open and poured gin down her throat and chased her down the street until she screamed that she wished she were dead. Half of Juniper Green crowded in to watch Mary Ann lie drunk and senseless on the hill-side behind Woodhall Mill. Margaret Wallace could vouch for how much Mary Ann had had to drink. In the end it was his own solicitor, Alastair Remy, who finished Mary Ann off. He noticed the poker by the grate. He pressed it into her hand and made her stab herself once, twice, thrice.

The women in the public gallery were herded out and with a clinical and detached precision, Remy detailed Mary Ann's more serious injuries. The news-papermen whispered to each other and printed the words clearly in their notebooks.

Edwin covered his face with his hands.

Your life or mine, Edwin dear? If anyone deserves a bastard verdict, it's you.

Mr Remy had stopped talking. Something was happening. The jury was leaving the court.

★ ★ ★

The public gallery seemed fuller and the chattering had subsided. Edwin searched the faces of the returning jurors. None of them would look at him. The Lord Justice Clerk asked one of the men in the jury for the

189

verdict. The man passed a piece of paper to the Lord Justice Clerk. He read it and then turned to Edwin.

'The jury finds this prisoner guilty by majority, but unanimously recommends him to mercy, in consequence of the great provocation he received.'

Edwin doubled over with relief. Guilty by majority but with a unanimous recommendation for mercy. Alastair Remy hadn't talked about that. Maybe this was another kind of verdict. The jurors understood how difficult it had been for him living with a wife in the grip of drink. He could go home, after all.

'You have been found guilty of the foul crime of murder,' the Lord Justice Clerk continued. 'Regardless of the recommendation to mercy, the court's duty is to pronounce against you the last sentence of the law.'

The Lord Justice Clerk picked up the black cap. Something in Edwin's mind seemed to come loose. He struggled to hear, to understand: '. . . place of execution . . . hanged by the neck . . . dead.'

Men hit the oak walls and shouted at the jury. Women nodded to each other so slightly that their husbands didn't notice. A clerk called weakly for order.

Edwin leapt to his feet and looked to the public gallery. Eliza had gone.

* * *

A constable shoved him into a small room where a warder and a man wearing a suit waited. The suited man introduced himself as the prison doctor and peered at Edwin through small spectacles.

'Clothes off,' the doctor commanded. 'Now.'

190

Edwin took off his clothes. The room was freezing. He shivered with shame. The warder smirked. The doctor looked into his ears and up his nose and ordered him to cough. He examined Edwin's hair for lice and measured his girth and height. He prodded the scar above Edwin's right eye.

The warder pointed to a tin bath full of water. 'Get in.' He handed Edwin a bar of soap that smelled of tar.

The water was icy, and he shrank from it.

'I said, get in.' The warder kneed Edwin in the back, shoved down hard on his shoulder and pushed him under.

* * *

News of the guilty verdict spread across the country and as far as Belfast. Petitions grew heavy with hundreds of signatures. Newspapers across England and Scotland filled columns to overflowing with Mary Ann's gin-sodden shortcomings, before declaring the long-suffering, unfortunate man's life should be spared. A juror wrote to the Home Secretary that the verdict was only eleven to four, and if any man in the room had honestly thought the court would ignore their recommendation of mercy, they would 'to a man, sir', have decided upon the verdict of not proven.

Edwin lay on the floor of the cell and tried to bury himself under the freezing air.

I bet you got lots of wishes now, my master.

The smell of Mary Ann's skin was all over him. She scrutinised him from every corner of the cell.

'For Christ's sake, woman, you were drunk. Dead drunk. What in God's name was I supposed to do?'

191

Edwin shouted at the walls. They stared back, blank-faced.

You're asking God? You should ask Dr Michael. He'll tell you what they do to murderers, my master.

Edwin shivered. Was this it? Strung up until his limbs stopped twitching, then carted away for anatomists and surgeons to pick apart before they buried the scraps of him in the unconsecrated ground of Edinburgh's gaol.

Go on. Throw your wishes in. Might as well. Nothing else to do.

As every day passed, Edwin's wishes went ungranted. No visit from Alastair Remy, no visit from Eliza, no word from his father. No last chance to remind his children that their mother had brought it on herself. He shivered and wept. He curled his knees up to his chest and tried to remember the buttery scent of her skin, the sound of her raw laugh, her beautiful hair, his own undamaged self.

★ ★ ★

Three days before Edwin's scheduled execution, a warder let the prison superintendent into the condemned cell.

'It seems Her Majesty has judged your blameless life worthy of being spared.' The superintendent dropped a letter on the floor. 'I believe you can read.'

Edwin looked at it, uncomprehending. He was dizzy from hunger.

'Did you hear me? The Queen has granted you mercy, Mr Salt.'

Edwin scrambled on the floor to grab the letter.

'Your death sentence has been commuted to penal

servitude for life,' the superintendent announced. 'The Scottish penal system congratulates such a fine, upstanding Englishman. Until we can make alternative arrangements, we look forward to funding your lengthy stay with us.'

In the distance, a steam train whistled. Edwin began to shake. He groped for the bucket and only just managed to pull it to his face before he vomited.

Agnes

Adelaide, 1892

Agnes's baby girl arrived late at night and much quicker than expected. Sarah fetched hot water and towels and looked after things. Florence dabbed cool water on Agnes's twisted face and talked her through it. Her voice was like a distant lighthouse seeing Agnes through a storm.

Agnes kissed her daughter's dark hair and counted ten fingers, ten toes.

They christened her Emily May. She was Em to Florence and Ernest and Sarah, 'our bairn' to George. At night they tucked her up in a pretty white blanket that Florence had sewn for Agnes's firstborn. On Sundays they walked along the jetty and Agnes talked to Emily to help her get acquainted with the world she'd been born into. She pointed out the fat grey gulls and swift white gulls. She looked through the railings at shadows of fish darkening the seabed. George pulled faces and made rude noises and Emily gurgled with delight.

When the wind picked up, they sheltered underneath the jetty and George pulled at the collar of her coat and kissed her neck and sometimes she let him kiss her like he did at night in their bed.

'I'd do anything for you and our bairn,' George whispered.

'You already did more than enough,' Agnes said, tapping her belly, and the wind pulled joy out of their mouths.

It was a sunny, cloudless day. Nothing unusual for Adelaide. At the port, George was among the men lugging bulging sacks of coal, their hands blackening and the dust coating their throats. For fun, some of the neighbours' children kicked around an old boot stuffed with newspaper.

The worst of winter was well behind them and as far as Agnes knew, none of the children had so much as a sniffle.

Sarah insisted on staying with Agnes that night. She prepared cold compresses and said in her firmest matron's voice, 'It's just a fever. Em will be perfectly well. I ought to know. Mothers always worry too much. Em is a tough little thing.'

Agnes and Sarah took turns throughout the night. Poor Emily shivered and screamed through the cold compresses. The heat from Emily's blazing cheeks dried up the wet cloths. Agnes flung the useless compresses on the floor and hugged Emily tightly to her.

'Put her down,' Sarah instructed gently. 'You won't help her by making her too warm.'

By the first light of dawn, Emily's cries had quietened to whimpers. Agnes ignored Sarah and held Emily close and whispered the few prayers she knew, every half-remembered hymn. She prayed to Mam, she prayed to Baby Cath, she prayed to all Mam's saints.

Emily seemed to be calming down. Agnes asked forgiveness. *Please, God, forgive me for being unable to let go of poor Emily, like Sarah says I should. Forgive me for taking money from Da's pockets and Annie's tin on the shelf. Forgive me for leaving Walter behind. Forgive me for being in the river while Mam fell asleep in the sun. Forgive me for giving Baby Cath to the nun. Please, God, forgive me for all the screaming and the leaving.*

Agnes kneeled on the floor and sobbed into Emily May's hair. Emily kept very still and quiet while Agnes held her and turned her face to God, who surely listened high above their street.

Sarah unfolded Agnes's stiffened, stubborn body and gently eased Emily out of her arms. Then suddenly came the chill of the great gaping space left by her taken-away baby. Agnes had never imagined there could be a pain worse than bringing Emily May into the world, but oh God, here it was. Come back, come back, come back.

★ ★ ★

Agnes stayed in bed all day. She clung to Emily's clothes and her daughter's special blanket. When she woke up, for a moment she felt like Emily was still with her. But as soon as she opened her eyes, she could see it gathering strength at the edge of her vision. She buried herself under the bedclothes and submerged herself in the terrible waves of grief. She cried the sheets sodden and Florence made Agnes get up every day so she could change them. The sun baked the loss of Emily hard into the cotton. Every day Agnes asked Florence if there was a letter from home and every day Florence shook her head. The absence of a letter dug the grief in deeper.

Thank the Lord for the bell down at the port to signal the shift changes, to divide one day from the next, or else none of them would have known any time had passed. Agnes barely spoke to George, and he knew

196

better than to push her. He reached his arm across at night sometimes, but she rolled away from him.

One night, something changed. She pulled him towards her without speaking or making any sound of pleasure. It was a hollow sort of wanting that gnawed at her insides. It was almost like being alive but with none of the joy. She wanted him like this night after night. George whispered about wanting to bring the old warm noises from her, but she pushed his hands away and lay there until his own agony took him over. Afterwards they slept as if alone, sheets wedged between them.

Before long, Agnes felt sour waves in her gut in the mornings. She had been hoping for it. Hoping that, if she tried hard enough, she could fill her empty body with Emily May all over again, somehow unlock that tiny wooden box and wash the soil from Emily's blue little mouth and bring her home. But the morning sickness had a different character. Instead of relentless vomiting, this was a passing cloud of nausea that rarely came to much. Her body swelled and ached in different places. Even her dreams were new.

'Another bairn.' George rested his hand on her belly. 'Now everything will be all right.'

Agnes curled up against her husband and sobbed. Something foreign now grew inside her. Emily May was never coming back.

Edwin

Portland, Dorset, 1861

The Portland dockside teemed with carpenters carrying beams up gangplanks. Rain thrashed and wind rattled the ropes on the waiting transport ship, *Lincelles*. The tops of its masts poked into the clouds. Three hundred pairs of wet trousers flapped against three hundred pairs of freezing legs. Someone called an order and the line of men started to sway. Edwin's feet fell into rhythm with the lifer Mick McCarthy in front of him, the pimply youth Martin Smith in front of McCarthy, toothless stonemason Arthur Molloy in front of Smith and embezzler William Pullinger behind them all. The rain and wind got heavier. Three hundred identically dressed convicts trooped up the gangplank. Three hundred pairs of feet marching. It sounded like gunfire.

'With this wind we'll be in Trinidad by Thursday,' one of the guards said. There was a darkness about his tone. Below deck, all light disappeared and the sounds above were muffled. The air was sticky and warm. Men lost their footing, stumbled, cursed. Somebody groaned and the stench of vomit filled the air.

Once below it was clear what the carpenters had been doing. Crossbeams and long beams divided the empty cargo space between the decks into sections. Men unrolled their hammocks and fixed them to the beams. The ship forced itself against the swell, rolling first to port then heaving back to starboard. The

198

guards did their best to stay upright, in command, but they were no more accustomed to the undertow than the prisoners.

'Reckon a few of us could take them on, for certain,' McCarthy said.

'Bloody Irish, always seeing an uprising everywhere you go,' Edwin said. Smith and Molloy had to agree.

Five days later the *Lincelles* was still suspended in Portland harbour. Rain trickled down to the convict bunks. Rumours did the same. A convict heard from a guard who heard from the ship's doctor that, even though the *Lincelles* was one of the biggest and sturdiest convict transports ever fitted, it would not be safe to leave until the weather calmed. A dozen or so Irishmen were already whispering, agitating, whipping up dissent, so the captain and the ship's doctor implemented the shipboard routines immediately. Mick McCarthy was appointed a mess captain, along with half a dozen of the wide-eyed and terrified Newgate lads, a bit of responsibility to take their already fractured minds off what was ahead. School monitors were appointed from the best educated of the men. Edwin Salt for reading. William Pullinger for mathematics.

'You heard about him?' Smith whispered to Edwin. 'A proper celebrity. A quarter of a million quid nicked from the bank, they reckon. No trace of it ever found.'

A quarter of a million. Mary Ann tickled the back of his neck. Her fingers scratched like hessian. *Plenty there to set yourself up in the Swan River, Edwin dear.*

In the warm stillness of confinement, stories spread as freely as crotch fungus. Smith had heard about natives who would spear a man and boil him until his skin peeled off his bones. Molloy had heard there was exotic fruit that grew bigger than a man's head. One of the Newgate pickpockets said his uncle had been transported to Van Diemen's Land and had escaped, never to be seen or heard from again. A spotty-faced youth, sent away for stealing, said he knew a couple from his church who'd gone to the Swan River as free settlers. Made good, he said. But he was howled down. Everyone agreed the gaol would surely be paradise compared to what probably lay beyond the gates.

One night without warning, the *Lincelles* lurched forward. The swell rose angrily against the bough. The masts creaked. Up on deck the crew shouted. Winches screeched. Edwin clutched at his throat. Molloy whispered a prayer.

'Bon voyage, men,' Mick McCarthy shouted. 'May God bless the mighty *Lincelles* and all the righteous servants of the Lord who sail in her.' The other Irish cheered and the Newgate lads looked worried.

Pullinger retched and groaned.

'In the name of God, man, pipe down,' Edwin said.

'My apologies, good fellow. I think I am dying,' Pullinger mouthed.

Is that poor man keeping you awake? Mary Ann sat on the end of his hammock and rubbed a low, gentle circle over her stomach. *I know how he feels. I ache here also, my master.* Mary Ann drew a line with her index finger from under her breastbone to below her belly button. *Oh, how I ache.*

Below decks it already stank enough to make the doctor gag and keep him busy with powders and tinctures. The space was cramped but the routine was more suffocating. Dr Crawford ran the ship with precision, but still all kinds of danger festered. Talk of taking the ship was everywhere but the only convicts taken seriously were the Irish, and the guards never took their eyes off them.

In the mornings Edwin read out loud from books to the illiterate Cockney lads who parroted back the words when he pointed to them. In the afternoons, Pullinger talked and wrote numbers, and everybody listened. Even some of the crew and the religious instructor sat in on Pullinger's arithmetic lessons.

'A quarter of a million,' Mick McCarthy whispered as he slopped porridge in Edwin's bowl one morning. 'Where does a man hide that kind of money?'

It was almost a week before the weather calmed enough to allow the convicts up on deck for exercise. The air slapped their faces and sea spray burned their eyes. The blue-black sea rolled and lunged. Huge birds swooped and hung in the sky, and men who had killed other men crouched in fear.

The ship lurched and Pullinger fell heavily. The guards ordered the convicts to leave him be, let him find his sea legs. Edwin ignored them and helped Pullinger up. The guards scowled but did nothing.

'Thank you.' Pullinger shook Edwin's hand. 'Damned sea air. What a man needs is the stench of horse shit and burning coal.'

'Oh, for a whiff of the Thames. God's own personal privy behind the East India Company dock,' Edwin said.

'And to think my wife always complained I would never go so far as Brighton to take the waters,' Pullinger croaked.

Next morning, Edwin opened a book and prepared to read to the Newgate lads. He stifled a gasp in case any of the others noticed his reaction. The colour. The insignia. It was a crisp Bank of England note.

201

Mary Ann prodded Edwin in the ribs. *That's the way, my master. He looks the sort who'd help his friends. You always were the charmer.*

As a Cambridge-educated forger from London theorised one evening, William Pullinger might be guilty of little more than fiction: he'd told a wildly improbable tale of how much money his esteemed employer, the Union Bank, had deposited with the Bank of England. In truth, some of the cash may well have found its way into Pullinger's possession, but if nobody at either bank bothered to check, who was Pullinger to blink first? Molloy said he'd heard Pullinger's wife was now living comfortably in London. Perhaps Pullinger would send for her the moment he had his ticket-of-leave. 'I'd send for my wife and she hasn't got a penny,' Molloy said. 'You'd think Pullinger could have bought his way out of this rotten fate.'

★ ★ ★

In the weeks it took to battle towards the Cape, three hundred convicts prayed for calm weather. Edwin had personally begged God for it every night. Even the Irish talked less of how to take the ship and more about blessed mercy from the vagaries of wind and air pressure. When the sea stopped boiling, the crew cursed the convicts and changed sails and uttered old seafarers' prayers. Only an idiot landlubber of a city man would be stupid enough to think that calm waters made for an easier passage. The *Lincelles* heaved and strained. Dr Crawford ordered the convicts up on deck in shifts, and they lugged the boards from underneath their hammocks and scrubbed them clean, over and over, to pass the time.

202

Edwin kept his eye on Pullinger, gave him extra food, helped him walk on deck, and in return, he sometimes found a banknote inside a book or in his pocket. Edwin slept with the fold of money up his sleeve and he believed it kept him warm. He loved it when the lump of money woke him in the night. He hated the routine, the unending sea. The fattening wad of money was the only way Edwin knew for certain that days were passing, that he was still alive.

* * *

'Land!'

The cry pierced the monotony. Dr Crawford allowed the convicts on deck to look at the thin strip of land.

A single black bird materialised from the green water, its wingspan enormous. The men followed it with their gaze, watching how it chased the ship, drifting up and down on the same breezes caught by the sails.

'It wants to feast on our piss and shit and vomit,' Pullinger said airily. 'See how it stares at me?'

'Take it easy, old man,' Edwin said. 'They'll lock you in the black box for talking like a lunatic.'

McCarthy scowled at Edwin. 'What's it to you if they lock him up in the black box?'

That night in Edwin's dreams, Mary Ann sprouted wings and pecked his face, body, arms, then flew away, carrying parts of him in a tin bucket that rattled and glinted in the sun.

The next morning the land had disappeared. Air tickled the topsails and the mainsails hung flat. Riggers ran up and down the masts, letting out sails, pulling them in. The convicts grumbled that the island must have been a mirage, the weevils in the porridge causing hallucinations.

Pullinger hadn't appeared on deck. Nobody had seen him. Edwin flicked from front to back of the book he was reading to the Newgate lads, but found nothing.

'Damned wind,' a rigger shouted. 'Never known anything like it. Can't make up its mind if it wants to hold us back or spew us straight into the mouth of the Devil.'

Below decks, Mick McCarthy cornered Edwin. 'Pullinger's been taken ill,' he said. 'Looks like your bank will be closed for a while.'

McCarthy took something from behind his ear. It was one of Pullinger's banknotes. Edwin instinctively put his hand to the fold of notes hidden in his shirt pocket. From nowhere, two more Irish appeared. They each held one of Edwin's arms and McCarthy thumped him square in the guts. He struggled and tried to elbow one of the Irish in the face, but both men were too strong for him. In the time it took for the guard to notice the scuffling and cursing, McCarthy had grabbed the fold of banknotes from Edwin's pocket. The two Irish shoved Edwin to the deck and kicked him repeatedly in the back. Pain flamed through his middle.

See? It hurts, doesn't it, Edwin dear? Mary Ann held a pannikin of best whisky just out of reach.

* * *

Pullinger's condition worsened. Dr Crawford insisted it wasn't contagious, but for every morning Pullinger didn't appear on deck, half a dozen more men reported feeling ill. Dr Crawford swabbed ears and listened to chests. He ordered the mess captains and the school monitors to take shifts watching Pullinger. Edwin glared at McCarthy. McCarthy looked wary like a hungry dog.

Pullinger lay motionless in his hammock. His teeth chattered. The sores around his mouth were red and weepy.

'Jesus Christ,' McCarthy said. 'I ain't going near him.'

'Too late now. You've had your hands all over his money. You may as well be dead,' Edwin said.

'See you in Hell then, Salt.'

'I think we're already there,' Edwin said, and McCarthy grunted his agreement.

'Happy New Year, Pullinger.' Edwin shook his friend's hand. It was cold and clammy.

'Should old acquaintance be forgot.' Pullinger clutched his stomach. The ship rolled. The rattle of timbers signalled thunder. Edwin and McCarthy took turns in helping Pullinger drink his lime juice. A couple of the Newgate lads brought extra blankets. Everybody wanted to help the man who might have a quarter of a million stashed away.

'And what, sir, do you hope for in the year of our Lord eighteen — what year is it?' Pullinger's eyes were wide, confused.

'Eighteen sixty-two, sir.' Edwin put another spoon of lime juice to Pullinger's mouth. 'Since you ask, I first hope for good health.'

Pullinger winced and wiped his mouth with his hand. 'I pray for underthings not rotten with sea water and in which lice have not made themselves at home.

205

I pray for land under my rotten, stinking feet.'

'Shut up and drink your juice,' McCarthy said. 'You're no use to us dead.'

There was a loud crash and the ship rolled. Dozens of sleeping bodies fell from hammocks.

'I pray for the stink of horse shit in my nostrils and the continued good health of the auditors of the Bank of England.' Pullinger convulsed. McCarthy grabbed more blankets from other convicts and laid them over Pullinger.

You'd better pray for Pullinger, Edwin dear, because he doesn't look too good from where I'm stood.

'Shut up, woman!' Edwin shouted at nothing.

'Not you too, Salt.' McCarthy said. 'I'm buggered if I'm feeding lime juice to you.'

'I'll outlive you both,' Edwin promised.

Pullinger smelled like rotting meat. The ship heaved and rolled and there was the now familiar thud of convicts being thrown to the floor. Edwin held onto the beam that supported Pullinger's hammock. A rogue trickle of sea water lapped at his feet.

'Keep it together, Pullinger.' Edwin wiped the sick man's forehead. 'Talk is we're not far from Fremantle.'

'My ankles tingle in anticipation of the cool embrace of the irons,' Pullinger wheezed.

The ship lurched. The force of it flung Edwin and McCarthy across the floor and hurled Pullinger from his hammock. Edwin's head collided with a joist a few feet away. The puddle of sea water swilled around his face, his arse. Men cursed and swore, and somebody whispered about having a go at the guards before it was too late. McCarthy hissed that they might as well wait until they got to dry land and then make a run for it.

206

Edwin held tight and rested his throbbing head against the joist. Here he was, in the bowels of a sea monster. He was entrails, he was shit. He wasn't even human. His limbs creaked. His own timbers shivered with damp. The crew said it was just the weather south of the Cape, but Edwin knew better. It was Mary Ann awakening on the seabed, puffing air into the ragged sails, Mary Ann who made the sea rise, Mary Ann who made his brow sweat, who made him feel he was permanently up to his neck in water, inches from drowning.

Sleep, my master, while you can. It's blowing a gale up on deck.

* * *

By sunrise on the sixth of January 1862, William Pullinger was dead. At five o'clock that afternoon, Molloy, Smith, McCarthy and Edwin lifted his shrouded and stiffened body up to their shoulders. The weights that had been added to the shroud made it more difficult.

The religious instructor read a rudimentary funeral service. It was so windy on deck, his words had barely escaped his mouth before they too went overboard. The Newgate pickpockets snivelled, more for the looming fate of Pullinger's body than for the death itself.

Dr Crawford gave the order and the men swung Pullinger up, up and over the side. His emaciated body bobbed up and down. The sea bashed against the side of the *Lincelles*. In less than a minute, Pullinger sank without trace.

Molloy gripped Edwin's shoulder and he swung

around. He was shocked to see Molloy's eyes wide with fear.

'I killed a man with my bare hands, but I never seen nothing like that,' Molloy said.

'Turn your back on it.' Edwin offered Molloy some tobacco. 'Same as we do with everything that got us here.'

First chance they got, Edwin and McCarthy went below to take Pullinger's things apart. Some scavengers must have got there first because there was nothing left in his hammock, not even a blanket.

Not to worry, Edwin dear, Mary Ann said, squeezing his sleeve where the banknotes used to be. Isn't money the root of all evil?

Mary Ann mopped Edwin's forehead. She touched her icy lips to his flaming cheeks. *Poor Edwin. The captain says it's the toughest weather he's ever sailed through.* Edwin craved a whisky-blind sleep. Something kicked him in the guts. He bent his knees up to his chest and screamed at it to stop. It was faceless, cruel, it kicked without mercy.

★ ★ ★

The convicts, the crew, the guards, even the guards' wives, all trooped up on deck. They squinted at the bleached and ragged coast. The water was green. No, it was blue. It was a colour yet to be named. The light hurt their eyes. Birds cooed in the sky. Convicts stretched their arms out to let the warm air dry four months of seawater from their bones.

'That's it?' Mick McCarthy pointed at the view. 'I reckon I'll take my chances.'

Hundreds of legs. Hundreds of arms flailed in the

water. Hundreds of mouths cursed. It was Edwin's turn. He climbed into the water. Sea slapped his thighs. Convicts in front of him, convicts behind him. One foot in front of the other. They walked. Grit through the holes in his boots and a slimy weed that hindered his movement. He was part of the sea now, he was washed up, tidal, taking in air through his skin. Ceaseless light came off the water and the sky. Blinded and nauseated by the hot glare. They walked. Thigh deep, knee deep, ankle deep. One foot in the water, one foot at the end of the earth. He thrashed his arms at his feet and cut it all loose: Samuel Salt and Son, Saint Chad, Edinburgh, Sir Walter Bloody Scott.

A fumbling at his ankles, a burning pain and he was part of a ten-legged, iron-sinewed monster whose bones would one day be scrubbed clean and peered at behind glass. They crossed the white sand and lumbered up a track. Legs, flabby and unsteady, learning how to walk on this land.

Men in coats and hats, women — *women* for Christ's sake. A small boy pointed and Edwin shouted and waved. Albert and Eliza, waiting for him! But the boy screamed and the woman dragged him away and disappeared into the shade of a building. The building looked familiar, its pillars and classical lines in the middle of a sandpit. Jesus Christ, a courthouse. He started to sink. Someone shouted, 'Keep moving, keep moving,' but there was another building up ahead, a high wall, and he was drowning in glare, in light.

⋆ ⋆ ⋆

Edwin rested his aching head against the cool stone of the cell. His new prison uniform was scratchy and ill-fitting. His pockets were empty.

There was a bucket and a hammock and a pannikin of water and wailing and cursing from other cells. Everything was the same, everything was different. He waited. He drank the cool water. He waited for her to appear, to snatch the pannikin from him, to kick him in the guts and split him open, but she was gone.

Agnes

Adelaide, 1894

Agnes gave birth to a screaming baby girl in the middle of the night. Sarah cleaned the baby up and delivered her safely to the weeping mother. Agnes put her baby to her breast and held her very tightly while she fed. The child wriggled and kicked against the confines of Agnes's arms. Florence brought in Emily's old clothes. Agnes wrapped her new daughter in her lost daughter's blanket and the smell of the newborn girl mingled with the smell of the lost girl and Agnes loved them both in the one body. The baby wriggled.

'She's in a mighty hurry,' Florence said.

'I promise I'll never let you out of my sight.' Agnes blew little raspberry kisses on her daughter's pink cheeks.

Little Frances Johnson's hair was as dark as Emily's, but she had twice as much of it. It grew faster and curlier. Her eyes, pale like Emily's, darkened and eventually settled into a deep blue.

Frances grew faster, ate faster, crawled and talked sooner than Ernest and Florence's children had done. On the day Frances first walked, she stood up, wobbled, walked and then almost ran, before wobbling to the ground, picking herself up and walk-running again. It was a month after her first birthday, a windy afternoon on Semaphore Jetty.

'Even her name's too slow for her,' Florence said. 'We should call her something quicker to shout when she's running away.'

'Fan.' Agnes scooped up her squealing, wriggling daughter. 'Little Fan. You'll run all the way to Brazil before the rest of us have put our shoes on.'

* * *

Ernest's news about buying a house took them all by surprise. He grabbed Sarah's hands and danced her around the table. It was a four-roomed cottage in Rosewater, a newly made suburb with streets that ran as straight as tracks for the railwaymen and their families who could now afford a place of their own. George found his little family a tin-roofed cottage a decent walk back from the beachfront and about halfway between Largs pier and Semaphore Jetty.

The morning after their first night in their new home, Agnes made George bring Fan down to the beach. The sky was streaked with cloud and the beach almost emptied of sea. The lowest tide in weeks, George said. Agnes pulled off her shoes, hitched up her skirt and waded into the sodden sand.

'You'll sink to the middle of the earth,' George called, but Agnes was too far away to hear. She picked up a handful of shells. The sea looked shallow and benign and far away, but she aimed for it anyway.

One for Mam.

One for Baby Cath.

A heart-shaped pearl shell for her darling Emily May.

A handful of broken shells for Samuel the tailor, Sam Junior, James, Eliza and Mary with all her dreadful luck.

From this distance, Fan's hair shimmered blue-

212

black in the metallic light. Agnes ran through the weeds and shells that the tide had left behind, through the middle of the earth and back to Fan, George, her very own family.

News from Home

Fan

Fremantle, December 1906

Fan heard Grandpa before she saw him. That booming, storybook voice he used when he talked to her. Fan walked into the smelly hotel, her nose in the air, chin defiant.

'You must be lost, love.' A man let out a long, slow whistle. 'Does your mother know you're here?'

'I'm looking for my grandpa. Edwin Salt. I think I heard him.' She pointed into the dimly lit bar.

'Wait outside. I'll fetch him.' The barmaid eyed Fan. 'You're too young to be hanging about with his sort. Lord knows, you live in Fremantle for long enough and there'll be plenty of time for that.'

Grandpa emerged, looking thinner than he did at home. He leaned on his walking cane.

'It looked like rain. I didn't want to catch my death,' he said.

'The doctor reckons you're half-dead, anyway. Don't think this is what he meant by fresh air.' Fan grabbed his sleeve and dragged him along like she did with Ned when he was being stubborn. The sky was darkening with purple clouds. In Port Adelaide it would've meant a storm. Dad always said that harbours were the first places to feel the weather, and maybe it would be the same here.

'What you doing in there anyway?' Fan asked. 'They looked like the sort Ma says to stay away from.'

'Let's just say I was pleased to attend a reunion of

old friends,' he said.

'You ain't been in Fremantle long enough to have old friends,' Fan said.

'Some friendships stand the test of time, Miss Johnson.'

By goodness, he talked some rot.

'In any case, you must be pleased you found some mates to talk to,' Fan said.

'Their conversation is not a patch on your witty banter, Miss Johnson.'

'But of course, Grandpa,' Fan said in her best posh voice. 'What's your mates like? Where they from?'

'They hail from across the globe.' The grog had made him talkative. 'What would you say if I told you I once knew a fine gentleman who had a quarter of a million in the bank? Or someone else who had killed a' — he hesitated, thinking — 'a *lion* with his bare hands?'

'I'd say can you get your hands on that quarter million by teatime? 'Cos Ma's in a terrible state about you going missing.'

He snorted. 'I'll make enquiries, Miss Johnson.'

'Any of your mates from . . .' Fan tried to say it lightly, 'New South Wales?' She hooked her arm through his. 'You know anybody in New South Wales?' She said it again slowly to be sure he understood.

'What a curious thing to ask. No, Miss Johnson, I do not know anybody in *New South Wales*,' he said, mimicking her.

They reached home just before the rain started. But that was nothing compared to the storm brewing in Ma's eyes.

'I found him for you,' Fan mumbled.

Ma grabbed Fan's fingers and she flinched. Then

she realised Ma wasn't squeezing. She was pressing a blue ribbon into Fan's hand.

* * *

Ma's silence lasted for days. She didn't even say good-bye when she left the house. Fan dug her nails into her palms to give herself something else to think about.

'You left quite a mess,' Ma said eventually, while she was splitting pods and hurling poor innocent peas into a bowl. 'But I tidied everything up. I doubt he'll know.'

'I'm so sorry.' Fan burst into tears. 'Are you going to tell him?'

'Not unless you do such a thing again. Do you hear me?'

'I promise, I promise.' Fan wiped her eyes, but the tears wouldn't stop.

'What kind of stories is he filling your head with?' Ma glowered.

'Nothing, Ma, honest.' Fan held Ma's gaze as best she could. 'Honest,' she repeated for good measure. 'He complains about things. The heat. The sea air. His feet. Your cooking.'

'Ungrateful old man.' Agnes snapped the backbone of another pod. 'I have told you time and time again. Your grandfather's mind and heart are failing. He has nothing to do with us besides food and lodging. And now you've turned into a sneak and a thief. I don't want you bothering him anymore.'

'But Ma, I was only —'

'No, Frances.'

'What if I'd found out where my Uncle Walter is?' Fan blurted.

'What did you say?'

'I reckon I know where Uncle Walter is.' Fan's mouth had gone dry. 'He's in New South Wales somewhere.'

'Oh, my Lord.' Ma sounded like someone had their hands around her throat. On the stove, a blackened pot bubbled. Ma threw peas into the boiling water and watched them rise and split, wiping steam from her eyes.

Edwin

Fremantle, 1862

Like other gaols, the Convict Establishment smelled of piss. It kicked men out of their hammocks and made them bathe twice a week whether they needed it or not. It fed its men lumpy porridge and salted beef and sometimes the slower men went hungry. It shoved its men to their knees on Sundays — Catholics on one side, Protestants on the other, and guards with their eyes on the men, not God. It had corridors and locked doors and a laundry and dark cells and secrets. It howled at night. It had strict routines: up at dawn, breakfast, inspection, instruction. If it was stew, it was Thursday. The routine trapped you inside, the routine saved you from the asylum. Sometimes Edwin woke up believing he was back in England and had a tiny glimmer of hope that somebody might visit him or that there might be a letter from Eliza. They rationed even that. They rationed contact, letters, news, and they doled it out in meagre portions like the porridge.

Like other gaols, it dispensed discipline. Warders prowled the corridors, their eyes opaque with cruelty or fear, you could never be sure which. If a warder didn't hit you just to see if you'd hit him back, one of the other convicts would. The convicts knew that warders would take marks off for insolence, disorder, disobeying rules, talking, blaspheming, stealing. A convict knew he needed a blank slate to get his

221

ticket-of-leave, and too many marks off would add extra time to a sentence. A ticket-of-leave was easier to get here than in England, everyone knew that, and because the colony was so desperate for workers, they'd forgive a man just about anything. Somebody noticed a couple of the Portland men, Watts and O'Neill, seemed to have gone missing, and Edwin joked they'd survived the voyage only to drown in knee-deep water. Turned out they'd stepped off the *Lincelles* and been given their tickets straight away. Everybody went quiet when a warder told them that. Nobody expected ever to see Watts or O'Neill again.

Everybody knew a warder would take off a mark if you so much as looked at him the wrong way and he didn't like the look of you. Thanks to Mick McCarthy stealing tobacco from the wrong man, the *Lincelles* men learned early that the place was really run by a pig-faced, toothless Londoner transported for armed robbery five years earlier. McCarthy's split lip and bruised eye took a week to heal and the man in charge, Comptroller-General Henderson, locked him in a dark cell for a couple of nights just to make an example of him. McCarthy's absence for those two days made the atmosphere taut with some unnamed fear and all the whispers were of the lash this and the lash that. When they let McCarthy out of the dark cell, he swore it was the gaol water affecting him; after so long at sea, the shock of fresh water had sent him mad. Edwin told him to keep quiet if he didn't want Henderson on his case and the cat on his back.

The rule in the Convict Establishment was silence at all times, but like some seeds and some settlers, silence had never really taken root. Before the first week was out, the *Lincelles* men knew which convicts were here for murder, which were here for robbery, who had stolen a sheep and who had first got their tickets years ago but kept getting into trouble with the Fremantle magistrates. Reoffending was a contagion, a Cornish forger told Edwin. Stick with a reoffender too long and you'll catch it from him. You should have swung, and you're so close to freedom now. For Christ's sake, don't fuck it up.

Once a day, in the early morning, the convicts were herded out to the exercise yard. They cursed and squinted in the sudden glare of daylight. The heat was unbearable. The sun reflected off the white walls and made their eyes water. There was always the smell of fire somewhere in the distance. Edwin didn't complain. He turned his face to the sky and soaked it up. He walked in a circle and willed time to pass. Some days he ran as fast as he could around the yard until his lungs hurt. McCarthy just stared and talked to himself. The Irish congregated and whispered and smoked. A man didn't need to be a lag to smoke with them, but he did need to be Irish.

On some mornings, the breeze was already ripping in hard off the ocean. On these days, Edwin had to be pushed and threatened to take his exercise. The smell of the sea. The roar of it in the background. He hated it. Even on the days when he couldn't hear it, he could feel the stickiness of the salt air on his skin. With the smell of the sea came unsteadiness under his feet, sickness in his guts and the nightmares of Mary Ann dressed for the grave. Her bruised eye, her split lip. On bath day he scrubbed his skin red raw to get rid of the smell of the sea. Other men had never seen anything like it and wondered if the new English lifer might be more at home in the asylum.

223

Like other gaols, this place had a wall, but that's where the similarity ended. Over the wall was nothing but sky. No London streets teeming with thieves and vermin, no piss-ridden docks. There were hills in the distance, Perth town was a few miles away, a scattering of frontier towns lay over the hills and goodness knew what was beyond that. Somebody said they'd heard there was an inland sea, but nobody had been there to find out one way or the other. The lads from London and Newcastle couldn't believe how much nothing there was. They couldn't stop talking about it. In the yard, the warders, too, liked to put their faces to the sky and talk about home or what might lie over those hills.

A newly arrived convicted murderer stirred the slime at the bottom of the pond. Edwin was placed in the gaol's tailor shop on account of his trade, but he proved less than helpful. On his first day, a Cockney armed robber grabbed him and held a knife to his throat. Edwin managed to wriggle free, only to be kicked in the stomach by two other men. He begged for mercy. The two men kicked him in the back again and again. One landed his boot hard on Edwin's hand. He shouted in pain. Two warders watched and did nothing.

Edwin tended his bruises and patched up his hand. He refused to see the doctor. In the end he left the tailor's shop and got thrown in with the labourers. The worst of the worst were in the tailor's shop, somebody told him. Even stone-breaking would be better than that.

He forced himself to keep his fists in his pockets and his head down. A couple of the warders goaded the hardest men to take on the newly arrived murderer,

224

pushing him to crack open. Edwin shoved them away and stared straight ahead at whatever life might be possible over that wall.

They'd all heard that the powers that be considered the land beyond the walls worse than Hell itself. That's why they sent convicts out on work parties to Perth and Guildford and York to build roads and bridges and gaols and courthouses. Once a convict had a taste of the evil that lived out there, he'd be begging to be let back into the Establishment quicker than you could say 'Not guilty, your Honour'.

Henderson was in charge of the gaol, but all the rumours were about the man they'd just appointed the new governor of the colony. Hampton had made quite a name for himself in Van Diemen's Land. His reputation among convicts didn't so much precede him as run, screaming, miles out in front. Talk was that Hampton was obsessed with the lash, that he slept with a cat-o'-nine-tails in his bed and kissed it every morning. More backs broken in Van Diemen's Land than anybody would believe. Hampton would order a hundred lashes if a convict was out of his cell at the wrong time, or if a lag gave backchat to a warder. Talk was that every man who wore the broad arrow had reason to fear Hampton. So, what difference did it make whether any of them kept their heads down or not? It might not keep them safe from the lash. What did any of them really have to lose? At least this was how McCarthy explained it to Edwin the day they left for York and a few of the convicts decided to plan their escape.

★ ★ ★

They clung together on the dilapidated barge that carried them up the river to Guildford: warders Paterson and Brennan, a Cornish policeman called Lissman and a dozen convicts. The light was fierce and the horizon further away than anything they'd ever seen. The warders chained the convicts at the ankles, even though there was nowhere to go except into a river that was lumpy with jellyfish. Nobody talked. Eyes scanned the riverbanks. The warders braced their rifles on their shoulders and stared fiercely at the eyes they imagined were staring back at them through the dense scrub. The river weaved ahead of them. It looked like a giant snake swallowing them whole, Smith grumbled. This water was nothing compared to what they'd seen on the *Lincelles*, but they felt every inch of the unbearable slowness by the passing of trees. The occasional curl of smoke broke the blueness of the sky. How much further was there to go into this godforsaken place? The irons made it hard to keep their balance. They steadied themselves and cursed.

Once they were safely off the barge at Guildford, the convicts watched McCarthy. McCarthy watched the warders. The sun was hot. One of the policemen pointed his rifle towards a red-dirt track.

'Look at those clouds.' Molloy pointed east towards a mass of dark blue gathered on the horizon. It was impossible to see what, if anything, lay beyond them. 'Never seen nothing like it.'

'They're not clouds.' Lissman gestured with his rifle. 'They're hills. We're walking towards those hills.'

'How long's that going to take?' Molloy said hoarsely.

'Plenty have done it before you.' Paterson took a tin from his supplies. 'Mutton fat. Rub this in. There've

226

been complaints about the state some men's feet are in by the time they get to York.'

In chains, the men struggled to walk: they fell and stumbled and swore. The warders threatened and shouted and prodded the convicts with their rifle barrels. They fell into step and the more they walked, the longer the track seemed to stretch. The track ran flat for a while but then started to climb at the foot of Greenmount Hill. The trees got denser. Paterson and Brennan watched the men. Lissman watched for Aborigines. Every now and then he fired shots into the scrub. The air crackled and birds flew, screeching, from trees. They had to get to Greenmount road station before nightfall, or so Brennan kept barking at them. Dusk brought kangaroos out from shadows, and they looked so comical and frightening, nobody could decide whether to make fun of them or shoot them. One of the Wakefield lads said he'd heard kangaroo meat was tough as old boots, but there was plenty of it out there if you were brave and starving. The men watched the darkening sky and waited for a signal from McCarthy.

* * *

It was nightfall when they reached the road station. It was little more than a couple of stone huts and a clearing. The men pulled their boots off and groaned and swore. So did Lissman, Paterson and Brennan. Paterson passed around a pannikin of rum and they all slugged a mouthful to calm their nerves. They smoked. Half of them were asleep on the ground before the fire had been lit.

'Are you in or out, Salt?' McCarthy kicked at the

blood-red ants that crawled over everything. He gestured to where Lissman, Paterson and Brennan talked quietly. 'Those three look scared out of their wits. We can make a run for it.'

McCarthy was right. The men in charge looked more scared than the lags. And no wonder. The stars sprayed across the blackest sky Edwin had ever seen. It looked unearthly. His feet throbbed, his head ached and he was hungry. Whatever was making that hissing noise in the trees was roaring in his ears. It made him wonder if he had in fact swung from the gallows and was already dead.

'Where would we go?' Edwin put more mutton fat on his feet. 'Look at this place, McCarthy. Where in God's name would we go?'

'Suit yourself.' McCarthy planted his boot into the crowd of ants. 'You and the screws might be the only ones who make it to York.'

* * *

Four days walking and still no signal from McCarthy. Their feet blistered and bled. On the few occasions anyone saw a house or a curl of smoke above the trees, convicts and warders alike stopped and stared. They didn't see a single person. The trees were monotonous and hid kangaroos and who knew what else. Their ankles bled from the chains but by now everyone had forgotten the pain. Lissman shouted an order and veered to the left down a narrow trail. Again, the smell of fire, but this time it mingled with the sound of men whose words they understood. In front of them loomed a wide waterhole.

'Saint Ronan's Well,' Lissman announced wearily.

228

The land around the waterhole had been cleared except for a scattering of skinny trees near the water's edge. A group of travellers were camped nearby, their horses drinking from the waterhole. Paterson opined about Sir Walter Scott and Saint Ronan's Well and did whoever named this godforsaken swamp ask the great man for permission to use one of his finest storybook places? The mere mention of Sir Walter Scott reminded Edwin of his trial and he spat at the ground. Lissman said that it had nothing to do with the Scotsman, the Aborigines had a name for this waterhole, and what's more, different sorts of trees grew close to water, and that once one of the Aborigines had explained the land to him, it sort of made sense. But none of the men were listening. Brennan unchained the men, and everyone took off their boots and pulled up their trousers and limped into the water.

Edwin's feet had never hurt so much. The sun was still burning.

'Civilisation.' Molloy pointed to a rough-hewn building, more like a hut, fashioned from lumps of stone.

'That's a police station,' Lissman said. 'A convict road gang built that a few years ago.'

'Thank the Lord, a police station out here in the middle of nowhere,' McCarthy observed. His face was badly sunburnt. 'We can all sleep safe in our beds tonight.'

The ants bit them. The mosquitoes bit them. Sweat mixed with dust ran in rivers down their faces. The night sky was impenetrable and the birds were loud. One of the Irish lads tapped McCarthy on the shoulder, whispered about making a run for it, but at Saint Ronan's Well, even McCarthy was too tired to think about anything but sleep.

They woke up with drizzle on their faces. Finally, the hills were behind them. In front was flat, red land, divided by rows of trees and dotted with farmhouses.

'That's York?' said a Wakefield man. 'It don't look nowt like the York I remember.'

★ ★ ★

It was crowded in the small depot. They slung their hammocks up in the cramped space. Edwin, McCarthy and Smith volunteered to sleep outside and put their hammocks up between trees. The stone-breaking would continue every day from dawn until dusk, come Hell or high water, Brennan bleated, because they were finishing this stretch of road to York on Governor Hampton's instructions.

'We're already in Hell,' Edwin said, 'and we've seen enough high water for a lifetime.'

The ground was hard. The stone was harder than anything he'd encountered in Portland. Fortunately, Edwin had stores of rage to unleash. Smash one for his father. Smash fifteen for the jury. Smash the biggest one into tiny pieces for Mary Ann. Lissman had never seen anyone break stones like the English lifer did.

Once the stones were broken, the convicts hammered the pieces into the ground. 'It's got to last for a hundred years,' Paterson said, tapping the barrel of his rifle into the dirt to make his point. Nobody listened. The road inched closer to the town. At night the convicts shared smokes and rum with Lissman, Paterson and Brennan, and everybody talked about home. The hot days were followed by chilly nights.

230

Edwin shivered through fitful sleep. Molloy's nightmares kept them all awake but Smith seemed better rested than the others. A couple of times Edwin woke in the night to hear low voices, one of them Smith's. The other didn't sound like English. Smith was either brave or stupid, but he swore it wasn't 'like that'; it was just Lissman who knew a couple of natives and they'd given him a sweet flower to crush and sniff to help with his sleeping. Smith said his tobacco was more than even trade.

* * *

The April rains began without warning.

The ground turned to rust-coloured sludge. The clay smeared their clothes and faces. The hammocks outside were soaked through. The land turned to river and those tall, skinny trees were suddenly growing in the middle of a glistening lake. The stones wouldn't stick in the road, but the warders made them keep going. 'Come Hell or high water,' Brennan shouted again from the comfort of his hessian shelter.

A few of the convicts began to grumble. Edwin shivered in his sodden hammock.

'McCarthy,' Edwin hissed. 'Wake up. I've been thinking. Let's give it a go. Steal that idiot Lissman's rifle and make a run for it.'

McCarthy made no sound.

'Wake up, man.' Edwin stared at the hammock. McCarthy had disappeared.

* * *

McCarthy almost made it to York before the local policemen caught him. They took him to the York depot in irons, McCarthy screaming that all he'd wanted was a whisky, a woman and a proper bed. Lissman hit him hard in the back with the butt of his rifle. That soon shut him up. They put McCarthy on the next police cart back to Fremantle.

Once McCarthy had gone, Lissman, Paterson and Brennan grew wary. They stopped sharing tobacco with the convicts of an evening. They moved all the hammocks back inside the depot and chained up the doors at night.

'It's this damned land,' Brennan said to Paterson one evening. 'It lures you in. You don't know where you stand. You forget who you are, who they are and who's in charge.'

★ ★ ★

Houses, farms, people appeared in their sights. Settlers continued to cut trees and plant crops. They agreed such heavy rain was a curse from God, but it would surely coax something out of this land. The road gang heard whispers of local shoemakers, blacksmiths, builders, farm labourers, men who'd arrived as convicts but had got their tickets so long ago and built so much of the place that nobody thought it necessary to dwell on their origins. It was easy, Lissman said, to start work and just get on with it, because on land like this, everybody needed everybody else's help.

'We may have arrived on different ships, but we're all in the same boat now,' Edwin quipped, and they all grunted their approval.

232

Just as the road reached another creek, the orders came to return to Fremantle. They were back behind the piss-stinking walls of the Establishment before the week was out.

★ ★ ★

The silence was new, as was the following of warders' instructions. It was Hampton, McCarthy whispered. McCarthy didn't look like a man anymore. His back was so scarred and infected from repeated flogging that he couldn't stand upright. He'd lost more teeth and had an unearthly pallor from being locked in the dark cell. Poor Smith started to recite frantic prayers at the sight of him.

They all had nightmares about the lash. Edwin kept his head down and said yes sir no sir, no matter how much bile rose in his throat, and made McCarthy do the same.

'You're so close now,' Edwin said. 'You haven't survived all this only to die from your own stubbornness.'

★ ★ ★

A man who could read, let alone a man the other men liked, was rare among lags, Hampton said, so they made Edwin the school monitor at Perth Gaol after the previous man got his ticket-of-leave. Edwin made McCarthy swear to keep his nose clean until he got out. McCarthy agreed, but neither of them believed McCarthy could commit to keeping himself out of trouble.

Edwin didn't think it would be possible for a prison to be darker inside than Fremantle, but Perth Gaol

233

was like night itself. This was where they threw the town drunks, the whores, the illegal grog runners, the transported convicts who'd spat in the eye of freedom and somehow couldn't keep their sorry arses out of a magistrate's court. Perth Gaol reminded Edwin that the law was around every corner in this godforsaken place. It whipped his resolve into shape. He gritted his teeth and kept his head down. He taught idiots and drunks and lunatics to read Defoe and Dickens and Dumas. He read aloud, and the words he didn't understand, well, he threw in a few of his own. Sometimes he put the names of his children into the stories just to amuse himself. Sometimes he told his pupils the stories were written by someone other than the rightful author. *You will be pleased to know your book* A Christmas Carol *was well received by the intelligent gentlemen at Perth Gaol*, he wrote to Eliza.

On the ninth of December 1864, Edwin Thomas Salt put his ticket-of-leave in his pocket, his few possessions in a swag and walked out of Perth Gaol.

Agnes

Adelaide, 1898

'Fan!' Agnes screamed, not for the first time that day. The other walkers shook their heads at the dark-haired toddler who ran past them with wobbly determination.

'Now she thinks it's a game.' Florence held onto her hat. It was almost three o'clock and the breeze was up. 'She needs a bonnet, Agnes. She'll catch too much sun.'

'She has one. At least she did when we got here. Goodness knows where it is now.' Agnes caught up to her daughter and scooped her up. Fan screamed and kicked.

'Can't you be still for just a minute?' Agnes kissed Fan and put her down. Fan wobbled on her fat legs. She glared at Agnes before turning around and running back up the jetty towards the beach. Agnes spotted a man standing alone at the beginning of the jetty, wearing a dark coat, too heavy a coat for a sunny day like this. He slouched and grinned at the little girl who seemed to be running towards him. The man was smoking a pipe, and he tilted his head back to puff a heart-shaped smoke ring into the air.

'Oh, sweet Jesus.' Agnes left Florence in her wake and ran so hard to catch up to Fan she had a pain in her side from the effort. She picked Fan up. The man shivered despite the sunshine and the coat.

'Everything all right?' Florence caught up to them

235

and scowled at the stranger.

Agnes nodded. 'Florence, this is my brother, Walter.'

★ ★ ★

It had taken Walter a few weeks to get to Adelaide — Agnes didn't ask how, and Walter didn't volunteer the information — but once he'd arrived, it had been easy to find out from men at the port where Ernest lived. Sarah had almost fainted when he told her who he was, but once she'd gathered her wits, she'd told Walter Agnes's address, and that he would probably find her at Semaphore today, like most Sunday afternoons.

Agnes made Walter have a bath and a meal. He needed the bath more than the meal, and he really needed the meal. Afterwards, he took out a tobacco pouch and a pipe. The cinnamon smell of tobacco filled the air, and it was as if Da himself had somehow leapt out from behind the folds of Walter's clothes.

'You took his pipe?' Agnes asked. 'He loved that thing more than any person.'

'It's not his anymore.' Walter took another puff and savoured the moment. 'It's mine now. He took something of mine, so I've taken something of his.'

'I'm glad you're here.' Agnes spooned more food onto his plate. Walter was pale and thin, and his eyes were bloodshot. He was crumpled and whisky worn.

'Will you stay?' Agnes ventured. 'You can stay as long as you like. George will get work for you.'

'I know, Ag — I could be swimming in money.'

'So you got my letters.'

'I suppose.' Walter smoked.

236

'Why didn't you write back? I was worried sick. I just wanted to know you were all right, you know, after . . .' the memory caught in her throat. 'After the day I left.'

'I was all right. Annie patched me up. Da kept out of my way, mostly.' He coughed. 'You know me, Ag. Not one for writing things down.' He coughed again, rougher this time.

'What's wrong, Walter? Are you ill?'

'Jesus, don't fuss.'

'Sorry,' Agnes said. 'Walter, what happened? You can tell me —'

'For Christ's sake, Saint Aggie.' He sent clouds of smoke aimlessly into the air. 'Let's just enjoy my unexpected holiday in Adelaide, shall we?'

Walter slipped into their lives easily. He went to bed early and got up late; he said he hadn't been able to sleep without half an eye open in years. Agnes didn't care what time he surfaced, messy-haired and stubble-faced. The house felt different while he was sleeping in it — still and calm somehow, like it had when Fan was a baby — and she never got tired of it. She fed him porridge, and warm bread with fresh butter, and meaty stews, even though it was summer, and pinched his cheeks with delight as they grew plumper. George welcomed him generously, getting out the good rum in the evenings, and they discussed lofty subjects such as working conditions for wharf men and the prospect of the colonies agreeing amongst themselves to form a nation. The two men sometimes stopped talking mid-sentence when Agnes walked in, but she didn't mind because she wanted them to know each other, to share men's secrets.

Fan took an instant liking to her uncle. She sat

with him on the front veranda when he smoked and whacked him on the arm when he fell asleep in the chair. She even followed him to the outhouse until Agnes told her off so severely that she cried. Walter relaxed even more when he mucked about with Fan, cooing and tickling behind her ears until she giggled the house down. On Sunday afternoons on Semaphore Jetty, Walter whizzed her around in dizzying circles and pretended to throw her over the rail. She squealed with delight and insisted he keep doing it long after his exaggerated protests about being a weakling with skinny arms.

They all trod carefully around the things that Walter never talked about. Agnes didn't ask about Da or Annie or anything about home, no matter how hard it was to hold her tongue. She knew better than anyone that if Walter wanted to talk, it would only be when he was damn well good and ready.

★ ★ ★

Walter sat outside on the back step, an empty glass nearby, his head in his hands.

'Any chance of a refill?' he yawned.

'Haven't you had enough already?' Agnes put her arm around him.

'Bugger off, then.' He shoved her away.

'Oh, come on, Walter, I didn't mean anything by it.'

'Oooh, I didn't mean anything by it!' Walter mimicked her in his old way and pushed her harder. 'Saint Aggie.'

'I suppose you're going to hit me next,' she said, standing up. 'Don't end up like Da, Walter, all your anger coming out of your fists when you're full of grog.'

238

'Christ, Ag, I'm sorry.' He gestured to the step next to her. 'Come back, sit with me.'

She sat down and put her arm around him again. This time he leaned into her.

'I'm sorry, Ag. It's just . . .'

'Whatever it is, you can't keep it in.'

'Dunno what you're talking about.'

'Oh, come on, Walter. I'm not blind.' She looked him square in the eyes. 'Whatever you're not saying, it's killing you. Tell me, don't tell me, don't ever speak again for all I care. Stay here with us forever — we're your family. Just don't let him win all over again.'

'Bloody hell. You don't give up, do you?' Walter sighed so hard, he seemed to deflate like a carnival balloon. 'All right, you asked for it. You still like those silly family stories? This one'll make your hair turn white.'

A stranger had come home with Da from the Western one night, Walter told her. A miner from the Murchison, down on his luck — a stranger with ink on his forearms, hair the colour of wet sand, stark blue eyes. A stranger, but there had been something familiar about him all the same. Annie made him a bed for the night but a fortnight later he was still there. It was nothing like when Ernest visited. This man was tense, tightly wound, like a rifle cocked and loaded and just waiting for some poor unsuspecting thing to shoot at.

Annie never took her eyes off him, and Da, well, Walter had never seen him like this. Scared. Da said he'd known Eddie's father in England, and he was to be treated like family. 'You mean, treat him like shit and slap him about after too much grog?' Walter said, but Da didn't see the funny side. Da and Eddie spent a week fixing the fence. Eddie started cutting down trees at the bottom of the block where they'd never cleared trees before. Da dug in new fence posts while Eddie did bugger all except smoke and drink Da's rum. Da's usual cronies at the Western were silent on the subject of the house guest from God-only-knew-where. Eddie said he had brothers, that his ma had died when he was little, and he'd been drifting ever since, waiting for his ship to come in.

'My mam died too, when I was little,' Walter said, and Eddie got the strangest look on his face and said, 'Do you remember her?' Walter said, 'Not really, although sometimes, a smell, or an Irish accent,' and Eddie said, 'Me too. I remember the smell of her hair.' Eddie kind of leaned towards him and for a moment, Walter thought Eddie was going to hug him, or shake his hand or something. Walter said, 'For strangers, you and me got a lot in common,' and Eddie said, 'More than you think,' and the moment passed.

Walter caught Eddie swigging Da's best whisky — 'mother's milk', the smug bastard called it. Walter clenched his fist ready to teach him a lesson, but Eddie just smirked and said, 'The old man owes me.' Eddie showed Walter some papers. It may as well have been double-fucking-dutch for all Walter knew, but he could read pictures well enough, and he knew the shape of their land like his own self. And there it was: an official line drawn right where Da and Eddie had put those new fence posts.

Agnes shook her head. 'I'm sorry. I can't take this in.'

'He gave Eddie half his land.' Walter's face was taut and shiny with anger. 'Land that should have been mine.'

They sat, not talking, for what seemed like an hour.

'Eddie has something big on Da, and Da wants to keep him quiet,' Walter murmured. 'I kept all his miserable secrets for my whole miserable life, and this is how he repays me.'

Agnes let out a long, slow breath.

'Da had a wife,' she said. 'Before Mam.'

'What?'

'I saw a picture. Mary Ann. She died, and that's why Da came to the Swan River.'

The look on Walter's face was so peculiar Agnes thought for a minute he'd had some kind of attack. 'What do you know about it?' he said.

'Nothing, not really. Sarah said she died. It was a baby, I suppose. That's what it usually means.'

'Why didn't you tell me you knew about his wife?' Walter said slowly.

'You never wrote to me. I didn't know where you were. There didn't seem any point.'

Walter loosened his collar.

'Are you all right?' Agnes asked. 'You're scaring me. What do you know about Mary Ann?'

'Nothing. Plenty of them had wives — kids too, probably. Talk was that Mad Molloy had a huge brood back home.'

'Plenty of who had wives?'

'Nobody.' Walter kissed her forehead. 'Anyway, Eddie got the useless bit of scrub down by the river gums. Come winter, that stinking river will rise right up through the ground. It'll be like living in quicksand.' Walter stood up. 'What's done is done. Let's talk about something else.'

★ ★ ★

241

Walter did cartwheels on the soggy sand and pre-tended to fall over, sending Fan into squeals of mirth. Fan grabbed Walter's hand and tried to pull him up, but he pulled her down and she rolled in the sand, giggling. He hauled her up on her pudgy feet and Fan ran off ahead of them shouting, 'Un-kel Wa-ter. Wa-ter. Wa-ter!'

'She's saying your name.' Agnes slipped her arm through his. 'You're officially part of her family. Fan's given you her seal of approval.'

They walked from Semaphore up the beach to Largs and back, taking it in turns to carry Fan. The sun trailed reds and yellows as it sank into the hori-zon.

'We should talk to Sarah and Ernest. See if they can tell us anything more,' Agnes said. 'Sarah knew about Da's wife. She had a picture of them.'

'It's probably best left.' Walter shielded Fan from the breeze. 'He gave his land to a man he met at the Western. Neither of us are ever going back. Does it matter now?'

'No, Walter. I want to know.' Agnes turned her face towards the shore. 'Let's go tomorrow.'

★   ★   ★

Agnes knew by the quietness of the house. When the sun had risen enough to send darts of light through the window, she got out of bed and padded quietly to the kitchen. At least he'd left a note on the table, scribbled and messy. In all these years, it was the only letter he'd ever written. Agnes could've given him a clip around the ear if only she wasn't crying.

242

Sorry Ag not sure were Im goin but will let you know were I am promise. What you got here is real good. Dont mess it up by looking back. I dont want to look back. Give angel Fan a big kiss from me. W.

Walter had drawn a picture of Fan running on the jetty, her little arms stretched out and her dark hair flying behind her. Underneath, Walter had written in careful, neat script, *My Angel Fan.*

Agnes's eyes stung. George told her gently that if Walter wanted to leave, there was nothing they could do about it, except welcome him with open arms if he ever decided to come back, because he'd always know where to find them. Fan started to howl as she did every morning, but today her cries were harsher, as if she knew Walter had gone.

★   ★   ★

To the north, Largs and the port. To the south, the rest of Adelaide town, and in front of her, the jetty slicing the ocean in half. Left and right. Then and now, she thought.

George insisted on walking along the shore to keep watch. He went on about sailors and the power of the sea and how you were better off giving in to it than swimming, but she said, 'Don't worry, George, I'll hardly leave dry land.'

Agnes waded in. Children stared and whispered, but she ignored them. She dug her feet in to anchor herself and when she felt the swell lift, she sat down in the thigh-deep water and dipped her head under. She shrieked with the shock of the cold, then stood up and wiped the sea from her eyes. George shouted

243

something about mad women, but his voice was light.

The sun bounced back at her off the upstairs window of Mrs Jensen's seafront house. What was it Mrs Jensen had said? Everyone here was from somewhere else. Adelaide had Germans in the hills, English on the beachfront and Irish in the taverns. Now Adelaide had Miss Salt of the Sea with her father long gone and her mother long dead. She wished Walter would come back. But right now, she was Miss Salt of the Sea, with Fan, George and a house of her own. Ernest, Florence and Sarah were all the family she needed.

She held George's hand tightly all the way home.

Edwin

Perth, 1864

Henry Wood was still a youngish man, whippet-thin with black hair and a scar on his left cheek. His tailor's shop in Perth town was squashed between lodging houses and taverns on Barrack Street. Black paint peeled off the door and the small front window was so clean that Edwin was tempted to reach in and feel the tweed on the jacket he had on display.

Henry had been sent out a couple of years earlier, he told Edwin with a grin, but he never talked about that unfortunate business anymore.

'A misunderstanding, that's all it were.' He inspected Edwin's hands. 'You better be a good tailor. I don't want no ham-fisted Portland stone-breaker tearing holes in my best Indian cotton.'

Henry pulled back a thin curtain to reveal a small room at the back of the shop. A lumpy hessian mattress took up almost all the floor and there was a water jug under the small window.

'Welcome to freedom,' Henry said.

After so long sleeping in a hammock, Edwin had forgotten what it felt like to stretch out flat on his back. He'd looked forward to it, but that first night, after what felt like hours, he was still wide awake, shifting from one side to the other. He opened the tiny window and listened to birds, animal sounds, the shouts of drunks. As the moon rose higher, the noises subsided. He'd never heard such a rush of silence, not

245

even working on the York road.

The next time he opened his eyes the room was filled with the fresh light of sunrise. He threw on his clothes, found his pipe and tobacco and left quietly.

The sun was already bright enough to make him squint. The morning air smelled of peppermint. It was December, but it didn't look like any December he knew. He walked down Barrack Street past a church and a couple of taverns, stepping over a sleeping drunkard. He followed a track to where it finished at the river's edge.

Birds that looked like swans, but with black feathers and red beaks, waddled into the water. Funniest looking birds he'd ever seen. Across the water on the other side of the point, the trees seemed to move. It must have been a group of natives. He tipped his hat in their direction, wishing them good morning. They didn't scare him. He'd seen so much to scare him in gaol and on the *Lincelles*, he doubted they would ever have worse to throw at him.

Edwin lit his pipe. The tobacco tasted all the sweeter for being smoked in the fresh air with no other man looking to barter or bash him out of his supply. Edwin tried to remember the last time he'd been anywhere without some other stinking body nearby.

He threw his shirt and trousers under a white-barked tree and ran shrieking into the river, beating his chest like a storybook savage. The cold made him gasp, but he waded in anyway. When the water reached up to his chest, he spread his arms out wide and dug his feet into the silt to stop himself from thinking about drowning. He imagined poor old Pullinger watching from Heaven, or wherever in the afterlife he had washed up.

How did people swim? Edwin shut his eyes and pressed his nostrils together for good measure. Then the man who'd never in his life stuck his head underwater in anything deeper than a bathtub let himself sink until his buttocks hit the rough stones of the riverbed.

Edwin stayed submerged for only a few seconds before he leapt up like a bloated fish gasping for air. Was this how it was for Pullinger as his weighted-down body sank under the waves? Poor Pullinger, shackled until the end. Did his soul manage to fight its way out of that burlap coffin and float up to Heaven? Was Pullinger looking down on him, McCarthy, Smith and Molloy, watching them struggle to escape the coffins of their own making? Was Pullinger in fact the only one of the three hundred *Lincelles* men who got the freedom they were all hoping for?

Edwin swung his flabby arms about. The sunlight twinkled on the water. Then, without warning, the memory of Mary Ann rose up and he choked so violently he thought he was going to die.

★　★　★

Edwin expected to see gentlemen who'd given their names to roads and vast tracts of land, but Henry Wood's tailor shop wasn't that kind of establishment. He smiled and nodded at the land speculators from New South Wales with their mongrel accents and their oiled hair and their nonstop chatter about profit. He talked amiably about York with farmers who were up in town for a dance or a meeting about roads. None of them asked how such a fine tailor had come to be in the colony, but before they took their leave, they

247

checked their pockets.

It stuck in his throat, hearing his own voice mimic Samuel's grovelling 'Thank you, sir' and 'As you like, sir' to men no better than himself. But what every man wanted from a tailor: well, Edwin knew that better than anyone. He soon remembered the feel of a needle and how to look at dark fabric under weak lamplight. He stitched every man a straighter spine, a broader shoulder, a collar so clean and snug that even a gentleman whose suits were made in London would see that this, too, was the work of a craftsman. Henry kept a close eye on him; after all, Edwin was the ticketer and Henry was the boss, but soon Henry began to give Edwin more of the work while he disappeared most afternoons to the Western.

One stinking-hot day, a man appeared, and the shock of a once-familiar face made Edwin spill his pannikin of water. It was young Joe Watts, one of the Portland lads who'd got his ticket as soon as he stepped off the *Lincelles*. Watts still had the wiry body of a young man, but his leathery skin and sun-whitened eyebrows made him look like somebody's grandfather. Watts shook Edwin's hand and pointed at the serge he wanted for his new jacket. A week later, Watts stood in front of the mirror and admired the cut of his newly stitched self.

'My own mother wouldn't know me,' he said.

'You could pass for Governor Hampton himself,' Edwin said.

'Next stop's the Lands Office.' Watts unfolded a pile of banknotes. 'If I bump into Governor Hampton, I'll tell him he can kiss my free-pardoned arse.'

Joe Watts was the first Portland man to wash up in Henry Wood's shop, but he wasn't the last. Word

248

spread among a certain kind of man that the ticketer working for Henry Wood had a keen eye for precision and he got the job done at a good price. In the months Edwin was ticketed to Wood, and in the year that Henry kept him on, the work kept coming from liars, thieves, forgers, bigamists and thugs keen to cast off their ragged histories and make themselves anew.

Henry paid Edwin fairly, more or less, and Edwin wrote down the hours he worked, and what he was owed, but he never quibbled with Henry over a shilling here or there. He locked away as much money as he could in a tin hidden under his mattress.

In summer, the heat at night brought the smell of the swamps from the east. It pressed in on his chest. Edwin slept in the yard and got bitten by mosquitoes. His limbs swelled and he couldn't work for five days. Mrs Wood gave him a jar of ointment for the blisters. Henry docked his wages.

Edwin cleared his head in the mornings by walking to the river. He rinsed his calloused and pinpricked hands in the water, and stood in it until his swollen feet didn't hurt anymore. Sometimes he stood for a couple of hours and felt the tide creep up his shins. He began to notice the different tones of colour that flowed in the trenches and in the shallows. Everything moving, nothing standing still. Not even him. He thought about the growing pile of money he had locked away in that tin.

If a mug of tea waited on the table when he returned, he knew his nightmares had kept Mrs Wood awake again. He never remembered them. He felt only a vague sense of unease when he awoke, as if somebody had just left the room. Henry and his wife exchanged looks and Mrs Wood told Edwin he needed to get settled, find a woman who was keener to take the hardworking man who stood in front of her than ask about the criminal who'd left England.

Edwin drank himself sleepy at the Western Hotel on Howick Street with Henry Wood, Mick McCarthy, Smith, Molloy and a few others. The Western could have been the Anvil or Wallace's gin shop, if not for the heat and the light. Edwin felt at home around the smell of tobacco and rum. They talked of grog, or women, or land, and if any man were idiot enough to start some talk about the *Lincelles*, or Portland or Newgate or Fremantle or England, Henry Wood or Mick McCarthy silenced him with a glare or a swift kick.

'You escaped with your life. Don't never look back.' Henry's voice was steady, but his eyes had the look of the hunted.

★ ★ ★

In the Swan River colony, months were marked off by ships arriving and ships departing. Every ship that stopped in Fremantle brought food and building materials and fabric and clothes and the sweetest sustenance of all: news from home. People stood in streets with their heads bent over letters, unable to wait for privacy before they ran their hands over their loved ones' words. On mail days, the hotels on Howick Street were hushed, with little noise except the sound of the landlord pouring drinks. Men who had persuaded themselves that their wives and children were dead stared out of windows, dealing mutely with the resurrection of feeling.

When Edwin wrote to Eliza, he pretended he was

holding court again at the Anvil, or Wallace's gin shop, or that damp tavern in Galway whose name he no longer remembered. He told his stories with humour that a young lad might find amusing if the letter happened to be read aloud. He invented man-eating natives and serpents and trees that flowered grotesquely in the winter. He told of his own growing reputation as a tailor to a certain kind of man.

Months passed with no replies, and he fought hard not to feel his own irrelevance. He wrote knowing another part of himself would disappear in the coal fire at the back of the shop or in the freezing-cold privy or wherever Samuel destroyed his letters. But imagine if Eliza or one of his sons risked Samuel's anger, even if it was just curiosity, to find out how his story ended?

In the colony a tailor is as good as a magician, he wrote to Eliza. I take one sort of man and turn him into another. The air stinks of swamp and the mosquitoes could kill you in your bed, but there's the promise of land for the likes of me.

★ ★ ★

'Want to be a real man? Get home to your feckin' children.' A dark-haired woman stood between a red-headed woman and one of the Irishmen. The man stood up. The redheaded woman covered her face.

'I said, leave her alone.' The dark-haired woman put her hands on her hips. The other Irishmen stared into their drinks.

'Damned Irish.' Henry gripped his glass so tightly his knuckles went white. 'How many taverns are there on Howick Street? You'd think they'd find somewhere

251

of their own to drink.' He stood up. 'Somebody wants to teach 'em how to keep their women in order.'

'Leave the fighting to the Irish.' Edwin gestured for Henry to sit down. 'Haven't you seen the inside of enough gaol cells in your life?'

'Wouldn't say no to one of their fine ladies.' Smith licked his lips. 'As long as she didn't talk. The accent wittering in my ear all night.' The others mocked him. Smith's own Devon accent was as heavy as clotted cream.

The dark-haired woman stood her ground, her arms folded. Her pale face was rosy with anger.

'Come on, Deirdre.' The Irishman gulped his drink and grabbed the redhead's hand. 'Don't want you mixing with the likes of this whore.'

'You keep drinking like that, Jimmy, and a whore'd be a big waste of your little wage packet.' The dark-haired woman's eyes flickered to Jimmy's belt buckle. Edwin sniggered, despite himself.

The dark-haired woman turned around and walked slowly over to where Edwin stood with the others. She stood so close he could smell the starch in her brown dress, see the roundness of her breasts. Her eyes were the same colour as her hair, blue-black.

'You think it's funny, Englishman?'

'N-no.' Edwin felt his cheeks flame.

'You're blushing.' The woman reached out and touched his face. Her skin was rough, but her touch was light. 'You got a stutter, Englishman? You afraid of a poor little Irish girl?'

'No and no,' Edwin said, holding her gaze. 'And I can see you're not afraid of anything.'

'A few years in this place and I got no fear left.' She was smiling but her voice had an edge. She followed

252

Deirdre and Jimmy out of the door.

'By God but she's got a mouth on her,' Smith said, and Henry guzzled his drink.

★ ★ ★

Long after he'd left the Western, long after he'd done what he needed to do to get to sleep, Edwin's skin still tingled from where she'd touched him.

'There are so many more men than women here in the Swan River,' Mrs Wood told him the next day. 'Be kind to a woman who hasn't seen much kindness, and she'll forgive you much more than you'd imagine.'

'In the Western they keep kindness on the top shelf and it costs a week's wages,' Henry said.

It was weeks before he saw her again, but he was ready.

'May I buy you a whisky, miss?'

'A gentleman? In the Western? You must be lost.' She smirked. 'By the way, I'm not a miss.'

'Oh. My apologies, madam.'

'I'm not staying. Specially not for some layabout lag.' She gazed around the crowded room. 'Checking up on a friend.'

'What a fortunate friend. Tell me, madam. Are you from Cork or Dublin?'

'You a seer as well as a lag?'

'A few years in Ireland taught me a few things.'

'But not when to give up.' Her eyes shimmered with mirth. 'County Cork, thank you for asking.' She wiped her forehead with her sleeve. 'It's like an oven in here. All right. One whisky.'

Edwin ushered her to a quiet corner and fetched two glasses.

'My, but aren't you the answer to a girl's prayers?' She picked up the glass and turned it upside down. 'You're a bigger fool than I'd reckoned on. It's empty.'

Edwin felt warm, but not from the sun.

'I was told that in the colony, the way to win a lady over is with kindness,' Edwin said. 'So that's what I offer you.'

'Is that all you got? Don't look like much to me.' She stood up to leave.

'Please.' Edwin grabbed her hand.

'Oh, very well,' she said, looking from his boots up to his eyes. 'But only because I feel so damned sorry for you.'

Fan

Fremantle, December 1906

It rained all week. Humidity settled heavily inside the house. Ma left the windows open all the time in the hope of a breeze, but it never came. Animal smells wafted up from the wharf. Fan couldn't sleep. She got up and sat in the kitchen and listened to the faint rhythm of the sea in the distance.

Fan felt a warm wave of air. It was Ma in her nightdress, her hair unwound down her back.

'Jesus, Ma. I thought you were a ghost.'

'Language, Fan.' Ma pulled up a chair. 'Is there any breeze?'

'Not a whisper.'

They both stared out of the window.

'Turn the lamp up. I want to show you something.' Ma handed her a piece of paper. Fan blinked into the light. It was a sketch of a small child running, her hair flying out behind her and her arms out like bird wings. A small child running down a jetty. The wooden structure looked as familiar to Fan as her own mother. It was obviously Semaphore.

'That's you.' Ma pointed to the child. 'Your Uncle Walter drew it the last time I saw him. He came to Adelaide when you were very small.'

'I met my Uncle Walter?' Fan's eyes were hot. She tried to recall something, anything. 'I knew him?'

'He lived with us for a while. You wouldn't remember.'

255

'Jesus, Ma.' Fan ran her finger over the sketch of her younger self.

'Your uncle was — is — the bravest man you could ever meet.' Agnes's eyes glistened.

'Grandpa says he was a liar and a thief.' Fan frowned. 'Why would Grandpa say it if it's not true?'

'You and Walter took such a shine to each other. He would want you to have this picture, I know he would. I hoped he would stay with us in Adelaide, but I got up one morning and he was gone.'

'I reckon Grandpa would tell you where he is,' Fan said.

'Walter and your grandpa had a terrible, terrible fight.' Agnes squeezed Fan's hand. 'So I don't think Walter would be in touch with him.'

'People fight and say they're sorry. Me and you, we do it all the time.'

'Some things can't be fixed with sorry.' Ma's voice prickled. 'Fan, listen to me. It can't be Uncle Walter in New South Wales, because Walter told me they'd fallen out. Your imagination's run away with you. I keep telling you, your grandfather's mind is going. You can't trust anything that man says.'

★ ★ ★

If she shut her eyes, the smell of the sea made Fan feel like she was home, but, when she looked out across the uninterrupted blankness of water, she ached with homesickness. She pulled off her boots and clothes. The costume she'd worn underneath was already beginning to feel tight around her hips and up top. Nothing was the same shape anymore. Fan walked in up to her waist and slid underwater.

She swam out a little way and kept one eye on the shore. Her hair spilled out. It was better to be in than walking on sand, even if the current was unreadable. She swam deeper to where she couldn't touch the bottom.

This was the peace she craved. Fan opened her eyes. Underwater, it was easier to escape Ma, Grandpa, Uncle Walter or whoever-he-was in New South Wales. The current was strong, and she let it carry her deeper.

A clump of yellow weed swirled and billowed, brassy in the fractured light. The seabed seemed to shift, and something thumped her back. The sand clouded around her legs. Fan thrashed and panicked before her feet touched sand and she crawled up to the shallower water.

The strip of white beach gleamed. Foam bubbled up to the shore. The wave that hit her was stronger than she was used to at Semaphore. Fan spat out water until her heart stopped pounding. Then she turned back to the ocean and swam in the direction of the straw-gold seaweed. In a single breath she dived under, grabbed a piece and dragged it up with her to the surface.

Agnes

Fremantle, December 1906

Tom was obsessed with building that stupid contraption in the yard. Charlie's mum had complained
that Tom had whacked Charlie's ankle with a hammer. Tom stubbornly defended himself, said it was
Charlie's fault, Charlie got too close to where he was
hammering, but Tom would never have dreamed
of even picking up a hammer before they came to
Fremantle. Ned had started saying 'Jesus' and 'for
God's sake'. That lovely young lad, Lee, had taught
Ned some rude words in Chinese. Ned had recited
them to Lee's mother, who had given Agnes a lecture
about taking better care of her children. And as for
Fan . . . Agnes sat down and read through a list that
sounded like a charge sheet. Fan had ransacked her
father's room like a common thief — left the window
open, taken the lid off the wooden trunk and spilled his
papers everywhere. Agnes had packed everything up
as best she could, as quick as she could, without looking — she didn't want to know. Fan wasn't interested
in school and it was obviously because her grandfather was filling her head with ridiculous stories. Fan
had become slow to answer her mother's questions,
speaking carefully, as if she was making sure her lies
would hold water.

'It's him. It's all happened since he's been in our
house,' Agnes told George. 'He's bitter and ungrateful. He's made up all sorts of terrible stories about

258

Walter. He's not as ill as Annie led us to believe. I can go into Fremantle and find him a room in a lodging house.' She stood up, as if she meant to do it this minute. 'You said we could look at how things worked out once we got here. Well, that's how things are working out. I want to go home.'

George took hold of Agnes's hand and kissed it. 'I love you, my Agnes, Miss Salt of the Sea,' he said, his words nuzzling her palm. Then he ran through a list of his own. He was well in with all the foremen at Fremantle. After a shaky start, he was getting shifts every day because he'd made it his business to prove himself. The foremen all knew he was strong, he was reliable, he was careful with cargo, he never complained. Things were getting easier. There was a union fund now, to look after lumpers' families. Agnes and the bairns would be taken care of, if anything happened to him on the wharf. He was happy to be working among Sunderland men and River Clyde men and good men from all over the world.

'We can't pack up and leave now, Agnes, love.' George kissed her hand again because that was all he was prepared to offer. 'I'm too old to go back to Adelaide and start again.'

'I miss home.' Agnes's eyes stung. 'Ernest and Florence and Sarah and . . . everything.'

'The boys are happy here. Why don't we get Fan into the brush factory or in service somewhere? She's old enough, too old to be in school. Girls are flighty. She just needs something else to fill her head,' George said.

'But you promised, George.'

'My back's giving me some trouble. It could go at any time.' George couldn't look her in the eye. 'As

Annie said, he probably doesn't have long. He could be dead in a month. We need to stay the course.'

Agnes let go of his hand. 'I'm writing to Annie tomorrow, to tell her to take him back.'

'If you think that's best, love,' George said. 'And it's not a contraption. I had a look under the tarp. Tom's not building a contraption. It looks like he's building a boat.'

Edwin

Perth, 1865

Her name was Cath Curtin. She'd come to the Swan
River with her husband, 'dear Johnnie', on the convict transport *York*. Johnnie had come home from
the Crimea with a banged-up leg and a mind shot
through with the horrors of war. Everyone agreed that
the fresh air and sunshine in the colony might ease his
troubled spirit, and as a guard on a transport he got
free passage for his family. Cath gave birth on board
the ship — in the captain's cabin no less — just as
the *York* headed into the rough waters off Fremantle.
Everyone said a boy born on board would bring good
luck, but the poor little mite didn't last the summer.
Johnnie went last winter with consumption. Now she
worked six days a week in the governor's laundry and
on the seventh day she sat with Johnnie in the church-
yard up on the hill come rain, hail or shine.

'Holy Mother of God, you took little Christopher
and my lovely Johnnie.' Cath raised her third glass to
the sky. 'When you coming for me?' Her tone was as
dark as her hair.

'Not this evening, I hope,' Edwin said.

She slid her hand into his.

Every hour Edwin spent with Cath, his past cut
itself a little freer from its moorings. His vision was
filled only with the roundness of her hips, her long
black eyelashes, the roughness of her washerwoman's
hands.

261

★ ★ ★

Edwin spotted Cath from the bottom of the track that led up the hill to the cemetery. She was kneeling. He tipped his hat to a white-bonneted woman who stood next to one of the large headstones near the church entrance.

Cath bowed her head, crossed herself and wiped her eyes. He felt uneasy, as if he was spying on her while she bathed. He coughed politely and kneeled next to her. She glared at him but turned back to fussing with the small wooden cross, scraping her fingers in the dirt to straighten it up, pulling out weeds. When she'd finished, she clasped her hands together and murmured a prayer. Edwin closed his eyes and said 'Amen' with her and afterwards she wiped her eyes again, leaving a streak of dirt on her cheek.

'Let me help.' Edwin took a handkerchief out of his pocket, spat on it, rubbed her face.

'Don't be daft,' she said, but she closed her eyes and let him finish.

'Something else, if you'll let me.' Edwin fished around in his pocket. 'Give me your hand.'

'Edwin, what are you doing? Johnnie's watching.'

'He won't mind. Give me your hand.'

'Come on, it's a bit soon ain't it?' Cath said, but held out her hand anyway. 'Plenty of men in the colony, I'm sure I can do better.'

'Don't be so cocky, pretty colleen. I haven't picked you yet.'

Cath laughed, loud and rough. From his pocket, Edwin took out Mrs Wood's jar of eucalypt ointment. He gently rubbed the peppermint-smelling cream into her palm, the back of her hand, her fingers, then her other hand. Her skin drank it up. When he'd finished, he did both hands again, then rested them back in her lap.

They sat in silence for a long time.

'Kindness,' Cath said.

'Anything for you, pretty Cath.'

On the walk down the hill from the cemetery to Howick Street, the sun warmed their faces.

'So, you got some witch of a wife saving her pennies for a passage out here?' Cath said. 'Jimmy sent money for Deirdre. God only knows where he got it, and everybody knows better than to ask.'

Edwin stared at the horizon. 'Nobody's coming for me.' His neck felt tight. 'I haven't heard from my family since I left England.'

They reached the bottom of the road that turned into Howick Street. Noise from the taverns drifted into their ears. The afternoon light made Cath's skin look even whiter, her eyes blacker.

'You lot are worse than a secret society.' Cath pulled away from him. 'You tell me your story, Edwin Salt. I don't care what it is, but I better hear it from you and not the likes of Mick McCarthy.'

Edwin sat down on the side of the road. He'd walked much further in much worse heat, but he was sweating so much he half-wondered if he'd wet himself. Cath sat down next to him.

It felt like spitting out pieces of rotten apple, but Edwin gave Cath the story he was sure she wanted. His poor wife Mary Ann had died of a fever. His grief had sent him mad and taken him far away from home, and his children. A stupid bit of thieving, a bit of a mouth on him when he drank too much and here he was, marooned on colonial shores.

263

The river in front of them glinted in the sun.

'You get some land and I'll marry you tomorrow,' Cath said, her eyes on a group of men strolling down Howick Street.

'No. You marry me tomorrow,' Edwin said, his eyes on her hips. 'I'll get my land before the year is out.'

* * *

Edwin paced to the eastern corner. Small lizards scattered in the wake of his boots. He walked to the bottom of the block to where the land sloped away to the river. The jarrah trees gave way to pale-barked river gums where the water ran unseen under the ground. To the west was a sawmill, and the sound of saws cut through the noise of crickets.

He stared from the deed of title in his hand to the land in front of him and back again.

'Victoria, by the grace of God. To have and to hold,' he read out loud from the paper.

The transaction had been signed into existence by old Governor Hampton himself. He'd shaken the clerk's hand and promised himself he'd never again hear a bad word about Hampton, his son or his second cousin twice removed for that matter.

To have and to hold. As if he owned a woman, not a half-acre of snake-infested river gums and stumpy little grass-headed trees that smelled of rum when they burned.

To have and to hold. He certainly would, until death did them part. Samuel Salt and Son, unwilling tailor, feared excise officer and condemned man, would spend the rest of his days as lord of the manor among the magnificent swamps and slaughterhouses.

264

Cath stood in the middle of the only patch that had been cleared.

'I present to you the vast empire of the tailor of Water Street.' Edwin strode towards Cath, his arms outstretched.

'Is this the best you could do? Downwind from the tannery and slaughter yards,' Cath grinned. 'I wouldn't be surprised if blacks still lived here.'

'Don't be daft. They're long gone.'

'So you've got the land even the natives born on it don't want.'

'Nothing but the best for the likes of you and me.' Edwin pulled her closer.

'The luck of the Irish.' Cath kissed him.

The sun was directly above them in a cloudless blue sky. Edwin ushered Cath under a tree. With the heel of his boot, he dug a line from Cath to the last river gum that marked the boundary of his land.

'You call that a fence?' Cath called, her eyes shining.

The sun burned his face, but he didn't care. Molloy and Smith and a few others he knew had bought land up here already, but he couldn't see another house or another person anywhere he looked. The huge jarrah trees dwarfed him, and the sun blinded him so much that when he looked up, he couldn't tell where the trees ended and the sky began.

Cath teased him, said he was a damn fool fit for the insane asylum. He whooped like a little boy. He was a giant and he was no bigger than the ants scrambling over his boots. He was condemned and he was saved, reborn in this light with the help of this woman, her hair shining blue, her arms open to receive him.

265

They lived through summer without a proper roof on their four-roomed cottage. Edwin worked days and nights. Henry Wood went out of business, then started up again. Cath ran chickens and kept a cow and planted vegetables. She spent long hours digging in the heat and dust. Some days she was out there until dusk but came in smiling. She dug her sweat and her homesickness into the dirt and made it sweet and rich with shit from her cow and the chickens. She stood guard with hessian and wire to protect her little rows of potatoes and beets from the heat as best she could. 'It smells like home but without the hunger,' she told him. Cath's plot was the envy of the Smiths and the Molloys and all the others until a heatwave sneaked in and killed everything. Edwin planted it over, even though the seasons were all wrong, because the sight of Cath smiling made him forget the blisters and calluses on his tailor's hands.

At the end of summer, Cath gave birth to a tiny boy. Edwin insisted they call him Albert. Cath thought it would be bad luck, but she was too tired to argue. Little Albert must have known his name was already taken because he died without warning. Cath screamed and thumped her fists into Edwin's guts so hard he spent a night at Molloy's until the urge to smack some sense into her subsided. Edwin worked more days and nights. Despite the trouble on How-ick Street between Mick McCarthy and some of the other Irish, Edwin gritted his teeth and grudgingly tipped his hat.

They lived through rain that dissolved Perth's dusty roads to grey dirt that stuck to boots and hooves.

Cath's belly swelled with another baby. She was slower on her feet, but her eyes were bright with hope.

One rainy day a parcel arrived.

Edwin saw the postmark and made a noise like he was being strangled.

'What's wrong? Who's it from?' Cath asked.

'My sister.'

'Oh, Jesus,' Cath said. 'After all this time.'

Edwin poured himself a glass of best whisky and unwrapped Eliza's parcel. Inside was a letter and two smaller parcels. He stared at her handwriting. Neat, evenly spaced, like her stitching. She always was the best at everything.

He opened the envelope and Eliza rushed at him, talking fast and precise as she always did. It took him by surprise, the force of it, the nearness of her.

My dear Edwin.

Da says you are as good as dead to the family but, like progress, I choose to pass him by! I found your letter by the fire. I am supposing he must burn them, if you have written before.

I was pleased to read about your wife and your land. I am glad you are making a life in the colony. They say the climate is good for improving the temperament of a certain kind of man. I pray very little these days, but I pray you will find it a healing place.

There is some sad news. Our mother died soon after you left for the colony. She didn't suffer. Da gets some help from young Amy Bullock next door.

267

He pressed the letter to his face. The smell of the coal fire, the scent of bread. Many months at sea in a calico mailbag and the paper still held traces of home. His chest hurt. He put the letter down. It was too much to take in. He poured another whisky and picked up the small package. He tore off the paper to find a piece of light-blue cotton, about a foot square. He unfolded it.

Eliza had sent him a summer day at Lichfield Cathedral. Tracing his finger over neat stitches, he followed the road past the Crown Inn, up Dam Street, up the curved path to the small door, the three spires. Eliza had embroidered the cathedral outline in white thread and under each spire, an initial: A, E and M. Albert, Edwin, Matthew. His three sons.

One last thing: a cloth pouch. He opened it and the sweet smell of old tobacco smacked him hard in the chest. He knew without looking what it was, but he made himself open it anyway.

Something to remember me by, Mr Wishless.

A small lock of straw-gold hair tied with twine. Edwin laid it on the table and it curled into a question mark.

The sunny cornfield of their days.

He lifted the memory of Mary Ann to his cheek.

'Throw it away.' Cath's voice was sharp. 'Don't look back.'

'For Christ's sake, you're dripping wet. Why have you been outside?'

'I didn't like the look of you in that foul mood.' Cath shivered.

'You must be freezing. You'll catch your death.'

'I'm fine. It's only rain.' Cath shook her wet hair.

'Don't do that, woman. It'll end up soaking in here as well as outside.'

'D'you know your mate Molloy's got a wife and an army of children back home?' Cath put her hands on her hips. 'He don't talk about 'em, and he's better off for it. Like I said, don't look back,' she repeated.

Edwin put the letter back in its envelope.

'All right,' he said.

'It's best for everyone. Most of all, for you.'

'I know. Go and change your dress. I'll throw it all in the fire.'

The blue embroidered church. The lock of straw-gold hair. He waited until Cath had gone to the washhouse and then he locked them up in the tin where he kept his money. He poured another whisky and read the rest of Eliza's letter.

★ ★ ★

Mick McCarthy looked surprised to see Edwin so early in the day, but he made room for his mate and beckoned to the publican for more rum. Edwin matched Mick drink for drink, which had everyone shaking their heads. Mick asked him if there was anything in particular that was bothering him, but Edwin shook his head and bought more rum. Edwin drank until he couldn't stand up. He drank until he couldn't hear Eliza whispering in his ear. He drank until he could feel the sea breeze and not think it was Mary Ann whispering at the back of his neck.

In Howick Street after closing, a Scottish carpenter bumped into him, and Edwin cursed and lashed out. He barely noticed the thud of his knuckles on the man's

269

cheekbone, but by Christ it felt good. The Scotsman swore and punched Edwin in his face. Edwin hit back again and the other man fell. McCarthy and Molloy tried to hold Edwin back, but he shoved them, too. They stood back. The look in his eye told them that whatever had possessed Edwin wasn't finished yet.

* * *

The magistrate raised an eyebrow and brought down a gavel and declared, 'men with your dubious moral character, Salt,' were bound to end up back in gaol sooner or later, and 'given your history' frankly he was surprised he hadn't seen Mr Salt before this day.

Molloy said he'd tell Cath about Edwin's sentence of one month with hard labour.

* * *

Thank goodness Mrs Molloy called in when she did, because she found Cath in agony on the floor. Cath gave birth to twin boys and instead of asking the good Lord to bring her husband some peace of mind, Mrs Molloy saved all her prayers that night for Cath and her tiny newborns. It was winter, yet the air was sticky and warm enough to smother both infants in their beds. Cath washed her babies and wrapped them in clean cloths. She buried them alongside Johnnie and little Christopher and the boy who should never have been called Albert. Mrs Molloy stood next to Cath because somebody had to, and Cath's no-good drunk of a husband still had a week left to serve. Mrs Molloy made a point of telling Edwin all this on the morning they let him out of Perth Gaol. She waited for him at

270

the bottom of the track that led up from the road to Edwin's house, her arms folded, her face like thunder. 'Johnnie's widow's too good for you, Edwin Salt. Say what you like about my Arthur, but at least he never hit nobody on account of drink. I dunno what set you off, but you make damn sure it don't happen again or else God forgive me, I'll throttle you myself.'

★ ★ ★

Edwin looked around for signs of birth, or death, but the house looked exactly the same as it had a month and a day ago.

'Oh. You're back.' Cath appeared at the door. She had soil on her face and hands. Her dress was shapeless and roomy on her. 'Sorry I'm late for your homecoming. I've been working in the yard.'

Edwin stood up and tried to speak.

'For the love of God, Edwin, shut your mouth. You trying to catch all the flies in the colony, or just one or two?' Cath wiped her hands on her dress. 'Oh, there's trouble with the well. Smith took a look. Reckons we need another one dug.' She went back outside and slammed the door.

★ ★ ★

He dug until his arms hurt more than they'd ever hurt breaking stones in Portland. He dug until the blisters on his hands dissolved into raw flesh. He tore into the black dirt harder than he'd torn into anything in his life. He dug deeper than a grave, than two graves, than all the graves Cath had kneeled by. He dug to the rhythm of her name — *Mary Ann, Mary*

Ann — because no matter who had pardoned him and who had sold him land and who had borne him more children, she would not leave him alone.

He dug until night fell and for hours after. Another shivering summer night in a crooked country where a day's heat could burn you alive and its darkness could freeze you to death. He continued to dig long after the lamplight up at the house had been dimmed and he could no longer distinguish his house from the blackness that surrounded it. He dug until the shovel hit the cool river that slept underneath his house and his bed and his crooked freedom. He dug until he stood knee-deep in the water that coursed through all his borrowed days. He dug because there was rum in the house for when he finished digging. Rum and a walk to the cathedral and the feel of straw-gold hair against his cheek.

Family

Fremantle, 1907

By mid-February the full force of summer hit Fremantle. There was no breeze. Wooden beams creaked as they dried out and the sickly whiff of decaying fruit began to smell normal. In yards where nobody thought they'd be seen, women stripped down to their underclothes and flopped in the shade with their limbs at indecent angles.

In the airless nights, Fan was sometimes woken by the low, wordless wailing that leaked out of Grandpa's sleeping mind. Once, Tom whispered across the room, 'Can you hear that, Fan? What's wrong with Grandpa?' Fan heard herself whisper, 'Don't worry about him; he's an old man and his mind is failing,' and she wondered which side of Grandpa's secrets she stood on. In the mornings, nobody mentioned his nightmares, especially not Grandpa, but everyone watched him carefully.

Grandpa seemed to stay out all day at the Commercial. Sometimes he even whistled when he left the house. One morning, after the breezeless heat had kept the whole town awake, Fan waited until she heard him leave the washhouse and close the front door. She put her bathing costume on under her dress. She glided into Grandpa's room. She pictured herself underwater: fluid, noiseless.

The lid of the trunk lifted off easily. Fan took out the leather bag and removed the bundle of letters and the blue embroidered church. She put the bag back underneath some of his other rubbish and carefully put the lid back on the trunk.

'Fan, where are you?' Ma's footsteps grew louder. 'What are you doing?'

'I'm nowhere, Ma. I'm not doing anything.' Fan could hardly speak, her mouth was so dry. She fled into her room, hid the letters and the blue cloth under her bed and pulled out her notebook.

'Your face in a book?' Ma stood at the door. 'What a turn of events, Frances.'

'You're letting me stay at school — I want to make you proud of me,' Fan beamed at Agnes. 'I promise.'

Ma raised her eyebrows at the idea of Fan applying herself, but left her daughter to it. As soon as Ma was back in the kitchen, Fan headed for the beach, the bundle of Grandpa's letters tucked under her arm.

The water was blue-green with no hint of current, and the air was completely still. A few fishermen dotted the shore. She found a protected spot in the dunes and took off her shoes, then her dress, and spread it out like a blanket. Fan felt tight in the chest and sick in her stomach, but she made herself push on. She'd come this far. She'd kick herself if she was too chicken to see it through.

She laid out the letters in the order they were postmarked. She read them in the order they were written. 'Coming, ready or not,' she said to the secrets, and plunged in.

There were some old-fashioned words she didn't know, but once Fan got used to the handwriting, Eliza's voice seemed so clear it felt like she was whispering in Fan's ear.

My dear Edwin.

Da says you are as good as dead to the family but like progress, I choose to pass him by! I found you letter by the fire. I am supposing he must burn them if you have written before.

I was pleased to read about your wife and your land I am glad you are making a life in the colony. The say the climate is good for improving the tempera ment of a certain kind of man. I pray very little thes days, but I pray you will find it a healing place.

There is some sad news. Our mother died soon afte you left for the colony. She didn't suffer. Da gets som help from young Amy Bullock next door.

Albert and Edwin Stewart are settling in with D although it is very cramped. They go to the churd school and learn writing and arithmetic. Matthe is living with me. He is a sickly boy with a consta cough.

I took them to the cathedral last Sunday and show them our childish old games. You will be glad to kno that I outran them, and that Saint Chad is still dea

I told your boys I always beat you in our silly rac but they did not believe me. I always knew you let r win, old man.

I made a keepsake to remind you of home. Da clear out so much after our mother's funeral, but I am sen ing you all that remained.

With love from your sister Eliza.

Your boys. Did Grandpa have other children in Lichfield? He'd never talked about them. Did that mean Grandpa had a wife in England? She opened Eliza's next letter.

I am sorry to tell you your son Matthew died of consumption. While it was the consumption that got him, I believe in my heart it was the terrible loss of his mother, and then his father, that killed him.

Albert does not ask me anything and so I leave him be. Edwin Stewart asked me what happened to you and so I told him you are making a new life in the Swan River colony. Da still refuses to have your name spoken in the house.

Albert is learning tailoring, but he shows little skill. Da could be more patient and Albert could try harder. Edwin Stewart has run away again. People blame him for stealing a horse from outside the Cross Keys Inn but nobody saw him do it, and he has not come back to defend himself.

The snow is lingering. The children are freezing and have colds as their clothes are constantly damp. I am expecting another child but am not so well with this one.

I hope you are doing well. There are always stories of men out there making good, even men with your unfortunate start.

She opened the next letter, a different, less educated handwriting. The news got sadder the more she read.

I regret to inform you Eliza died in her confinement this July past. The child a girl died with her. My husband your father Samuel asked me to inform you of this sad news as a duty nothing more as she confessed she were writing to you.

She were buried next to your son Matthew. It were a great turnout to see her laid to rest, Eliza were much loved even with her odd ways.

Samuel said to tell you he will never have your name spoke in the house on account of your hand in the dreadful death of poor Mary Ann.

He said to tell you Albert joined the Navy and vowed never to come back. Edwin Stewart goes by Eddie now and he left too. Good riddance after the thieving the whole town knew was his doing. Talk was he headed for the London docks but we never heard a peep from him.

You were spared the gallows but your father will never forgive you for the shame you put on his family.

Samuel says now all traces of you are gone from Lichfield you do not send any more letters on account of Eliza's sad passing there be nobody here to want them.

Mrs Samuel Salt (Amy Bullock)

Fan prayed for a different ending — for Eliza and Matthew to suddenly pull through, for Samuel to want Grandpa's name spoken in the house.

On account of your hand in the dreadful death of poor Mary Ann. Who was Mary Ann? Grandpa had never talked about her. And what was *spared the gallows?*

Fan opened the letter from New South Wales, the one she'd reimagined so often in the middle of the night, the one she was sure had been written by Walter.

I am grateful for your kindness with the land all those years ago or else I could not of bought my land were I now live. I hope my poor mam can rest in peace now. You will always have a place with us but if you cant beg my forgivness this is the last time you shall hear from me.

Your son.

She re-read Eliza's letters, and then the letter from Amy.

. . . on account of your hand in the dreadful death of poor Mary Ann.

She traced her finger over the scrawl on the back of the envelope from New South Wales. It looked like it was Something Farm, then the name of a river, in New South Wales. The round, fat script, and the one letter with a curly tail that dropped down below the rest.

Fan's finger wrote and rewrote the scribbled address until the name resurrected itself. The hairs on the back of her neck prickled and she suddenly understood.

280

The address was Maryann Farm. She compared the word with the shape of the words in Amy's letter. She was certain.

It was still early but the sun was beginning to glare off the sand. The dreadful death of poor Mary Ann must have been years ago, years before Ma and Walter were born, before Grandpa came to the colony to seek his fortune.

So, Ma must be right. It probably wasn't Walter in New South Wales. Who lived at Maryann Farm? Was it Albert or Edwin Stewart — Eddie? Did the lock of hair belong to Mary Ann? Fan hugged her knees.

What did Grandpa do? What were gallows and why was he spared them? Did Ma know any of this? And where on earth was Uncle Walter?

Fan's limbs ached for Semaphore, its familiar currents and breezes, the jetty that always reminded her how close she was to home.

★ ★ ★

Everything was the same. The big house at the top of the road, three joined-up houses, Grandpa's old boots on the step, with their holes in the toes and sagging ankles. Everything the same: the sound of hammers and the boys' voices in the backyard, Ma shelling peas.

Everything the same, except Grandpa wasn't in his room. He was sitting near the unlit stove in a chair, reading, with a wet cloth on his head and his feet in a tub of water. Fan waited for a twitch in his neck or a tightening of his mouth. She waited for him to recognise the inky stains of Eliza's and Amy's words all over her hands. She waited for something, anything, about the dreadful death of poor Mary Ann to rise up and

281

live in his face, his eyes. But it was the same twinkly eyes as he said, 'Hello, Miss Johnson,' his fingers tapping on the cover of his book.

Fan thought she was going to be sick. She pressed her hand to her mouth and ran.

★ ★ ★

In the outhouse, she read by the very weak light. It was the only place she was sure she wouldn't be disturbed. These days Ma was always looking over her shoulder or walking into a room so quietly you'd swear she was a ghost. Fan read the letters over and over and whispered names and words to herself to help her remember them later. The next time she heard Grandpa whistling in the washhouse and the tub being filled, she tiptoed barefoot into his room and carefully put the letters back where she'd found them.

In the kitchen, Agnes was slicing potatoes. Fan sat down and started helping. Agnes murmured her thanks.

She heard Dad on the front steps, so she went out to meet him.

'Dad, what's gallows?'

'It's where they hang murderers in prison,' George said, pulling off his boots. 'Why?'

'No reason. Something at school today.'

'You finally paying attention in class, young lady?' he sounded pleased.

'Yep, Dad. Finally.'

Jesus, Mary and Joseph, Fan had never been so scared in all her life.

Fan had never taken much notice of it before, but now the wall that separated the gaol from the rest of Fremantle was everywhere she went. The creamy, rough-hewn stone soaked up the sunlight. It was higher than trees. The shadow of it followed her home to Ellen Street. That wall was everywhere, except in people's talk. The only place it didn't follow her was under water, into the cool sand of the seabed.

* * *

Edwin didn't know or care what the barmaid at the Commercial put in that ale, but these days he felt like a different man. His feet still hurt when he walked, but he stood straighter and he smiled more. Every morning he dressed up like it was a special occasion, in his good jacket and a waistcoat. When the wharf bell rang at midday, signalling the shift change, he bid Agnes goodbye with a tip of his hat. Agnes responded with a cheery 'Goodbye! We eat at five,' but she hardly looked up and never stopped what she was doing.

The men who drank quietly down the back at the Commercial spent the afternoon enquiring about each other's families, each other's ailments. Sometimes, one of them would have news of a mutual friend — usually involving arrest, absconding or death, but news nonetheless — and these anecdotes unaccountably cheered Edwin. 'The sore-footed tailor was outrun but not outlived,' he could imagine Eliza saying.

He was always slower on the walk back to Ellen Street, but it gave him an appetite for whatever mess his daughter served up for dinner. He and Fan had invented quite a few new names for Agnes's cooking. Gristle pie. Crucified mutton. Starvation pudding. Fan would open the door with her face screwed up, her hands around her own neck, saying 'Jesus, Mary and Joseph, Grandpa, are you still alive?' He'd pretend to spit onto the plate and say, 'You must give me the recipe for stewed socks, Miss Johnson. I don't know how I've lived this long without it.' Then they would laugh and laugh and laugh, putting their fingers over their mouths to remind each other to be quiet in case Agnes heard them. After Fan collected his tray and said, 'Sleep well, Grandpa. Let's hope we survive the night,' he'd pour a drink, as had always been his custom. But for the past couple of weeks, he'd left Eliza's letters unopened and the past where it belonged.

* * *

'Salt! Is that you?' A toothless man with a boil on his cheek limped towards his table.

'I don't believe it. Look who the Fremantle tide washed up.' Edwin shook the man's hand, recoiling slightly at the flaking skin. He hadn't seen this pock-marked face since he left the *Lincelles*. 'Is it O'Neill?'

'The very same.' O'Neill beckoned to the barmaid with a tobacco-stained finger. 'Will you celebrate with me? It's my birthday.'

'Most certainly! Every birthday in this godforsaken place is worthy of celebration. To you, O'Neill.' Edwin lifted his glass. 'It's a miracle you're still alive.'

'Ah, but folks like you and me, we believe in miracles, don't we, Salt?' O'Neill wheezed. He reeked like a corpse. 'In our case, the miracle of the merciful pen

284

of Her Majesty Queen Victoria.'

'To our most merciful queen.' Edwin raised his glass. 'In fact, to mercy itself. In all the guises we may find it.'

★ ★ ★

Fan got to the beach just as the first brightness of day hit the sand. She took her notebook and copied down what she could remember as best she could, but pictures came easier and faster to her than words. Perhaps she took after Uncle Walter, whose drawing she had stuck in the back of her notebook. Fan made a page for Grandpa's Lichfield boys: Albert, Eddie and Matthew. She made a page for Grandpa and Uncle Walter and Ma at East Perth and put a family of Aborigines under a tree at the edge of the page. On the page next to it she sketched a river and Ma's face on top of the water, a single stick-arm waving above her head.

Maryann Farm needed two pages. She drew a stick figure and called it *Albert or Eddie*, and a blank-faced woman for Albert-or-Eddie's wife. She gave them a long and winding river that stopped at their door.

The seaweed that reminded her of Mary Ann's hair — for that's how she had begun to think of it — had dried and crackled. She put it in the front of her notebook and on the first page wrote: *the dreadful death of poor Mary Ann.*

After she'd copied everything she could remember, Fan swam. She let the shoreline be her guide. She pushed herself to swim a little further around the curve of beach. She swam until the ache in her limbs made it impossible to think of anything else.

285

Agnes was surprised to see Fan sitting at the table long after everyone had finished.

'Are you going to fetch your grandfather's dishes?' Agnes asked.

'Nah. I asked Tom to go instead.'

'Have you and Grandpa had a falling-out?'

'Ma. He's about a hundred years old.' Fan rolled her eyes. 'I made some friends from school.'

Agnes ruffled Fan's hair. These days, it was permanently frizzed up and sticky with salt water. 'I'm glad, Fan. It's about time.'

Fan pushed Agnes's hand away. 'We go to the beach. There's a group of us. I'm the best swimmer, though.'

'Of course you are.' Agnes kissed her daughter's hair. For once she was pleased about Fan's fickleness. There would always be much more in the world to occupy a young girl's attention than a grumpy, infirm old man.

★ ★ ★

The day of Tom's great unveiling dawned clear and breezy. Tom, Charlie and Lee fussed with the hessian sacks they'd used to cover up the boat. It was about six feet long, maybe more. Longer than Dad was tall. Grandpa stood in the thin oblong of shade by the back door, dabbing a handkerchief to his shiny forehead. Tom tapped a hammer against an oilcan and everyone stopped talking.

'Ladies and gentlemen.' Tom bowed like a circus ringmaster. 'Charlie, Lee and me would like —'

'And me,' Ned said, and everyone smiled.

286

'The real shipbuilders and my pain-in-the-neck brother would like to show you our fine boat.' Tom's sun-browned face widened into a white-toothed grin. 'She'll be the best boat on the water, thanks to our dad and the secrets of the Sunderland shipyards.'

'Get on with it, lad,' George grinned.

'Ladies and gentlemen, I give you the SS *Semaphore*,' Tom announced.

The boys pulled away the hessian sacks. Everyone gasped and clapped. Light broke through where some of the boards weren't held together properly. The inside was almost flat, and the little keel looked like a fishtail.

'Some of your joins are all over the place.' George ran his hands along the timbers. 'More gaps than boat in this boat, bonny lad.' Even after twenty years, George still said boat like a Sunderland man. *Boouat.* 'I'm dead proud of you, though, Tom.'

There was enough room in the boat for all four boys to sit comfortably. In the breeze, a calico sail flapped on the mast. And below it, something else.

'What's that?' Fan pointed to the thing fluttering underneath the sail. It was blue and about a foot square. Fan stepped into the boat, reached up and examined it. Three spires and three letters. Neat stitching that had yellowed with time. Sweet Jesus.

'Bloody hell, Ned. Where did you get that?' Fan asked.

'Tom said we needed a special flag to tell people who we are.' Ned climbed into the boat and stood next to her. 'I looked the whole house up and down, and the yard. Found it under your bed. Tom reckons it's just right.'

Fan's heart pounded. Grandpa leaned on the side

287

of the boat. The ropey muscles on his neck stood out.

'Where did you get that, young Ned?' Grandpa pointed up the mast.

'From under Fan's bed, Grandpa.'

Grandpa's eyes were cold. He turned to Fan.

'Did you take something from me, Miss Johnson?'

'I — well I didn't put it up there, honest to God —'

'I thought we were friends, Miss Johnson. Are you a liar as well as a thief?'

'I'm sorry, Grandpa.' Fan bit her lip.

'Do you know what they did to liars and thieves in the old days, Miss Johnson? They put them in boats just like this one and sent them straight to Hell.' Grandpa lifted his cane.

'Don't hit me!' Fan screamed and jumped out of the boat. Everyone stared at them.

Grandpa's face seemed to crumble. His cheeks sank, his mouth twisted. He blinked and looked away from her. He shrank like a bag of bones in his old-fashioned clothes.

Fan began to cry. Leaning heavily on his cane, Grandpa limped back to the house.

★ ★ ★

'You said you didn't know nobody in New South Wales, but I know different. Is it Uncle Walter in New South Wales?' Fan's voice shook, but she didn't care.

'Miss Johnson. I excuse your rude interruption.' Grandpa was putting on his good jacket.

'Is it my Uncle Walter in New South Wales? My ma would want to know.'

'Walter was a good-for-nothing liar and trouble-maker. I neither know nor care whether he is alive or dead.'

'That letter from New South Wales said, Your son. If it's not Walter, is it Albert or Eddie? How many sons you got?'

'Stop bleating, child.' Grandpa put his hat on. 'I am late for an appointment at the Commercial Hotel.'

'Were all those stories you told me true?' Fan shouted louder.

'In their way, yes, they were true.'

'They're either true or they're not.'

Grandpa began putting his books away in that old trunk. Jesus, was he packing?

'Whoever it is in New South Wales says you're his father and he lives in a place called Maryann Farm.' Fan's voice was harsh, her eyes fiery. She repeated it for good measure.

'Maryann Farm. And someone called Amy reckons you had a hand in the dreadful death of poor Mary Ann, whoever she was. So, did you? Did you have a hand in the death of poor Mary Ann?'

Grandpa's mouth was grim-set. He said nothing.

'Answer me or I'm getting Ma.'

'It's all right, Fan, I'm right behind you.' Agnes's face was white. Fan hurled herself into her mother like Agnes was one of Ernest's windbreaks on a blustery Semaphore afternoon.

'I think you'd better answer my daughter's questions,' Agnes said.

★ ★ ★

Nobody spoke. Agnes sat on one chair, Grandpa on the other. Fan sat on the end of the bed, kicking the wall with her boots.

289

'My son,' Grandpa said eventually. 'My esteemed second-born, Edwin Stewart Salt, now calling himself Eddie, who made it his business to take away the only thing I had left. Mary Ann was his mother.'

'Why did Amy think you had a hand in the death of poor Mary Ann?' Fan's kicking got louder. 'Why?'

'I saw a picture of her once,' Agnes said quietly. 'Mary Ann died. That's when you came here, wasn't it?'

'What does Amy mean by you been spared the gallows?' Fan was circling, merciless. 'My dad says the gallows is only for murderers in prison.'

Agnes pulled Fan closer to her.

Grandpa shook his head.

'Tell me it's not true,' Fan said. 'Tell me, Grandpa.'

'They got it wrong.' Grandpa stomped his foot and Fan flinched. 'It wasn't like you think. They got it wrong, I tell you.'

'Was she beautiful?' Fan could hardly see for tears.

Fan stood up, pushed open the wooden trunk, took out the leather bag and unwrapped the lock of hair.

'I said, was she beautiful?'

Agnes made a strangling noise in her throat. 'Fan, leave us alone.'

'No, Ma.'

'Fan, I'm telling you to leave now.'

'Yes, Miss Johnson.' Grandpa stared at the floor. 'Mary Ann was beautiful.'

Fan dropped Mary Ann's hair onto Grandpa's lap.

'How much did you know, Ma?' Fan shouted, and ran from the room.

★ ★ ★

The air pressed in on Agnes's temples. She waited for him to speak. He mumbled to himself and fussed with his papers and books.

'I want you to tell me all about Mary Ann,' Agnes said. 'When you met, what she looked like, who she was.'

'There's nothing to tell. She took to drink. It was the drink that killed her.' His face grew redder.

'I bet your boys don't give you a second thought, but they remember their mam every day,' Agnes said tightly. 'I bet Edwin Stewart calls himself Eddie because he doesn't want to be called your name, just like I felt about my Ned. And I know what it's like to lose your mam.'

'Agnes girl.' Edwin held out his hand. 'She died of drink, I told you.'

Agnes stared at the old man in front of her, his blotchy skin, his calloused hands, his jacket worn through at the elbows.

'I'm not asking you what killed her.' Agnes grabbed the window catches and pushed it up so hard, the glass rattled. 'You tell me about her life, damn you. Her life.'

* * *

This much he told his daughter: the woman he first saw hurrying along a bridge, the woman with wishes and her hair that was the only gentle thing he encountered in Birmingham. He tried to remain steady, but when he said the name of her village, his voice cracked open with the so-long unspoken and he stammered like a child.

He talked bitterly of the hard years, being shipped

around like cattle, Mary Ann heavily pregnant on one of those terrible Irish Sea crossings. Mary Ann was afraid of water, said it didn't feel natural; she liked to have her feet on solid ground. There were so many postings he couldn't recount them all. Mary Ann grew to hate it. She cried whenever they arrived somewhere new because she knew they'd eventually have to pack up and leave, and the thought of putting down roots became more painful than she could bear.

He blamed the midwives who gave her whisky for the pain in her insides and the black fog in her head. He blamed the weather, the baby who died, the babies who didn't die.

He was a hard worker, a fast and reliable worker, he put food in their mouths and a roof over their heads. It was her job to be the wife, be the mother. He blamed the Dublin gin shop, the Edinburgh gin shop, all the gin shops.

The gin put anger in her fingernails and in her boots and made her sleep so much her children went hungry. She was so mad she once walked up the hill to the millwheel and threatened to jump into the icy water. He blamed that woman who helped with the children and who sat with Mary Ann in the afternoons, the pious-faced widow whose name he could no longer remember.

No man deserved that kind of wife. No child deserved that kind of mother. It wasn't his fault. He did the right thing. Mary Ann was in the grip of drink. She fell down all the time. One morning she fell down and didn't get up. He fetched the doctor. He did the right thing. Hundreds of people signed petitions. Hundreds of people tried to save him. I did the right thing, he shouted at Agnes again, again, again.

But this much he remembered: coming home after his shift at noon. Mary Ann lying on the floor. The freezing room. Her cough that sounded more like hiccups. He kicked Mary Ann from behind. Once, twice. He slumped to the floor and lifted himself on top of her, rested his head on her breasts. Her heartbeat fluttered like feathers. He shoved her dress up and grabbed her thigh.

Dull afternoon light washed the room, the kind of light that makes dust stand out, and suddenly it swarmed around them like bees. Dust, cobwebs, the shadows of three boys: large, medium, small. Cut from the same cloth.

Mary Ann whispered something and thrust her knee up hard between his legs. He swore at her.

The poker next to the grate was close enough for him to reach, if he wanted to.

'I told you, she died of drink. Everyone said. She died of drink.' He sank his head into his hands, but his voice was flinty and hard and still fighting.

★ ★ ★

Fan drifted — down High Street, down to the dockside, past the hotels. Everywhere she went, the wall of the gaol separated her from the place it hid. She peered into the faces of everyone she passed: the bonneted women, the squealing children, the well-dressed merchants, the man in a stained jacket who sat outside one of the hotels, a couple of coins in his upturned cap.

What did it look like, the face of a murderer? Did it look like the frail man who lived in her house?

The breeze ripped up the ocean and dozens of

293

white-capped waves tripped across the sea in a diagonal line to the shore. It was too choppy to be thinking about a swim, but Fan ached for quiet. She left her clothes in a pile and ventured in.

The sea shoved and pushed. It tried to pull her under, but Fan hit out against it, carved it up with her strong arms, kicked it away when it snapped at her heels. A wave slapped her in the back of the head. She struck out again, but cramps shot through her legs. It was no use. She waded up to shore but couldn't see her clothes. The current had carried her much further up the beach than she'd realised. It would be a long walk back. Her legs felt heavy. Her hair felt heavy.

Fan spotted her clothes in the dunes. She climbed up, stripped off her suit and put her clothes back on.

It was impossible to picture Grandpa as a young man with the beautiful woman whose hair was the colour of burnt straw. Grandpa was old. His hands shook when he ate. He couldn't talk without wheezing. His clothes smelled bad. As for his hand in the dreadful death of poor Mary Ann, Fan couldn't imagine. Sometimes Dad read things out of the newspaper about bushrangers or robbers or worse, but the terrible crimes always happened somewhere else. Not in her house, in her life.

How much did Ma know?

The setting sun pulsed low and pink. Fan shut her eyes and wished for a jetty to the left and a jetty to the right, something to swim towards or away from, a way to reclaim her bearings. But she saw nothing except the blankness of sky and sea. She lay down on the dune grasses and curled up in the warm stillness that the breeze couldn't spoil.

Agnes held the letter she had written to Annie a few weeks ago. It hadn't been opened. *RETURN TO SENDER!!* Annie had written in capitals and exclamation marks to make her point. Who could blame her? She's served her time, Agnes thought darkly.

She read Eliza's words out loud to the empty kitchen. Hearing them made it all real. After she'd read Amy's letter, her heart beat so fast she leaned on the table for fear of falling. She read Edwin Stewart's letter last, her hand at her throat. Edwin Stewart — Eddie. No wonder Walter had been so angry.

Grandfather Samuel, the tailor from Lichfield,
He was the old-fashioned kind.
Used needle and thread, 'til he dropped down
   half-dead,
And his eyes were all yellow and blind.

Sons, three in all: large, medium, small.
And daughters, useless, but fair.
Sam Junior the small, no tailor at all,
Ten thumbs and he just didn't care.

James was the medium, found tailoring tedium,
He spent all the profits on gin.
Eliza, Eliza, oh pretty Eliza,
To love her, some said, was a sin.

Poor Mary, so sad, lost her son, and his dad
And died broken-hearted one day

After all these years, she still remembered it. No

wonder Ernest invented something that could have been sung by a drunk sailor. The truth wasn't fit for telling. How much had he and Sarah known? Did any of it matter now?

The stove glowed orange. The letters burned quickly. Walter must have known everything. Did he leave Adelaide because he thought she was circling too close to the truth? Agnes stared into the ashes of her family's secrets until they were dust.

★ ★ ★

Fan woke up with a headache. She wasn't sure how long she'd been asleep. Her lips were dry, and her eyes felt gritty. It was raining. She peeled off her dress and ran to the shore in her underthings. In the time she'd been asleep the tide had peaked and was already retreating. A line of shells curved up the beach, marking the place the high tide had dumped them. It looked completely different now. Every day the beach washed itself and made itself anew. Is that what had happened to Grandpa? The others? Did they get off that boat and make themselves into new men?

The water was cold. Always take a big breath before you jump in. Uncle Ernest had taught her that when she was small, Ma watching them from the jetty, her forehead knotted with worry, Uncle Ernest's skinny chest puffed up like a pigeon.

What about Uncle Ernest and Aunty Florence and Sarah? Did they all know? Or did none of them know?

Fan swam underwater. It felt like forever before the water pressed hard on her ribs. She surfaced and then plunged under again, straight through a whirling cloud of sand.

Fan gasped. Something more powerful than a wave had hold of her body. The rip dragged her swiftly out. Her arms cut into the swell, she kicked, but that only made it worse. She struggled to the surface and fought the urge to cry. The rip had left her much further out than where she'd started. She kept her eyes on the white strip of beach and trod water to try and get her breath back.

★ ★ ★

Agnes didn't need to ask where Fan might have gone. She threw some things in a bag and headed for the beach. It was hopeless walking in the sand in shoes, so Agnes pulled them off and tucked up her skirt. A flicker of movement on the water caught her attention. Mermaid hair, two arms. She waved and shouted and ran towards Fan in the water. The sea heaved. The arms and hair disappeared.

★ ★ ★

Fan let her body slacken. 'Don't resist it,' Dad always said. In a battle between you and the sea, the sea will always win. A whale of a wave threw her into a patch of seaweed. The currents fought each other around her legs. The sea couldn't make up its mind if it wanted to save her or drown her. She kept her eyes on the shore.

A figure was striding through the breaking waves, shouting, waving. A woman with brown hair. Fan gulped sea water. She turned to the horizon. The sea swelled with a set of waves newly forming. If she could let herself be thrown forward, she might be carried close enough to make a dash for the shore. Or at least close enough to reach the screaming woman walking into the water in her clothes.

The woman waved more frantically. Jesus, Mary and Joseph, it was Ma coming to save her. Ma who didn't own a swimming costume and never so much as got her feet wet.

A wave picked Fan up and threw her forward. She shut her eyes and thought only of Ma, the strength of her arms, the sound of her voice, the smell of her hair.

* * *

Agnes kept her eyes on the horizon as the waves broke around her. One of these days she'd chain that girl to a post like a mongrel dog. One of these days she'd give her daughter such a hiding that Fan would never say boo without asking first. One of these days.

She screamed into the waves to try and scare away her fear. She summoned up memories of weightlessness and the peace to be found under an endless body of water. Agnes lunged at Fan and in a tangle of arms and legs and shouted prayers, she grabbed Fan's wrist. Their feet slipped and they sank. By the time the sea spat them out to the grey sky, they were waist-deep, coughing, and Agnes was pulling Fan along with a strength that surprised both of them.

* * *

Agnes wrapped Fan in George's jumper and put the blanket around both of them. She could feel Fan's heart beating rapidly against her own body.

'It can't be true,' Fan said. 'I wish I didn't know. I wish I didn't know.'

298

'I knew about Mary Ann. I saw a picture of her once. Sarah said she died and that's why he came to the Swan River.'

'To seek his fortune.' Fan's teeth chattered.

'That thing your grandfather and Walter argued about — it was him giving his land away. Your grandfather brought a stranger home, but it wasn't a stranger. Walter said it was Eddie. Da's own flesh and blood.'

In the sand, Fan wrote with her finger: *Albert, Eddie, Matthew.* She drew a church with three pointy spires like hats above the names. Agnes wiped the sand smooth and wrote her mother's name: *Cath.* She traced her finger over the letters until her mother's memory wore a deep groove into the sand. She told Fan about the pocket of river hidden between the bent-over trees, the way the light burned on the water. The nights of wishing for Mam to come back. Underneath Cath's name she wrote *Agnes*, *Walter*, and *Baby Cath*. The story spilled out of Agnes's mouth and her eyes. It doubled her over. It was so many years buried, but now the story rolled out of her in waves. Fan put her arm around her mother, but she wouldn't be comforted.

'What are we going to do?' Fan asked.

'Go home,' Agnes said.

'Dad will go spare,' Fan said.

'Don't you say a word to worry your father.'

'But —'

'Enough.' Agnes held her hand up in front of Fan's face. 'Your grandfather is an old man. In a few months, he'll likely take all this to the grave with him. We never have to talk about it again.'

* * *

That night, Fan woke thirsty and feverish, her night-dress soaked with sweat and her hands prickling with pins and needles. Ma would probably say she'd been stuck in the water too long or had too much sun or swallowed too much sea water, but Fan knew better. It was the secrets. She pulled her notebook from under the mattress and fumbled her way to the kitchen. Two big mugs of water and still the flames licked at her face. Fan scribbled what she could remember of what Ma had told her. Underneath her picture of Maryann Farm she wrote in big letters, *Eddie, my grandpa's son*. Near enough to Walter and Ma, she drew a little baby and wrote her name as Ma had said it: *Baby Cath*.

She thought writing it down would get it out of her, but it stayed stuck in her thoughts. She tiptoed outside to the pile of old scraps Ma kept for the chooks and thought about shoving the damned notebook under it, but she just couldn't let it go. The only thing worse than getting rid of it would be having no evidence and wondering if she'd dreamed the whole thing up. She padded back to bed and squashed the notebook under the mattress.

Sunstroke and sickness kept Fan in bed for three days. Dr Archer said she'd probably swallowed some-thing nasty in the water. Agnes didn't leave Fan's bedside. George came straight home and they took turns dabbing Fan's forehead with a cold compress. Agnes found Emily's old blanket. George said gently that it wouldn't be much help, but Agnes ignored him and tucked it around Fan's shoulders anyway.

When her fever finally broke, Fan slept for a full day. She didn't hear her grandfather bring in a jar of ointment. She didn't wake when he dabbed a tiny amount on her temples and whispered, 'Forgive me,

300

Miss Johnson.' Fan didn't hear Agnes wake suddenly in the chair, nor did she remember Agnes jumping up and shoving the old man away so hard he fell against the wall. Fan did not hear the low noise rise up from the place where all Agnes's babies were made: 'Don't you ever lay a hand on my children, do you hear me? I'll give you a damned roof over your head and keep your damned secrets, but you stay away from my children, you murdering bastard.'

★ ★ ★

Grandpa was asleep in the chair by the window. His hair had thinned these past few months and it was obvious he'd lost some weight. His waistcoat gaped where it used to stretch tight at the buttons. She'd never really looked at his hands — his tailor's hands, as he sometimes called them — but they didn't look like the hands of a craftsman. His knuckles were swollen, and the skin was covered in faint brown spots. That scar above his right eye. Fan opened the window.

'Nice and fresh for you, Grandpa? I know how you love the smell of the sea.'

A blast of cold breeze had him rubbing his eyes and muttering.

'Ma reckons I'm to leave you be and you haven't got long, so all your secrets may as well die with you.'

'Your mother is right, Miss Johnson.'

'First time I heard you agree with Ma.' For all the anger etched into his face, she didn't feel afraid of him. 'Your Eddie got pretty lucky, didn't he? A nice bit of land for keeping quiet about you.'

'It was nothing more than a swamp. You wouldn't raise a dog there. That's why they sold it to the —' He

301

folded his arms. 'Tailors and builders and the like.'

'All the same, I reckon I deserve something too.'

'A price for your silence?' Grandpa said. 'I have nothing left, Miss Johnson, unless you want to ask Annie for my house, and she is more frightening than all my stories put together.'

Fan named her price. She was surprised at the sureness in her voice. He took his time, but he hobbled across the room and took it out of his coat pocket.

'Of all the punishments,' he said, his eyes glassy.

★ ★ ★

His room felt colder than usual after Fan left. Edwin sat in the draughty quiet until the family noises in the rest of the house died down. The light outside the window changed unnoticed until he blinked and realised it must be almost dusk. He flexed his hands in and out of fists to warm them up and reached for his cane propped against the back of his chair. At least he didn't have to walk far to reach that confounded window.

At the sound of the predictable-as-dinnertime knock on the door, his shoulders relaxed and he called out, 'Come in, Miss Johnson!'

Edwin waited, but Fan seemed to be taking her time. Or was it his daughter? He leaned out of the window. Tom was in the yard, hammering planks together. Tom waved, then got back to his hammering.

The smell of the sea was everywhere. It got up his nose, in his mouth, into his lungs. It tickled the back of his neck. He swallowed hard and shut his eyes and held the window frame to brace himself against everything the sea brought with it. Nobody was coming.

For the rest of the summer, the wharf bell continued to ring every morning and George continued to get shifts at the port. The beach launch of the SS *Semaphore* met with the cheering approval of even the most pessimistic Sunderland shipyard man. Tom skippered his boat with guts and backbone and earned the wordless respect of the other young captains. Ned regularly fell overboard, and Charlie and Lee regularly hauled him up like a wriggling herring.

Edwin continued to have nightmares and Fan continued to tell Tom and Ned it was nothing to worry about. They got Dr Archer back a couple of times and Dr Archer gave Edwin more powders. Agnes ran the house like an army general. It had never been more spotless.

Fan went to the beach every afternoon and swam alone until sunset. She didn't bother lying about going with friends because it seemed so pointless, compared to the other lies she was party to. Her limbs tamed the currents. Her skin became permanently puckered and her face burned red, then brown. No matter how far she swam, the secrets murmured at her from the deep channels way out where the cargo ships came and went. She thought taking Mary Ann's hair would feel better than it did, but it gnawed at her insides. Having it turned out to be worse than not having it. She trailed piles of sand into the house every day and ignored Agnes's shouts about good hidings.

'Why don't you just have me strung up from the gallows and be done with it,' she said once in front of Tom. Agnes left her alone after that.

Agnes continued to write to Ernest and Florence

and Sarah, using the thick, creamy notepaper she'd spent a fortune on. It was the kind of paper that would stand the test of time. She wrote more or less the same news every week, except for the week she made a special request. On her way home from the post office, Agnes took a detour and bought two train tickets.

Each evening, Fan looked at the lock of Mary Ann's hair folded in her notebook. Great sobs rose from her guts and she cried for the woman whose hair was the colour of straw. Fan cried for Ma, she cried for Cath, she cried for Eliza, she cried for Walter. But most of all, she cried for Mary Ann.

★ ★ ★

They got as far as the track that led to the house before Agnes stopped. The fences were wooden, new, they meant business. Ahead of them, the afternoon sun reflected off a tin roof.

'You all right, Ma?' Fan squinted. 'So many trees.'

'Not as many as there used to be,' Agnes said. Her chest was tight, but it wasn't from the walking or the heat. Looking into the faces they passed outside the tavern and the bootmakers and the grocers, she'd half-hoped to recognise Daisy Smith or one of the Aboriginal children, all grown up and with children of their own. The only person who paid her any attention was a frowning, white-haired woman standing at the door of what used to be Henry Wood's place.

'Are you Mrs Wood?' Agnes called, uncertain.

'What's it to you?' the woman shouted, then slammed the door.

'Jesus. What a welcome,' Fan said. 'We going up there?' she pointed up the track.

304

Agnes nodded. Fan held her mother's hand.

The trees, the track, everything seemed smaller, and Agnes strode like a giant towards the house. The tin roof gleamed, and a curtain flapped at the open front window. It looked like a doll's house. Agnes stared at the neat fence, the curtain. She slowed down and Fan walked ahead of her.

'Stop, Fan.'

'Hurry up, Ma!' Fan had almost reached the gate.

'Come back.' Agnes stood, hands on her hips. 'I changed my mind.'

* ★ ★ ★

Agnes barely heard Fan's complaints about what a waste of a warm day it was to come all this way for nothing. She was listening to the sound of wind through leaves, the high-pitched calling of grey birds. When they reached the top of the road, past the overgrown ruin where Mad Molloy's house had been, when they should have turned left because that was the direction for Fremantle, Agnes pulled Fan the other way to where the track gently sloped towards river gums and the faint trickle of water.

Agnes took off her shoes and her hat and sat down on the riverbank. Fan did the same and sat down next to her.

Agnes looked out to the deeper water where Mam stood, her pale skin and blue-black hair beautiful as always. Mam singing, waving at Agnes, beckoning her in. Melting. Everything was the same, yet everything was different. Was it Mam's laughter, or was it the grey birds?

'You want to go in?' Fan said. 'It looks a lot shallower than you made it sound. I reckon we could walk all the way across and the water wouldn't even come up to our thighs.'

Agnes didn't say anything, she just held Fan's hand and stared into the river. She rested her other hand on her heart. In, two three. Out, two three. They sat like this until the sun dropped behind the trees. Then Agnes stood up and started to put on her shoes.

★ ★ ★

Fan ripped the parcel open. Sarah and Aunty Florence had packed up some clothes handed on from Florence and Ernest's two: a couple of shirts for Ned and one for Tom. Florence had also included two beautiful swimming costumes. One was plain blue, but the other made Fan squeal in delight. It had white piping and a hint of a shimmer. She held it up to the light and it looked shot through with silver-green. Fan held it against her body and imagined gliding through the water.

'Bugger,' Fan said. 'It's going to be too big.'

'Language, Fan,' Agnes said. 'It's not for you. It's for me.'

★ ★ ★

It was choppy out where the boys were sailing, but close to shore the water was blue-green and still. Fan couldn't take her eyes off her mother in that suit. She looked beautiful and when she walked, she left deep footprints.

'You'll be all right,' Fan said. 'It won't get rough 'til the breeze comes in.'

'Someone's got to keep an eye on you,' Agnes said.

Fan took her mother's hand and led her into the water. They walked in up to their waists. Agnes shimmered and gleamed. Fan slid under the water and her hair soaked it up.

'It's wonderful,' Fan said as she came up for air. Agnes hadn't moved. She stood with her arms folded across her chest. Fan pointed out to the horizon. 'You coming?'

Agnes shook her head. 'Next time, I promise.'

Fan dived down as far as she could. The sea opened up and welcomed her. She looked back at Agnes, who shone in the light, her pale arms waving.

Fan swam out beyond the ridge to where the seabed sloped down into deeper water. The patch of brassy-coloured seaweed made wavy patterns in the clear water. She trod water for a while then reached into her bathing costume where she had hidden the lock of Mary Ann's hair. It was sodden and dark.

A big breath in. Fan dived down, her eyes open. She dug around in the sand and gently, quickly buried it. One last cloud of sand and the lock of hair was gone.

Fan took her time swimming back to shore. Agnes glistened: born for water, light bouncing off her curves and pale arms. Her mother was a different woman these days. She wanted no reminders of that business in the house, she'd said. Except for Grandpa himself of course, but he hardly left that smelly old room anymore, and when he did, he didn't look anyone in the eye. He even stopped going to the Commercial. Ma had started taking him his meals, wouldn't hear of any of them helping her. Sometimes Fan forgot he was there.

Ma grew bigger and more shimmery the closer Fan

swam and for a moment she wondered if she should tell Ma about her notebook, hidden away between the bed and the mattress in an old pair of underthings. But maybe Ma wasn't the only one who could decide what got buried and what got saved. The sunlight caught her eye and she dived under, where the thought disappeared in this beautiful water.

Author's note

The Silence of Water is a work of fiction informed by historical research.

It is based on some aspects of the life of convicted murderer Edwin Thomas Salt, tailor, excise man and convict number 6101, who arrived in Western Australia on board the *Lincelles* in 1862. The research included genealogical records; case documents from the National Archives in London and the National Records of Scotland; police, prison and colonial government records from the State Records Office of Western Australia; along with rate books, newspapers and a range of other records, all of which are publicly accessible.

The main characters, events in the public domain and major geographical locations are based upon real people, events and places. Edwin Salt was born in Lichfield, England, and was married three times: to Mary Ann Hall, Catherine Curtin and Annie Edwards. He died at the home of his daughter, Agnes Johnson, in Fremantle in 1910 after a period of estrangement from Annie.

Mary Ann is buried in Colinton churchyard. According to Colonial Secretary's Office records, it appears Catherine died of natural causes. Annie survived Edwin and was living in their house in Victoria Park, Perth, at the time of his death.

Agnes Salt married George Johnson at Ernest and Florence's home in Adelaide. They had their four children in South Australia. In the novel, Tom and

Ned swap birth order, and Frances is called Fan by her family. I have also made slight changes to the children's ages.

Ernest Salt married Hannah in Derby, England, before he came to Australia. He spent some time in Perth before moving to Adelaide. One record indicates the real Ernest may have travelled to Adelaide before Perth. I have begun his story with his trip to Western Australia to meet his wife from the emigrant ship *Kapunda*. Hannah Salt perished on board the *Kapunda* and Ernest later married Florence in Adelaide. The tailor's tale recited by Ernest is invented, and includes some genealogical research into the Salt family.

The infant Catherine Salt ('Baby Cath') was taken into the Girls' Orphanage by the Sisters of Mercy, and records indicate that she died there.

Walter Salt drifted in and out of Agnes's life. He spent time as an itinerant worker and traveller in the goldfields and the north of Western Australia. In this novel, his trip to Adelaide is imagined.

Eliza Salt became a teacher in Lichfield. Eliza corresponded with the authorities while Edwin was in prison and revealed herself to be an intelligent, articulate woman who cared about family. I've taken some licence to make her slightly older and given her some unconventional experiences. Based on the archival material, I imagined Eliza as the family letter-writer. Jane McKenzie and Margaret Wallace were real Juniper Green residents and are mentioned in the documents pertaining to Edwin's trial.

The timing of some events in the novel, including Edwin's departure from Lichfield, Agnes's departure for Adelaide, Agnes and George's return from

Adelaide, the arrival and departure of Ernest and his mother, Eddie's arrival and departure, and some characters' births and deaths, are imagined.

The case of Edwin's *Lincelles* shipmate, the embezzlerWilliam Pullinger, is famous and well documented. The scenes on board the *Lincelles* that involve Pullinger bringing money on board are invented.

William Crawford was the surgeon on board the *Lincelles* and part of his role was to keep a journal of the voyage. The convict Mick McCarthy shares a name with a real convict who was transported to Western Australia — however, the fictional Mick's experiences are imagined. The other convict characters, court personnel, police, doctors and other supporting and minor characters are either invented or composites created from experiences detailed in historical records. Henry Wood was a tailor to whom Edwin was 'ticketed' upon his release from Perth Gaol. I have based Henry's character on the real Henry, but changed a few details. Where there were several real people with the same name, some names and details have been changed.

Edwin Stewart Salt was the second son of Edwin and Mary Ann, and Edwin did transfer part of his East Perth land to a man calling himself by that name. The reasons for this, and the character called Eddie, are invented, as is Eddie's departure for New South Wales. Maryann Farm is an invention sparked by one of the more interesting trails of research breadcrumbs.

The courtroom scenes are drawn from some information in the case documents and newspaper reports of the trial. The report in The Scotsman on 15 February 1860 describes the courtroom as 'crowded' and that there was a 'sensation' at the jury's verdict. I have taken some licence with placing Eliza in the public gallery. Some researchers note that in the nineteenth century, women regularly occupied public galleries at trials, and others note that women were likely to have been removed from the court, or barred completely, if evidence of a sexual nature was presented. I like to think my fictional Eliza would have talked her way in.

I have chosen to leave out some details, events and people that aren't relevant to this story. Where there are gaps, questions and ambiguities in the records, imagination fills those gaps.

Lichfield Cathedral, Stowe Pool, Minster Pool, Semaphore Jetty, the Jetty Hotel (later the Federal), the Exeter Hotel, Greenmount convict station, Saint Ronan's Well, Wallace's gin shop and Woodhall Mill are, or were, real places. The Western Hotel is inspired by the pub originally called the John Bull Inn on Howick Street (now Hay Street in Perth) and later redeveloped as the Criterion. The Crown Inn in Lichfield is based on the George Hotel on Bird Street. While the Swan River (Derbarl Yerrigan) runs through East Perth, the stretch of river in this story where Agnes and Cath swim is created from images and archives relating to that area. The beach at Fremantle is based on my favourite stretch of South Beach.

While records indicate that Edwin Salt brought letters and books with him to Western Australia, the family letters and keepsakes are imagined, as is Fan's notebook. The discussions between convicts on the York road gang, and on board the *Lincelles*, are all imagined; inspired by information in convict archives and secondary sources. The family visits to Semaphore beach are all imagined.

As historical archives are increasingly digitised

and made more widely available, it's exciting that the depth and diversity of what we can read about aspects of the past is always growing. However, it's important to remember that some kinds of people were either heavily classified and controlled via colonial archives, or ignored completely. Some were written about in ways that dehumanised, demonised or marginalised them, reflecting the biases, exclusions and power structures of the era.

A list of sources that informed *The Silence of Water* can be found on my website, www.sharronbooth.com.

Acknowledgements

Writing *The Silence of Water* took many years, including a period of several years when it sat untouched. I can't adequately express my gratitude to everyone who has helped to bring it into the world.

The majority of this novel was written on Whadjuk Noongar land. Parts of it are set on Whadjuk and Ballardong lands in Western Australia, and the lands of the Kaurna people of the Adelaide Plains in South Australia. I offer my respects to Elders past and present and acknowledge Aboriginal peoples' continuing connection to land and culture. Depictions of Aboriginal people in this novel reflect some of the attitudes of colonial times; I have attempted to write these with sensitivity and dignity. The flower used to help Smith with his sleeping during the walk to York was based on information in the book *Noongar Bush Medicine: Medicinal Plants of the South-West of Western Australia*, written by Vivienne Hansen and John Horsfall, published in 2016 by UWA Publishing in Western Australia.

The title of this novel was drawn from José Saramago's *Small Memories*, published by Harvill Secker in 2009.

The two verses of Robert Louis Stevenson's poem, 'Keepsake Mill', come from my treasured copy of *A Child's Garden of Verses*, Chatto & Windus, London, 1919.

An earlier version of *The Silence of Water* formed part of my doctoral thesis completed at Edith Cowan

University (ECU). I am grateful for an Australian Postgraduate Award scholarship, an ECU Excellence scholarship and a travel bursary which gave me the time and resources for research I would otherwise not have been able to undertake.

I am so incredibly grateful to the City of Fremantle Hungerford Award judges Brenda Walker, Sisonke Msimang and Richard Rossiter for shortlisting *The Silence of Water* in 2020. The Hungerford is a major opportunity for unpublished Western Australian writers and to be part of the Hungerford tradition is an honour and privilege. Richard's early encouragement of my writing was instrumental in my decision to start, and eventually finish, this novel.

I would like to acknowledge the many librarians and archivists who dealt patiently with this rookie researcher. In particular, staff at The National Archives in Kew, the National Records of Scotland, the Lothians Family History Society, the Lichfield Record Office, the City of Port Adelaide Enfield Library, the Western Australian Genealogical Society, the State Records Office of Western Australia, the J.S. Battye Library, Landgate, the Archives Office of the Catholic Archdiocese of Perth, the Family History Centres of the Church of Jesus Christ of Latter Day Saints and many UK registry offices.

I was fortunate to be awarded a residency at the Katharine Susannah Prichard Writers' Centre at the very start of this journey. Apart from the inspiration and peaceful writing time I found there, I discovered an old bird's nest in an overgrown bush in the gardens. That moment was the inspiration for the nest that Edwin finds in Stowe Pool, and it set the story in motion.

Thanks to Ffion Murphy, Jill Durey, Ian Reid, Leigh Straw and Ari Chavez for insights, constructive feedback and encouragement over the time it has taken to grow this story from a thought to an idea to a manuscript to a novel. In particular, Ffion steadfastly believed in my ability to be a novelist and to write this story, even when I lost faith in myself.

My grateful thanks to Fremantle Press publisher Georgia Richter who understood what I was trying to do. Georgia's thoughtful questions encouraged me to think even harder about the characters, and find ways to be a better writer. Thanks to Armelle Davies for the astute conversations, commitment to this story and a keen eye. To Jane Fraser, Claire Miller and everyone at Fremantle Press, thank you so much for championing the work of Western Australian writers and helping local stories find their way into the hands and hearts of readers. I have always felt this novel has been in very safe hands. I am blown away by the support and care shown to my manuscript, and to me as a first-time author. Thank you also to Nada Backovic for the absolutely beautiful cover design.

I am deeply grateful to Amanda Curtin and Kiera Lindsey for endorsing this novel. Amanda's exceptional novel *The Sinkings* inspired and educated me about the Western Australian convict era and was the catalyst for this book. Kiera's engaging and considered feedback on my doctoral thesis, and her own work in bringing the stories of colonial women to life led to improvements in my work that wouldn't have happened otherwise.

To my Atlantic College family, thank you for showing me what was possible. I'm so proud I get to call myself one of the class of '83 and I love you more than I can articulate. In particular, big love to Maz, PV, Nicola, Ragini, Daz, Sarah, Sam, Amal, Silla and Tanya W for always encouraging me to write.

Thanks to my parents for having the courage to let their sixteen-year-old daughter travel twelve thousand miles to an extraordinary school, and for always being proud of me.

Special mention to the Women Who Walk and Whinge, without whom the past few years would have been impossible to live through. Also to Elda, Renee, Cindy, Lissa and Clare for soul-sustaining friendship when I really needed it.

My brilliant boyfriend, Adam. Thanks for going all the way to Semaphore before our second date, just because I told you about this book. And for the unconditional love and moral support, the hours spent reading, the really useful feedback and the many writerly conversations about story and character that have helped me do a much better job.

Biggest thanks of all to my sister Caroline, who is my role model and my rock, and Phil, Lilly and Beth. None of this would be worth doing without being able to drive to South Fremantle, sit in your kitchen and share it with you.